No Ordinary Love

Reviews

"Loved the poems, the storyline and enjoyed the characters…"
B. J. Stevens Author of Singing Soprano

"There were twists and turns that made me want to continue reading just to find out what was going to happen next…"
Dawn Abrams for Asta Publications

"Loved this book, couldn't stop reading it. Characters were so real I felt that I could identify with these women…"
Avid reader of romance and fiction

No Ordinary Love

A NOVEL
By

Elaine L. Allen

Perfect Perceptions Publishing
www.perfectperceptionspublishing.yolasite.com
perfect_perceptions02@hotmail.com

ISBN-13: 978-0615538341
ISBN-10: 0615538341
LCCN: 2011962489

Published by and for Perfect Perceptions Publishing

Cover Art By: Nu-Image Design
www.nu-imagedesign.com

Printed in the United States of America

*This book is dedicated to the memories of the man that
helped create me;
My Father: Thomas M. Allen
And
The woman who created him;
My Grandmother: Eloise Allen
They both believed that I could be whatever I wanted
I hope I'm making them proud*

*And to my everyday motivation to be more:
Aniyah A. Kennedy*

Amir A. Shepard

ACKNOWLEDGMENTS

Giving thanks is one of the easiest, yet one of the hardest things to do because you don't want to leave anyone out. My first thanks goes to Allah SWT for nothing would be possible without the gift of life and forgiveness. Follows with my mom, Elaine who continues to be a mother in a way only she knows how. To Latoya, the first person to ever read my writing when I was still using notebooks to put my thoughts together, to Marlon the second person to read and who reminded me every time I saw him that he always thought of me as a real writer. To my IUP Girl Squad of friends who back then supported me by reading and listening to all my ideas. Even if we don't talk like we used to when we were in college, I still remember those times and hold them dear to my heart. Special thanks to my current circle of friends and family for whom I would be crazy without: Crystal, Aimee, Kira, Shalom, April, Adrienne, Lauren, Anthony, Jamel, the man who showed me how to love with an adult heart and my future husband; Lonnie, and my children; Aniyah and Amir to whom I am a Superwoman. Thanks to Create Space for making self-publishing easy for me, to my editor, cover artist, and all the participants in my focus groups. Thanks Francavilla for that last minute re-read. Thanks Mrs. B J. Stevens for the corrections. Hope I didn't forget anyone but if I did it's because I have too many thoughts.
Love you guys, hope this turns into something good.........

PART ONE

Back In Those Days

Constant trials prove that my strength

is unattainable and is only passed down

from battles that didn't weaken

but made me stronger

Life has its ups and downs

and like many people say,

the future is not foreseen,

but revealed day by day

through living

Casey Moore 1995

Chapter One
You're Not the Only One

Casey

August 1995

The sound of the pouring rain against the panes of the church's stain glass windows served as a reminder that it was a gloomy occasion for their presence in the massive building. No sunlight shone through the darkened picture of God seated on his thrown, but the gold of his crown still managed to shine without it.

The death of nineteen year old Thomas Moore had brought a small North Philadelphia Community together in mourning. Sniffling, wrestling of tissues and coughing could be heard throughout the sanctuary. At least a hundred teens and their parents filled the pews of the Temple of Divine Love Church as Pastor Haddon delivered the reflection of the young man's life.

It was a life that had not been filled with much joy and had been marred with sadness of seeing so much struggle and loss at an early age. Many of the mourners had known him as the loving pre-teen who had run in and out of their homes during the summer months with their own children. Others saw him as the larger than life tough guy he had spent his later teen years becoming after the death of his mother two years prior.

Although the deceased Georgia Moore had been a dedicated mother, grandmother, friend, and retired elementary school teacher; Tommy had been attracted by the streets in a way that his mother was not able to pull him back from. It was an issue that had resulted in his untimely death.

The news of Tommy's stabbing death in broad daylight on the highly populated Susquehanna Avenue bustling with heavy foot traffic was met with heartache and the underlying notion that when you live in the streets; you die in the streets. None of the mourners were willing to admit they had foreseen his life ending there. Those who had, held on to their children tighter hoping that their own journeys through life would be enough to set the example for a straight and narrow life.

There were those who didn't care anything about his past actions or drug affiliations. To a small group of people he was just Tommy, their child, uncle, brother, and friend. His lifestyle and unwise decisions had not carved or shaped their feelings or emotions towards him into stone. It was those people who his loss affected deeply. It was those people who were closest and loved him that mourned the most.

It was the terrible feeling settling at the bottom of her stomach that had fifteen-year-old Casey Moore doubling over in pain at the sight of her Uncle Tommy, who was only four years older than she, nestled in a coffin. The agony of another death was too much for Casey to deal with. She wanted to scream in outrage and at the same time find solace to heal her young wounded heart.

Next to her sat Daemon Hicks, her uncle's best friend whom everyone called D. He sat there, his golden face pale but held tight as he forced his light eyes to stare at the coffin where his lifelong friend lay.

Daemon couldn't remember a time throughout this whole ordeal of losing his best friend when he'd broken down or taken time to grieve but his mother could. Serena Hicks watched with the trained eye of an observer yet with the thoughtfulness of a mother and remembered how he'd wept like a baby when the news of Tommy's death had reached him. Serena knew he'd just hold it in so he could be strong for Casey; the niece with no one in the world left.

Since the death of Georgia Moore, Tommy's mother and Casey's grandmother were both being raised by Serena Hicks. The two women had been very close to one another, though Georgia at least fifteen years older than Serena had been more like a mother and mentor.

When Serena had moved to Philadelphia from Virginia sixteen years before so that Daemon could have a relationship with his father and to start teaching at an elementary school, the older woman had taken a liking to her. She was a young single mother with a small son in a new place. Georgia had invited her to church and dinner; they had been friends ever since. Serena had supported her when Casey's mother had taken off leaving the one-year-old to be raised by her grandmother.

Georgia's death from breast cancer left Serena with the duty of providing love and care for the two children she'd left behind. She'd done it to the best of her ability. It broke her heart to see that even with the stable home and love she'd provided; Tommy's fate had not been determined by that. With a look at her son and the young girl, Serena prayed that Casey's and Daemon's fate would be different.

Daemon would be there for poor little Casey, she thought as she watched him lean down, grab Casey and wrap his arms around the fragile girl. Only at a time like this would the five foot eight, athletically toned but curvy female be considered fragile.

The fact that Casey's devastating but short past was enough to warm and soften any heart. Early in life Casey's mother made it a yearly practice to go on month long sabbaticals from motherhood whenever she felt like it. Casey had spent years being raised by her grandmother watching her mother walk in and out of her life. One day the door finally closed when her mother died from a drug overdose. She had no father to speak of because her mother had never named one. So Casey spent a lot of her time wondering who he was, where he was from and if she walked by him would either of them even know.

Casey had made a promise to herself to be more than the women who came before her. Her grandmother had spent her entire life helping the urban youth of their community but Casey never understood why she was unable to keep her own children straight.

Today Casey succumbed to the pain, today she would be fifteen, vulnerable, and yearning for the stability that every fifteen-year-old needed.

"Why, D?" Casey asked hoarsely. Glimpses of her brown eyes barely visible, her long dark brown hair tangled against her face as tears streamed down her mocha colored cheeks.

He shook his head, held her body close to his as he answered her, "I don't know." But he did, and so did she. Tommy had been a drug dealer and anything was possible when the streets were unpredictable.

In the pew directly behind them sat Tommy's other two friends, David and Tyree. The four of them were tight as any blood brothers could have been. They shared the same lifestyle as Tommy but none of them wanted to join him in death because of it.

"Trina, won't you take Case to the bathroom for a minute so she can get herself together," David whispered into his girlfriend's ear. Catrina nodded her head and wiped the tears from her hazel eyes. Casey was her best friend and she needed help pulling herself together. Catrina got up and went to gather Casey from her seat. Casey, the taller of the two was hunched over and had leaned into Catrina as they began their walk toward the back of the church.

"Won't you go with them," Tyree nudged his girlfriend Nyimah. She frowned, shook her head, and tightened her grip on his arm. Tyree sighed when she let out a disgusted breath. He didn't need a clue to figure out that she didn't like Catrina or Casey. It was only because she figured they were young girls grabbing all the eligible guys in her age bracket preventing her from getting her own friends hooked-up.

"Naw, I'm cool with you," she told him.

Tyree didn't press the issue because he knew she would get an attitude. It made no sense to him that she couldn't be friends with them. Tyree smiled when he noticed Briannah, the third member of their girl group get up to go with them. Briannah grabbed his hand as she passed by and whispered something comforting into his ear. He nodded and then she walked away. That didn't go over too well with Nyimah who almost broke her neck trying to stare after Briannah.

"What she say to you?" she demanded.

"Nothin'."

As Nyimah rolled her eyes and mumbled something under her breath, Tyree's mind went to what Casey was experiencing below.

There were mumbles coming from Casey as her friends surrounded her in a tight group in the small bathroom beneath the sanctuary. Both Briannah and Catrina attempted to ease her heart with soothing words.

"Case, we know," Catrina consoled her. Briannah held the sobbing Casey in her arms. Casey shook her head; surely no one else had ever felt the burning she felt in her heart. No one else had known Tommy as she had; as a brother, an uncle, and the only male in her family who'd cared for her when there was no one else.

Daemon, she thought and was positive that he felt it. Tommy had been his best friend since childhood. But he was being consoled already by some hot bodied tramp.

Damn it, Casey thought, *now is not the time for jealousy.* She needed to stand. Casey got to her feet and began to pace.

She was a pretty girl. Her long brown hair was styled in a wrap with bangs that covered her forehead and framed her oval shaped face. Her mocha colored skin had earned her the affectionate nickname; Co-Co when she was a child. She wore both her height and weight well. She would never be referred to as skinny. She had too many curves for that but she didn't quite make it into the thick category either. Her lean shoulders shook as she sobbed unabashedly in the mist of her friends; the only family she had left.

The black dress she wore was sleeveless showing off a pair of well-toned arms. It clung to a pair of breasts she'd finally developed, hugged her slim waist and stretched across her full hips and an even fuller behind before falling just below her knee.

The stress from this week's events showed in the darkened circles around her tired eyes. They were red with tears and heavy with sadness. The usual spark in them had been consumed by heartache and now seemed blank.

The anguish she felt was seemingly mirrored in the action of her two closest friends as they maintained their stance as her stronghold.

Briannah eased Casey into a fold-up chair and murmured words to her while Catrina fought the sick feeling rising in her throat.

"Not now," Catrina prayed when her mouth began to water. Instantly, her hand went to her mouth as she jerked forward to race to one of the stalls.

Alarmed, both Casey and Briannah followed her. They stood huddled together in the small doorway as they watched their friend throw her guts up. Despite tears, Casey and Briannah managed to smile at one another.

When Catrina found the strength to unfold her medium five foot six inch frame from the bathroom floor, she found them staring at her as if neither one of them had ever seen a girl throw up before. Catrina's heart-shaped face normally the color of honey had turned a light shade of rose. Her long black wavy hair started to curl at the temples as sweat beads began to form there. She pushed back the tendrils of hair behind her ears to display a pair of 1-carat diamond stud earrings.

Her arms were long and lean to match her height and build, her hands were a collection of long, lean delicate fingers. She made a daily practice to perform as much physical activity as she could to slim out the preteen weight she'd gained between the ages of ten and twelve.

The exercise had done her well. At sixteen she'd the developed body of a woman. She'd decided that being one hundred and fifty pounds suited her well regardless of what the BMI charts said.

She'd chosen a gray vest to go over the snug black V-neck T-shirt. The black skirt she wore was nipped at her small waist but flared out to flatter her large hips and behind inherited from her father's side of the family.

Catrina swiped at the front of her skirt to find something to do with her hands. The always perfectly arched eyebrows seemed to highlight a pair of distressed and sad hazel eyes. Above her left eyebrow she had a birthmark the size of the pad of her pinkie finger. Even when her full lips turned up in a sad smile to form a single dimple on her left cheek, she eyed her friends and braced herself for their questions and barrage of comments.

"So, is this a regular thing for you?" Briannah quizzed.

Casey gasped. "God, Trina, why didn't you tell me? I'm your best friend."

Catrina sucked her teeth. "Please, I have the flu," she explained. Well, she hoped it was the flu.

"So it's called the flu now?" Briannah asked sarcastically while Catrina rinsed her mouth with water at the sink.

"Shut up," Catrina told her, taking a seat.

Casey wiped her eyes and stood over her friend. "Are you?" she asked.

Catrina shrugged her shoulders. "I'on know. I've been nauseous for a couple days," she confessed, leaving out the important factor of her period being three weeks late. "I didn't tell you guys, 'cause so much is going on.   And, I just can't be pregnant."

"How late are you?" Briannah asked.

"Three weeks."

"Three weeks!" Casey exploded. "That's way before any of this even started."

Always the protector, Briannah interrupted, "Does Dave know?" She'd be damned if her friend would be the only one afraid.

Catrina shook her head as tears began to stream down her face. "I wanna be sure. I've been irregular since I started taking birth control. And it was making me fat as hell, so I stopped taking it. We've never been unprotected."

"Oh, Lord," Casey said when all this hit her. She knew that Catrina was pregnant, just had a feeling. "What you gon' do?"

Catrina put her hand to her face. "My parents are going to kill me. I don't even wanna think about it right now. Let's just go back upstairs."

"You sure?" both her friends asked in unison.

At Catrina's nod, Briannah looked at Casey. "You ready?" she asked.

She laughed pitifully. "No. I can't believe that he's gone. He's all the family I had in this world, y'all," She sniffed.

Her friends rushed to take her in their arms.

"No, Case baby, you'll always have us. All of us," Catrina assured her.

Though they differed in personalities, build, coloring, and family upbringing, they were as close as any sisters could be, Casey thought. At this point in her life, their bond was one of the most important things to her.

"I will, won't I?" she agreed.

"Yeah," Briannah said.

After they fixed their make-up, they all proceeded to go back to the sanctuary where they were having the final viewing of the body. Casey seemed to be holding it together emotionally until she reached the coffin. She broke down right there and Daemon was there to hold her and try to convince her that everything would be okay.

Catrina

The mosquitos are out, Catrina thought as she slapped at her calves. The sound of crickets could be heard, when it was quiet enough to listen. The occasional passing of cars added to what she liked to think of as her background music. She figured the darkness of the night and absence of street lights in combination of the low glow of the candles they'd packed had the insects thinking it was party time. Their blood was the liquor of the bug's choice.

As David pulled her closer into his body, Catrina closed her eyes tight to ward off the demons she felt had begun to plague her. The light September breeze made the air cool enough for them to come equip with spring jackets and blankets. David reached down with one hand to pull the blanket over their legs.

Catrina opened her eyes and let her head fall to David's shoulder. She was in her favorite place, with her favorite person. The combination of the two was always able to make her fears go away.

The place didn't seem to be much to look at. The only reminder of the deteriorated mansion was the long strip of hallway that still stood. The unpaved and broken section of street across from the historical concert hall; The Robin Hood Dell usually served as a parking lot for concert goers but served as her everyday sanctuary. She'd spent countless hours here, imaging her life making plans for her future. Reflecting on her past, indulging in her present. Most recently the loss of her virginity here this very summer would keep the place close to her heart and forever in her mind. Many of her evenings were spent snuggled with David in the dim light of his car's headlights shining from the parking lot into the large holes she'd decided must have been windows at some point. On some hot summer nights they'd been treated to free concerts from performing music artists. David was the only person she'd shared the space with. It was their spot.

The arms draped protectively around her shoulders provided her with the security she yearned for during an uncertain time. The fact that her period had elected not to make an appearance this month had her on edge. It was news she'd yet to share with David. That mixed with Tommy's death had rocked her world.

David's as well, she considered as he'd been one of Tommy's best friends.

"You okay?" David questioned as he squeezed her to him.

She had no idea where to begin. The fear of telling him that she may be pregnant kept her mind busy and her mouth closed. The poor and irresponsible choice to stop taking her birth control pills was also something she'd failed to share with him.

She'd made an appointment to see her doctor at Health Center #5. She was dreading visiting there. Everyone in their neighborhood went to 20th and Berks and on any given day she was bound to see someone she knew, someone her mother knew or worse; she could be seen by someone David knew.

Catrina bit her bottom lip to fight the urge to ask him to accompany her on the visit. She shook her head and cleared her throat. "I'm worried about you," she whispered, her throat so raw that it hurt to swallow.

David tilted her face up to his.

"Bey, don't worry. We gonna work something out. What happened to Tommy is not gonna happen to us."

He's being so naïve, she thought. It was so very easy for him to make promises that death would not take him. She figured it was very foolish of him to think that the same fate could happen upon him.

The love she felt for him rushed into her. Catrina moved inches away from him and took the opportunity to stare at his face. She loved that face.

David linked their finger together as she eyed him. She tilted her head to the side to study him. His skin was a shade darker than her own honey complexion. It was what she considered light caramel. His eyes were the same hazel as her own.

"What?" he laughed.

"I'm serious, Dave. You too smart for this drug shit. I'm scared. It's real when a crack-head can murder his dealer in broad daylight," she pressed.

David sucked his pearly white teeth. "Nigga won't be doing anything else."

Afraid to inquire the meaning of that statement, Catrina nervously looked away.

9

He squeezed her hand, brought it to his lips. "It's cool, Bey. We gon' be alright and I'm always gonna protect you."

She didn't let the hand peck sway her into agreement. "It's not. You're so much more than this."

"I am. We don't have to talk about it 'cause, it make you sad. I'ma show you. I got something for you."

Her eyebrows creased at his attempt to distract her. "Don't change the subject."

"I'm not," he said. He pressed play on the portable stereo they'd brought with them. The chorus to Ray Charles's version of *Unchain My Heart* began to play.

Catrina smirked. "Really though?" she giggled despite her mood. She absolutely loved this song. "What you got for me?"

Then she saw it, a blue bracelet box. The fact that it wasn't just any blue, but Tiffany's blue had her losing her breath and her heart skipping a beat.

She could now add the sense of dryness to the rawness feeling in her throat. When she opened the box Catrina saw the Tiffany's charm bracelet that she'd been eyeing for months encased in the velvet shelter of the box. He removed the bracelet from the box and revealed a silver heart locket charm and a key charm.

Touched beyond measure, Catrina let him place the bracelet on her wrist while taking time to admire it.

When she looked up at him she had tears in her eyes. "You bought the charms I wanted."

He nodded in response. "You've been sad the last week. I thought you could use a ray of happiness."

He was her ray of happiness.

"But it's so expensive," she murmured. She'd been trying to maneuver her father into buying it for her upcoming Christmas gift. She'd began dropping subtle hints around her birthday. If her father hadn't picked up on the hints, David sure had.

"You like nice things. I wanna do what I can to get you those things."

There it was. The excuse for him to continue to do what he did. It made her feel uneasy. She felt turning in her stomach and prayed that it didn't result in her vomiting.

She frowned waging a war with herself to give the bracelet

10

back. If she were pregnant, they would need the money. "I know you have your reasons but a man's environment does not ultimately have to determine his future."

"Trina, I know. Trust me, Bey. This not gonna be us forever," She did trust him. It was the outside world that she couldn't.

One week after Tommy's funeral, a visit to her doctor's office confirmed her fear of being pregnant. The hours she'd spent in the neighborhood clinic waiting to be seen were the most agonizing hours of her life. Even with the paperwork for prenatal care and prescription for vitamins tucked securely inside her notebook in her shoulder bag, Catrina couldn't get past the fact that she was carrying a baby. The doctor's voice echoed in her mind, *"You're Pregnant!"*

Catrina hugged herself close as she walked up 20th Street to David's mother's house. She'd tell him, and then they would break the news to her parents together. It was something Catrina was scared to death of. Neither Catima nor Terry Price were the accepting type. Both were working professionals, classic over achievers, and faithful Christians who strived for perfection.

Catrina knew they would be devastated. They'd also be disappointed; endlessly disappointed as their family had just gotten over the scandal of her cousin, Chantel having a baby with David's younger brother Chris. The sting of that betrayal of their trust still fresh, Catrina tried to think of something else but couldn't. She felt certain they'd give her a speech on what being the oldest child meant and how important it was to set positive examples for her younger sister and brother; that she was supposed to be patient and a faithful servant of God. She figured they would also chastise themselves for allowing her too much freedom, wishing that they'd hurry up and save enough money to build that house in the surrounding suburb of Montgomery County.

David's mother, Tyshina would be more understanding, Catrina assumed. Tyshina Johnson was the single mother of David and Chris who had started out as a teenage parent herself. She had struggled on welfare for many years before securing a job with the Commonwealth of Pennsylvania as a clerk for one of the county's welfare offices. The struggles David had seen his mother go through were something he kept fresh as a memory to fuel his ambitions in

11

life, Catrina knew. The rationale of being able to help keep his mother's lights on fed his desire to participate in the sale and distribution of drugs.

'*I want the money, money, money*', she could hear David saying. It was fast money David and his friends wanted but until Tommy's death none of them realized that it, like everything in life, had a price.

Catrina's parents had always taught her that the steady stream of income was always going to be more profitable than any splash in a pond. In other words; to her mind's thinking they'd meant that honest money lasted longer than a dollar earned hustling. Her thoughts on the longevity of selling drugs were something she constantly shared with David. Catrina had learned early, that type of life did not provide means for retirement, medical or social security benefits after death or disability. She did however accept what he did momentarily, hoping that his present would not be his future. There would be no way she'd be able to share hers with him if it was. Armed with that knowledge, she did what she could to ensure that David's life would be different. Catrina felt she had to, she couldn't imagine her life without him.

The two of them had spent countless summer nights on movie and dinner dates, cuddling within the halls of the mansion, taking long walks along Penn's Landing docks, and lounging on the grass at the Belmont Plateau discussing their dreams for a future together. None of those dreams included them becoming teenage parents themselves.

David was currently in his sophomore year of college at Temple University majoring in finance, while she was still in the eleventh grade at William Penn H.S. with serious intentions of earning a full paid scholarship to attend Howard University in Washington DC.

The thought that on one of those lazy nights in his campus dorm room they'd created a baby brought tears to her eyes. Catrina had no clue about the journey that they were about to embark upon. She was however certain that when you made life plans; that you needed to plan for detours. In some cases no routes were complete without at least one detour.

Shaking her head to clear it for one coherent thought to pass through it at a time, Catrina realized there were too many thoughts to count or file neatly in their place. She gave up trying and continued her journey down the cracked concrete sidewalks of 20th St.

A friend called out to her from across the street to find out if she wanted to join her and some other girls for a game of double-dutch jump rope. Catrina declined as she side-stepped the little children out playing in front of their doors as they crossed in front of her path. She listened to mothers yelling at their children for going too far, or doing something they had no business doing, some yelling just to yell. This street was not unlike any other at the close of summer and beginning of fall.

Catrina sniffled as she thought of new seasons and reached down into her pocket for a napkin. The thought of crying when she reached David was as unattractive as the action.

When she looked further down the street, she saw David's brother, Chris running up the street toward their house. Catrina walked a little faster so she wouldn't have to knock when she reached the door.

"Chris," she called

After spotting her, he stopped in his tracks and passed his house. "Yo, wis up, Trina?"

"Dave here?" She'd hate to have to walk the six blocks to his dorm room on Temple's campus. She knew that he had two morning classes but the majority of time he could be found at his mom's during midday.

Chris shook his head. "Naw, he ain't stop through today. I think he workin' on a paper or something he was saying."

"Shit, let me page him from inside, and when he call back you can tell him to call me at home," she asked.

He frowned. "I'll do it for you. Go head home. Tell Chantel I'll be up a little later," he said quickly.

Too quick, Catrina thought— then wondered if he was trying to get rid of her. She nodded in agreement. *He better not be being sneaky*, She thought.

"Tell him it's important," she said instead of the questions she was burning to ask.

"All right," Chris said as she turned to walk away.

Catrina looked back and found him staring at her. "Bye," she said with a wave as she waited for him to go inside the house. She shook her head. He was probably spying to make sure that she wouldn't talk to any of the guys on the corner, she figured. Like she was stupid. David would probably kick her ass, if she even thought about it. Thoughts of her with another man would invite his violent side. Just as it would hers vice versa.

Then she saw David and Catrina's heart sank. All six foot three inches of him, was there coming out of the house as he pulled on some short, thick, light skinned bitch. David, her man, the father of the child that lay resting in her womb, was smiling down at another girl, and she was looking up at him all wide-eyed. There was no mistaking that look, hadn't she herself looked at him that way millions of times?

Catrina's eyes watered instantly as she watched Chris murmur something to David. David looked straight into Catrina's watery eyes and let the girl's hand go. Her heart began to beat wildly in her chest, and drum in her ears. She laughed it off, and swiped the tears away.

No nigga gonna play me for a fool, she thought. Holding her head high when she wanted to lower it and run, she strutted her way back down the street towards him.

With all the red haze in front of her eyes, Catrina barely noticed David send the girl in the house or the fact that he was now walking towards her. She felt like breaking something, preferably his jaw.

Balling her fist up, Catrina took a swing at David when she thought she was close enough to his face. She missed, and was furious when he caught her arm and pulled her to the wall of an abandoned house.

"Don't fuckin' touch me," she yelled at him, yanking her arm away.

Catrina shook her head when he said, "Bey, it's not what you're thinkin'."

"How could you do this to me?" She hated the humiliating plea before it left her lips. Catrina was so sure she couldn't move. It felt as if her legs weighed a hundred pounds each.

There were words coming from his lips, but she was in a place beyond hearing. She pushed him away from her and began walking.

David pulled her arm. "Bey, let's go in the house—" David didn't care that he'd sent the girl in there.

14

"Don't fuckin' touch me!!" she yelled.

"Would you fuckin' listen?" he pleaded trying to hold her still.

"Don't ever try to touch me again! Stupid Nigga," she raged, successful this time in pulling away from him.

"Trina!" David called after her.

Catrina continued to walk, ignoring him. But it hurt. Huge tears dropped from her eyes and hit her cheeks with impact.

Nyimah was standing in her doorway when Catrina walked pass her house. She was smiling, of course.

Smug bitch, Catrina thought. *She better have the good sense not to say anything to me.*

She didn't.

"Ummm Hmm. Niggas ain't shit. Is dey, girl?" Nyimah laughed.

"How about you go ask your man?" Catrina flipped.

"Naw, it's cool. I think Dave is example enough," she laughed louder holding her stomach.

Catrina didn't give her the satisfaction of an argument. She called Nyimah a bitch and kept going with tears in her eyes and a broken heart in her chest. The disappointment more apparent when she realized that he hadn't followed her to the corner.

Chapter Two
Full of Decisions

The Meeting

The comfort of Daemon's kitchen had always been their secure meeting place. Serena always seemed to be off assisting with some after school program or church event that gave Daemon a large amount of freedom to do as he pleased.

Two weeks had passed since Tommy's funeral when Daemon, David, and Tyree decided that something needed to be done in the near future to ensure that what happened to him would never happen to them. They'd been given the opportunity to make a few extra dollars selling marijuana when they were fifteen. That led to selling cocaine and prescription drugs. In their neighborhood the four of them had gotten the reputation as the school boys. Except these school boys were the ones other school boys didn't want to be caught alone with in the hall after the bell rang.

They all had their duties within their small group. Daemon had the connection, it was his cousin Dametrius who they worked for. David handled all the money. Tyree was the muscle and location man; he was the only one of them to have his own place, they put the product together there. Tommy had been their daytime dealer since dropping out of Temple University his freshman year with no intention of going back. They all graduated from high school and the remaining three were attending college for various interests.

"So you saying that you'n wanna sell no more?" David questioned after Daemon suggested that they stay off the streets and hire some younger guys to place on their three block stretch of 20th St between Dauphin and Norris.

"He's saying that if we gon' stay with this drug shit we run our own block," Tyree explained. "This time it won't be the mills, for me and I ain't wit' that jail shit." At the age of fifteen Tyree had been sentenced to complete a year at Glen Mills; a Pennsylvania reform school for boys referred by the court system. Since then he made it his business to not get caught doing anything to send him back into the justice system of the Commonwealth.

Daemon smiled. "Thanks for the reminder, Ty."

"I'm saying it's a good idea. We all in school and we get to a couple dollars sellin' weed, pills and coke but we don't got time like we used to. Tommy was our day man and now that he's gone one of us would have to do it. And I'm figuring that this corner shit is old and beneath us."

"So we invest," David finished. He could see it now. Thinking in numbers was his niche, so the thought of investing easily appealed to his senses.

"Simply put," Daemon responded, tipping his bottled water to his lips. "I talked to Meat and he said as long as we ain't bullshitin' he's willing to give up the block to us for a small percentage of the profit." He could feel their disapproving stares.

Daemon tipped his water bottle to David. "You can go over some of the numbers, but I'm trying to negotiate the block as a gift. But the way I see it, in about five years we can drop this shit all together. All we gotta do is pour our money into this little project and invest some in stock. You could find something for us that's a sure thing, right?" he asked David.

David nodded. "You know that's right." His academic advisor and professor had an investment program for students that had been yielding record returns for the past eight quarters. David smiled as he went over the figures in his head. He'd had plans on investing his own money, but now their pooled money offered greater returns.

"I got a couple young boahs I trust that we can put on," Tyree murmured thinking about the desperate teens he knew who wished they could break into the drug game.

"Y'all down?" Daemon questioned.

Tyree smiled. "Yeah." He turned to David who had his own smile.

Having made one of the most important decisions in their lives, they all sat back and assessed what the changes of becoming investors would bring to their lives. There would be no more alternating late night shifts on the corner. They would have more time to dedicate to their studying and personal loves. There would be more money to spend on their desires and to spread around to their

17

families.

"So, how is Case doin'?" Tyree asked. He hadn't seen her for a couple days.

"She's okay. Been hanging out with Trina and Bri. You know how tight they all are so they keep her pretty much together. I be tryna be there for her but it's hard." Daemon winced as he thought of his arising interest in Casey. Those new set of feelings were currently being assessed by him, because it unsettled Daemon that they were anything other than brotherly. Up until recently Daemon viewed her as a relative with the faint knowledge that she was not. It was that faint knowledge that kept his mind wondering to thoughts of her being more than the little sister.

"I saw her in the mall with her boyfriend the other day. He treatin' her nice. She had a pile of shopping bags."

Daemon scratched his head, "Wit' who?" He asked disturbed. To his knowledge she didn't have a boyfriend. Now that he'd thought about it, she had been spending a lot of time on the telephone with guys from the neighborhood.

"The young boah Curt from 16th St.. You better watch her with that one. That nigga sweet talkin' more girls on their backs than a little bit." David laughed and tapped Tyree's arm.

Confused he looked at his friends, "Ya'll knew she had a boyfriend and ain't tell me."

Tyree chuckled this time. "Nigga, you betta open your eyes. Case is almost a woman-"

Daemon shook his head. "She is a little girl. My mom treat that girl like a goddamn queen and she'd flip if she knew that Case baby was going 'round here having sex."

"Yeah right. The only person agonizing over whether or not Case is a virgin is you."

"You niggas act like I'm just supposed to take advantage of her."

"Nobody ever said that, D," David replied.

"You wouldn't be saying that shit if it was your little sister."

Tyree frowned. "I think of Case as a sister. And every reason that you have for not messing with her that way is valid. You're a dog."

"Your best friend is a dog. I don't have a girl," Daemon

18

responded quickly.

Tyree looked over at David, nodded in agreement. "Definitely is."

"Whateva, nigga," David responded with a flag of the hand.

Daemon didn't want to continue with thoughts of the growing Casey and his uneasy attraction to her. He turned his attention to David, "I just want you to know that Trina been walking round here crying her eyes out all week."

David leaned back in his chair and folded his arms over his chest. "Trina misunderstood a situation and refused to listen to reason."

"I'on see no reason she should've listened," Daemon responded

Just when David opened his mouth to speak in walked Casey, Briannah and Catrina.

"Hey, ya'll, wassup?"

"Nothing," Tyree murmured. With his eyes on Briannah he added, "Wassup up with y'all?"

Catrina walked right past them without responding. She walked up the winding back staircase to Casey's room. Casey shrugged and followed, Briannah lingered.

"So when you gon' let me come see you?" Tyree flirted with Briannah.

Briannah smiled and shook her head. "I'm not," she responded as she disappeared up the back stairs after her friends.

"One day," he called out to her.

Briannah laughed as expected.

Tyree looked at David. "You not gon' go after Trina?"

David shrugged. He was tired of the silent treatment from Catrina but had been too proud to attempt to speak only to be ignored. Based on his previous attempts, he was certain he would be. "No, she doesn't want me to and I'm not about to kiss her ass. So, fuck it." He swallowed the last of his drink and got to his feet. Spent a couple seconds looking at the back staircase and sucked his teeth. "I got a date, I'ma see y'all niggas later," he told them.

One Question

Catrina paced the room, her arms folded over her chest, her head to the ceiling. Casey and Briannah watched her. When she'd called

19

them to inform them about what had happened between her and David, they had cast their opinions on her situation. They both thought it useless to get into it again but knew that they undoubtedly would because they were her best friends and friends listened.

Sorry that Catrina's heart was broken, they wanted to provide her with the support that each of them would need if they found themselves in her shoes.

"Do y'all think I'm overreacting? Even a little bit?" Catrina asked. She wanted to bite her nails, but wouldn't allow the strain of her frustration lead to the ruin her manicure. David's continuous calls to her had picked away at her resolve to delete him from her life romantically. She had been on the verge of contacting him when she'd walked in and seen his face. Her heart sank to her toes when he didn't speak to her.

"No—" Briannah shouted.

"Yes—" Casey admitted, with a roll of her eyes in Briannah's direction.

Briannah sighed. "I'm not saying don't tell him about the baby. Nobody deserves to be raised without their father around, and it's not as if he ain't gon' find out soon or later anyway." Her voice had softened but returned to its original tone when the next statement came out. "But if that nigga fuckin' with somebody else, forget him," she summed up.

Catrina finally lowered her head to look at them. Her eyes were glassy with tears. "I can't. He's been everything to me and I love him so much," she admitted. It was true enough, David had been her first everything. "I'm so scared to have this baby without him," she confessed, sitting on the edge of Casey's bed and putting her head on Briannah's shoulder and let the tears fall.

Casey's heart broke at the sight of Catrina's tears. "So work it out. A baby deserves parents who love and care for each other—"

Briannah frowned and interrupted. "That's just the point, Case baby, Dave is not acting like he cares for her, fuckin' around on her. I'on care how much beggin' he been doin' these past few days." In her opinion none of it was enough.

Casey shook her head. "You know he loves her."

Briannah shrugged. "So he loves her. Trina, you know that he is some bullshit, but you're having his baby and you love him."

20

Catrina lifted her head. "You think I should go talk to him?" she directed her question to Casey because she knew that she was more likely to agree with her out of the two.

Briannah frowned because she figured that Catrina would end up talking to David if she supported her or not. "You think you can deal with him the way things are?"

"No, I'm not the one for that. But I want him. I want us," she replied as more tears slipped from her eyes.

"Awww, go talk to him," Casey soothed, hating to see her friend so distraught.

"You're suddenly full of suggestions for Trina, Case. Don't see you going after D."

Catrina laughed as she wiped her tears away with a corner of her shirtsleeve. "Sure don't."

"D is scared of me, not the other way around."

Catrina nodded. "That is true. At least he has the decency to not want to hurt you—"

Briannah snorted, thinking of Tyree and all his overtures for her attention. "Unlike the rest of his friends."

"I know, right," Catrina laughed. "It must be a best friend thing 'cause Ty is a dog too. And he stay trying to get Bri."

Briannah smiled. She liked Tyree but he had entirely too much going on with his girlfriend and any of the other girls he was messing with on the side for her to add herself into the mix. Briannah huffed, didn't even know why she was considering him. She already had a boyfriend. "Nigga be trying hard too."

Casey laughed. "Nyimah is crazy. And she swear everybody want Ty cheating ass. She be like, 'Chase, why you going with dem? Who gon' be there?'" she mocked. "And she is ignorant as hell."

Briannah mentally agreed. She didn't want any drama. Checking her watch, she said, "I'm 'bout to go. Mark gon' flip out if I'm not ready." Her current boyfriend was taking her the movies. She looked at Catrina. "You gon' be okay?"

Catrina nodded and stood up. "Yeah, I'ma see if he still downstairs."

There was no time like the present.

Chapter Three
And Then Things Got Worse

Catrina

Since David left by the time she decided to talk to him, Catrina found herself walking down his mother's block. She'd decided that she would visit rather than page him in fear that he wouldn't answer her.

This was the right thing to do for the baby, for her and for him, she tried to convince herself.

Catrina shook her head; she still couldn't figure out why he would cheat when she tried to be everything that he wanted. Thought that she was everything he wanted. He called her his ride or die, down for whatever chick, and she had been that.

Damn, why couldn't he have spoken to her at Casey's? She'd have jumped right into his arms, but instead he'd treated her with the same indifference that she'd treated him with. Catrina quickly reminded herself that just because she wanted to talk didn't mean that things would go the way she wanted. She was hoping that the headache she'd been experiencing for the past couple days disappeared because she'd no longer be crying.

"Hey, Trina," one of the guys called from the corner as she walked by.

Annoyed, she looked back to find Kareem following her. "Wassup?" she asked him.

He smiled. It was the first time he'd gotten a chance to speak with her alone since he'd met her. After hearing about her breakup with David he felt confident that she might give him a chance. Still Kareem had lingering doubts, because when a high maintenance girl broke up with her boyfriend, she didn't hook up with guys below his status. Kareem himself was only seventeen and didn't have anything David had.

She looked up the entire block of closely connected rowhomes and dreaded every anticipated step. Meanwhile Kareem easily fell in step beside her and slung his arm around her shoulders.

Uncomfortable with being so close to him, Catrina rolled her eyes and pulled away.

The sun had already begun to disappear into the clouds and the sky had a purplish orange tint. The air was cooler than it had been an hour before. She rubbed her arms to warm the goose bumps that made an appearance and the nerves that came along with them.

"I really need to get going," she told Kareem.

"Hold up now, Trina"

Annoyance flashing in her hazel eyes, she looked up at him. "What?"

"I heard that you and Dave broke up," he admitted, which gave reason for his pursuit.

Gossip spreads like wildfire in this neighborhood, she thought. "No, we had an argument. I'm mad and he's mad," she allowed letting him know that she still considered David her man.

"Yo, dat's not what I heard." His voice was cool but somehow still seemed to shake with uncertainty.

"Yo, Reem," the shout came from down the block. "Get away from my brother's girl," Chris yelled, sprinting up the block towards them. "Yo man, what da fuck you think you doin'?" he demanded.

Kareem backed off and held his hands in the air as if Chris were the police ready to lock him up for doing something illegal.

"Damn, dawg. I was just rappin' wit' her for a sec," he admitted meekly.

Catrina shook her head and walked away from them both. She was still angry at Chris for lying and now even angrier that he thought he had the right to bust up her groove— had it been that type of situation.

"Don't let it happen again, nigga," she heard Chris tell the boy.

"Trina," Chris called, catching up with her quick paced walking.

"What?"

"Dave ain't home."

She stopped, arched a brow and then stared at him doubtfully. "You seriously want me to believe you after the last time?" she retorted.

He looked down at her. "Sorry 'bout that boop, but was I really

23

supposed to tell that he was home wit' some smut juhn'?"

Smut juhn'? Catrina liked how he categorized David's little friend. A smut juhn' was a female that dated and slept with a lot of guys. Was it supposed to make a difference if the girl was a virgin and attended church every Sunday? It made no difference to her what type of thing it was. Another bitch is another bitch was all she knew.

"Whateva, Chris. And I don't expect you to let me know if he in there wit' some otha bitch right now."

"I'm serious, he ain't here. He had some important thing with Ty and D. He might still be with them."

He wasn't, she knew but didn't argue. "If you lyin' we are done."

Chris grinned. "So you came down here to make up?"

She sucked her teeth. "I came down here to talk," Catrina clarified.

"Umm hmm. On the real, he misses you and he been tryna get you back, but your stubborn ass won't listen to reason."

She smiled. "You are so full of shit. You cheating on my cousin too?"

Chris frowned. "Never that. I love Chantel and my sweet baby Nyah and I would never do anything to lose them. Soon as I graduate from school and get a job, we gettin' married," he replied.

That made her smile. His talk of marriage didn't surprise her, because with Chris and Chantel marriage had always been on the agenda of things to come. Chris was so much more responsible than his older brother. Girlfriend, and child meant permanence to him— shit meant the same things to her now that she thought about it.

"I know."

"You want me to take you home?"

Catrina nodded. Her house was five blocks away and within walking distance but she felt she could use the ride. "You ain't doin' nothing?"

"Naw, I was gon' stop by your house a little later but I'll go now. The car is on the corner, cross the street," he said handing her the keys. "I got something in the house for Chantel that I want to drop off," he added when she gave him a doubtful look.

Once in the car she devised a plan to talk him into letting her drive home. Seeing how she was already strapped in the driver's seat, he would have to let her, she figured. Since obtaining her driver's permit David had let her drive his car all the time.

She was a responsible, cautious, and careful driver – A sharp pain in her abdomen disrupted her thoughts. "Ooow shit," she cried, her hand going directly to the source of pain.

Way too much stress. Just calm down. The doctor's words came to her now. 'Stress is not good for you or your baby so you'll have to maintain a good level of calm. Your blood pressure is very high.' "Ahh," she moaned and shifted in the seat taking three deep breaths.

She spotted Chris coming down the street the exact same time she recognized David's forest green Bonneville SSEi rolling up beside him. Catrina frowned as the pain in her abdomen eased a little and began to feel more like menstrual cramps. She unbuckled her seatbelt and got out of the car. She noticed Chris nodding his head towards his car before David got out of his.

David reached Catrina just before she had an opportunity to notice that there was a female in the passenger's seat.

"I wanted to talk to you," she started. David seemed impatient as he grabbed her by the arm and began dragging her back in the direction she'd just come from.

"Why you ain't page me, Bey?"

She shrugged and looked up at him. "I ain't think you was gon' call me back. I need to talk to you."

"You know I would have got with you," he assured her.

It took Catrina a moment to realize that he was pulling her in the opposite direction of his car. Frowning, she snatched her arm away. "What the fuck are you pulling on me for? You wanna stand out here and talk in front of all these nosy ass people?" she questioned.

David took her hands in his. "Bey, I missed you." He was hoping that Chris would be able to get rid of the girl before Catrina noticed anything funny.

As the pain in her abdomen began to intensify, she grabbed his forearm for support.

Something is wrong with the baby, she thought. Catrina winced, and dug her nails into David's arm.

David frowned down at her. He'd felt her change and was worried. "You okay?"

Shaking her head, Catrina let his arm go, and her hands went

25

protectively to her stomach. This had to be some type of nightmare. "Wait— No—" She could swear there was a haziness clouding her mind she couldn't see straight.

"Dave!!" The shouts were coming from behind them, and they were female.

While struggling to stay standing Catrina tried to look around him. It enraged her that she knew that voice. Struggling to put the face with the voice, Catrina squinted against the pain, dizziness, and the poor street lighting.

She recognized the girl walking towards them. Frowning, she took a step away from him.

"What are you doing with her?" Sharde questioned nastily.

David completely ignored her, studying Catrina, who now looked as if she was about to fall face first onto the concrete. It felt as if she were spinning and when she looked down at the sidewalk, it seemed as if it rushed up to meet her face.

Her pain was intense enough to make her cry but it was the realization of what was happening inside her body that had the first tears rolling down her cheeks.

"Chris!" she yelled.

Can't be angry. Have to get calm. Please get calm, Catrina.

David made a move forward. "This is not what you think—"

Catrina stepped away from him. "I don't care," she flagged. "This nigga is with this bitch and he act like I'm stupid," she stated when she reached Chris.

"You okay?" Chris asked as he slung a protective arm around her shoulders and pulled her with him. He shot his older brother a furious look for being caught again.

"Trina!" David called her.

"Please take me home," she cried to Chris.

"Catrina, let me take you home so I can explain," David pleaded.

"I don't want you to take me anywhere. You're so stupid!" she raged. She took a moment to wonder if her pain had stopped or if she was just too angry to feel it.

"I'll take her," Chris told David.

"David," Sharde called from behind them, "what are you doing?"

Catrina knew that Sharde was smart to remain where she was. She guessed Sharde figured the distance between them kept her safe. In this instance, she was correct. There was too much pain for her to take any type of action against the other girl. Although they were not friends, they lived in different hundreds of the same street and knew one another in passing. They were acquainted with one another enough that the girl knew that David was her boyfriend. Catrina would remember the girl's betrayal. It did not affect her deeply as David's did.

"Chris, take me home," she ordered. "And if I see that bitch on my block," she spoke of Sharde knowing that she would, "I'ma beat her ass."

He had to fix this, David thought. "Yo, she don't mean shit to me, Bey," David stressed.

"I don't wanna fuckin' hear it," she yelled, instinctively going over to push David.

Chris intervened by standing between his brother and Catrina. "I'll take her," he stated. "Give her a little time," he pleaded with David as a crowd of people on 20th and Susquehanna Ave. started to circle around them to watch.

Catrina walked away before David could see the tears begin to stream down her face. "You gon' be a'ight?" Chris questioned once he was seated beside her in his nineteen ninety Crown Victoria.

Catrina couldn't bring herself to speak so she just shook her head. She felt like she was losing everything. At that moment she stopped feeling completely. Then there was nothing, not the cramping or the ache in her heart, they both seemed to have disappeared.

Casey

The unexpected knock at her bedroom door had Casey stopping in the process of getting dressed.

"Who is it?" she asked checking her appearance in the full length mirror attached to the back of her door. She admired the subtle curves of her body and hoped that someday Daemon would as well.

"D," the answer came.

Knotting her the belt to her robe, Casey smiled and said," Come in."

Daemon entered her bedroom wearing his reading glasses and the boxing shorts and white-tee that had become his pajamas. He cleared his throat after taking in her appearance. He glanced around the well lit room.

The bedroom was all her. It was painted her favorite color; lilac. In the one corner she had named the wall of fame there were posters of R&B stars Usher, Monica, Xscape, and other various popular music artists. The 19 inch television and stereo both sat atop a black work desk next to a five tier black bookcase. It was filled with romance novels, fashion and hair magazines, school books, and a few childhood dolls that she had yet to part with.

The dresser, chest of drawers and night table were all adorned with small trinkets, nick-nacks, framed photos of those closest to her. There was a picture of her grandmother on the nightstand next her bed. He knew she kissed the photo every night.

R& B singer Monica's song *"Don't take it personal"* played through her radio speakers.

Casey stared blankly at him waiting for him to state why he was in her room. "What?" she asked with a smirk.

Frowning, he eyed the clothing that covered the top of her bed. The purple comforter almost lost beneath the mountain of clothing, stuffed animals and massive pillows she had on top of it. "My mom wanted to know if you wanted her to heat you up something to eat."

Casey shook her head. "Naw, I'ma get something while I'm out," she answered.

"Out? Where you think you going at this time of night?" he questioned angrily as his eye made contact with the digital radio reading of the time. He couldn't shake the notion of her having a boyfriend, or what he thought she was doing with this boyfriend.

Casey laughed and while secretly hoping to make him jealous she said, "Curtis is taking me to the movies."

Daemon sucked air through his teeth. "Do you know what time it is?" It was already after nine pm. "What movie you think you going to this late?"

Casey sighed and shook her head. "D, you are so funny. It's Friday night. Date night. I'm sure you remember what that is, right?"

Was it Friday already? He'd been so busy organizing and planning that the entire week had flown by without him even noticing it. Ever since he'd broken up with Tamika, his girlfriend of two years he'd been focusing all of his attention on his studies in Business Management, working in his uncle's mechanic shop and selling drugs.

"I guess it is," he murmured more to himself than her. When he looked over at Casey again, he was shocked to see her pulling her jeans over her hips. Daemon swallowed the lump that had begun to rest in his throat. Casey was going on as if he wasn't even in the room. Her friends were definitely having too much influence on her, Daemon decided. He made a note that he would have to speak to his mother about that.

It was easier for him to contemplate talking to his mother than thinking about how hard he'd gotten watching her little show. She didn't understand how much he fought with the inner male who just wanted to be let loose on the new prey. Daemon didn't know how much longer he'd be able to fight against it. If she slanted those seductive dark brown eyes his way like she was pleading with him to be taken, she probably would be. Daemon shook his head to clear it.

Casey was down on her hands and knees, searching beneath her bed for her boots when she finally looked up at him and said, "If you don't have anything else to say, you can leave."

Daemon felt the muscles in his stomach beginning to clench as he watched her tight behind strain against the denim.

"Well?" she inquired, standing up.

"I don't like what's going on with you, Casey," he began.

It's working, she thought and made a mental note that he used her whole name. "And what would that be?"

How could he explain it without giving up that he was attracted to her? "This new attitude you have. And a boyfriend? When you get a boyfriend?"

Casey threw her head back and laughed hard. "Are you serious? I'm not supposed to have a boyfriend?"

Either way he answered, Daemon knew they'd end up arguing. So he chose his words wisely and truthfully. "It's not that," he admitted. "I just realized that you're growing up."

Casey had to smile at that. She couldn't conceal the happiness

29

that radiated from her now that she knew he saw her not just as his best friend's niece but as a regular girl. "Have you?"

Guess I walked right into this one, he thought. "Yeah, I have. Casey—"

"You're not my brother, my uncle, or my cousin so why don't you just cut this act," she purred in a voice that was entirely too grown to be hers.

After that comment, Daemon pushed the pile of discarded clothes to one side of the bed, sat down on her bed and made himself comfortable.

So he'd touch her just this once, Daemon rationalized silently as he looked directly into her eyes. "And what is that supposed to mean?" he questioned her as she sat down beside him.

Smiling, she nudged his shoulder. "It means that you notice I'm not a little girl anymore," she invited, reaching out to touch his face.

"I noticed, Casey. It's just that I don't want every other nigga in the neighborhood noticing. I'on wanna have to fuck none of deez young boahs up. So make me feel a little better and don't get yourself trapped with some dickhead. All I'm saying is be careful," he advised, grasping the hand that had so recently caressed his face.

"I'm not doing anything, D," she confessed. "And when I'm ready, I promise you'll be the first one to know," she whispered.

Daemon could still smell the familiar scent of the Lancome's Miracle on her when he took her chin in his hands and turned her face so he could stare into her eyes. It was a mistake, Daemon knew, but he was lost.

There were foolish butterflies gliding around in Casey's stomach. She couldn't remember how long she'd wanted this. She felt the kiss before he cupped the back of her neck in his hands. Closing her eyes, she braced herself for the impact that she'd known it would have.

When his skillful lips captured her, she dug her fingers into his shirt and turned into mush. Daemon deepened the kiss, making her head spin.

He would stop Daemon reminded himself even as he murmured, "Move back."

Yes, he'd stop before they went too far, but ooh, not yet. Not when he'd yet to have the feel of her beneath him. There she was.

Her legs spread wide as he relaxed between them.

Casey tried not to show that her untutored body was no match for his, but she was entirely too excited. She wiggled and moaned in pleasure.

"I want you," she panted as he kissed the slim column of her exposed neck. She didn't know or care about where she'd gotten the heart to say such things when being with him was all she could think about. Daemon untying the knot of her robe and what would come after was all she could think about. Casey closed her eyes as he molded his hands to her firm breast, then sighed and arched her back, he bent his head to take her pebble of a nipple into his mouth.

It must be the man, Casey concluded. She'd done this before, and it hadn't felt this right. That's when she let all her lingering doubts on whether Daemon would be her first fade away.

Casey licked her lips as she felt the snap of her jeans give way to Daemon's tugging. She instinctively raised her hips so that he could slide the denim down her legs.

There were all types of alarms going off in his head as Daemon peeled away the white string bikini she was wearing. The faint whispering of Casey's voice had enticed him to go against his own judgment. His fingertips touched her most intimate part. Daemon delved inside her most sacred place, sending her into a whirlwind of hip moving.

Casey moaned and bit down on his bottom lip as her hips fought to keep up with on his fingers as they stroked on her nub that was now beating on its own.

Oh, God, he's kissing the inside of my thigh, she thought when his mouth began to explore her body.

"Just let go," he murmured when her legs began to clamp around him.

Daemon kissed her where she wanted him to the most and sent her into a shaking convulsion. He attempted to hold her still as he tasted her, little flicks that tickled her spine causing Casey's fingers to grip the bed sheets beneath her as she moaned.

"D! Casey?" the shout came from below.

The voice of his mother brought him back to reality. *Shit*, Daemon thought. *What am I doing?* Abruptly, he went to Casey's room door and stuck his head out. "She doesn't want anything to

31

eat, Ma."

"Oh, okay," Serena responded.

"Fuck," he muttered when he looked over at Casey who was now sitting up on her bed terrified after having almost been caught. Daemon huffed as he sat down at her desk... far away from her. He had to put the space between them. As guilt ate at him, he dragged both his hands down his face. "Damn."

Casey didn't want to think about what would have happened if Ms. Serena would have come in. It surprised her that she hadn't noticed that they were at risk of being discovered until Daemon pulled away from her. Watching him, she could see the guilt in his eyes, and she didn't want to hear him verbalize his thoughts.

"Don't say that you're sorry." She shrugged. "It happened, D and if your mom hadn't been here we would have finished."

Standing up, he sighed but didn't object. "God, Casey, you're only fifteen."

Since humiliation was already a part of it she said, "So what?" A latent reminder that she was naked had her pulling her robe closed. "I'll be sixteen soon and don't act as if you haven't fucked a fifteen-year-old recently," she retorted on the verge of tears.

Struggling not to notice the tears that came to her eyes Daemon said, "Case, you know that it is not that simple. I wasn't thinking with what I'm supposed to be thinking with. I would have taken your virginity if my mother hadn't-"

"Would it have been that bad? Evidently I want you to."

Daemon shook his head. "You don't know what you're saying. You wanna be like every otha little girl I don' fucked?" he snapped.

"It wouldn't be like that—"

"That's what you think. I won't take your virginity because I can't offer you the relationship or the type of love that goes with that gift."

Defiantly, Casey lifted her face to his. He didn't want her; she understood that now. It hurt to think that way but unless she was deaf, that was what he was telling her. "You don't want me?" They both realized that her question had nothing to do with the sexual, but everything to do with the emotional attachment that came along with the sex.

Daemon closed his eyes and cursed himself. He couldn't find

the right words to soften the blow. However, Daemon confessed that, he knew that he would hurt her. Then he answered her question, "No, not in the way that you want."

Casey remained silent for a moment. She nodded and smiled.

"You'll change your mind, Daemon." He'd be sorry if he didn't, Casey reflected when she found a man who wanted her in the same way that she'd always wanted him to.

He frowned. "You think it makes no difference that you're his niece? I just proved to you that it does. Otherwise, you'd be on your back with the hammer inside you and nothing to offer you afterwards. So be happy that I care enough about you not to take advantage of you that way."

Casey shrugged. "Maybe that's true. It still doesn't stop you from wanting me."

"Nothing probably will," he admitted.

"Okay, as long as you know. Now I'd like to get dressed," she said surprising him. She watched him, and smiled to herself. "I don't want make us late for the movie."

His eyes widened, and his anger exploded. "You think you still going out wit' some dude?"

"Why shouldn't I? You don't want me, right?" she challenged.

The Decision

Crying didn't seem to solve anything. Not the fact that she'd miscarried her baby, the fact that she'd completely disappointed her parents, or pretending that David never existed. It didn't help at all, Catrina concluded on day ten, even as the tears streamed down her light-skinned face. She almost seemed pale against the deep red of her sheets.

Restless, Catrina flipped onto her back to stare at the star covered ceiling. *'Aim for the stars.'* She recalled her father saying the day he'd uncovered her remodeled room at thirteen. Catrina honestly doubted that this is what he had in mind for her at sixteen.

Half of the room was painted sky blue with soft fluffy white clouds. The other half the room was painted midnight blue with silver stars creeping up to the ceiling to shine over her bed. There was a poster-sized black and white photo of Catrina blowing a kiss over her bare shoulder at her onlookers above the bed's headboard. Above the picture silver painted letters arched to spell her name.

Most of her things were color coded, separated and organized by type. There was nothing out of place. She was meticulously organized. Pictures of her family and friends decorated her desk and bookcase. Party favors she created for events that she'd planned were also out on display. Jewelry boxes were open to show off her prized collection of diamond earrings and bracelets.

Catrina caught a glimpse of herself in the full length mirror mounted on her bedroom door and sighed. The two braids she'd put in her hair had begun to fray. Her eyes burned with redness. The full lips that were usually glossy from thick layers of lip gloss were dry. Catrina licked them and felt the quick burn from the small cracks in them.

Hurt, she thought back to the way the on-call obstetrician had treated her, as if she were just another statistic. Some urban youth who got herself knocked up, one who'd been destined for nothing. It was in the way she spoke to her, the way she turned her nose up in the air.

Though the thought made her uncomfortable, Catrina figured she had no way of knowing that she was a straight "A" student, or that she was one of the top students in the city. No, she had no way of knowing any of that, because all she knew was that a sixteen-year-old girl had shown up, losing a baby. How many times in this day and age did that happen?

The reason, her family doctor informed her and her parents days later had been that during the cross-over of genes important information had been lost and without this information the pregnancy was doomed from the start. The baby had continued to grow until the needed information had come up missing, and at that moment, the baby inside her died without it.

"You don't know how I feel," Catrina moaned at Casey's insistence that everything would be okay.

How did she know? Catrina wondered. She'd never lost a baby, a boyfriend, and two years of her life in the span of a week.

After having read the do's and don'ts of helping a loved one cope with miscarriage, Casey was pretty sure that saying, "No, I don't, but I'm sure that everything will work out in the long run—"

was okay.

Catrina sucked her teeth. This moment in time was what she was currently concerned about. "Please don't start that bullshit."

"Trina," Casey gently pressed. "You can't lay in the bed for the rest of your life."

Sighing heavily, Catrina pulled the covers up over her head. "Ahhhaaaaaaaa," she yawned and stretched in a way that she hadn't stretched in days. "I know."

Casey smiled a bit when her friend uncovered her head. "Aunt Tima suggested that I get you out of the house for a few hours." Casey spoke of Catrina's mother suggestion. "She actually said, *'Peppa you and Spin take Salt out for a while to get her mind off things. ',*" She added doing an impression of Catima.

"She would tell you that," she laughed pitifully. To those who knew them they were affectionately called; Salt and Peppa after the all female rap group since they'd performed the group's classic track *Push It* in a neighborhood talent show.

The fact that she hadn't chosen to confide in her mother about this pregnancy had caused a rift between the two. Catima had been there for her, but Catrina couldn't mistake the look in her mother's eyes for anything more or less than disappointment. And beneath the disappointment there had been the hurt that her mother had been unable to disguise.

"She's worried about you."

The tears began to well again. This had been the only thing she'd ever been mute about and to think that her actions not only hurt herself but her parents as well was added stress. Catrina shook her head. "And she's hurt that I didn't go to her. She asked if there was anything wrong for like a week, and I kept telling her no. Then when I found out that Dave was cheating, I didn't tell her anything. She asked why I wasn't talking to him and where he'd been, and I -I lied." Catrina shrugged. "I guess that's all done with now."

Casey sat beside her on the bed. "Awww, Trina, I'm so sorry that all this happened to you," she mumbled wrapping her arms around her friend.

"Thanks," Catrina mumbled back, drawing from her friend's strength. She closed her eyes and vowed only to allow herself this one weak moment. And that once it was over, she'd be done with

David for good. "I loved him so much," she cried, tightening her grip on Casey's shoulders.

"I know. He thought you had an asthma attack. Your mom and dad wouldn't tell him where you were when you were at your grandma's. He was going crazy and is mad as shit that none of us would tell him what was going on."

She'd made the decision to not tell him about the baby. "So, he still doesn't know?" she asked. Just because she wanted it that way she really didn't expect for it to go that way, but since it was.... No need to fix it if it's not broken, she figured.

Having been against keeping the entire baby thing a secret, Casey shook her head and said, "No, he doesn't know, but that doesn't mean that you can't still tell him."

They'd been over this before, and Catrina was set on not telling him and cutting him out of her life. Casey saw that as her being stubborn. Telling him didn't mean that they had to get back together. She wasn't so naïve as to think that.

"Why? This will never be real to him. The baby was never real to him. It's not like I aborted it and decided not to tell him."

"I'on think that you'll be able to keep this a secret for long, Trina."

Catrina frowned as she thought up something cold and calculating to say to make this official. "As far as I'm concerned, when I stop bleeding, this entire mess will be over."

Casey doubted that and didn't hesitate to say so. "If that's what you believe."

She ignored her. "I'm not talking to him anymore."

I believe that one. Casey laughed because she knew that Catrina was serious. "You don't have to be that drastic."

Catrina shot her a look. "That is not drastic. I wanna be through with this and him."

Tonight she would go out, check the neighborhood to see who was having a dollar party, and enjoy herself like there was nothing on her mind. She couldn't have everybody talking about her like she didn't exist. There'd been entirely too much talk about David having broken up with her and in turn, made her hide out. There were things to prove. That's what she set out to do. And if she just happened to see David, then she would just happen to ignore him.

PART TWO

Letting Go of Yesterday

Saw it all as if it were part of a dream

Except then I remembered I lived through it

So what does that mean

I'm strong, I survived

And yes, I'm still living

But damn, I look back

And all I can do is remember

They say to forget it and just let it go

But that gets me confused

'Cause the past is all I know

Catrina Price 2001

Chapter Four
Big Girls Now

May 2001

Casey

Lazy mornings were what she'd dreamed of since childhood, Casey realized. She had yet to reach the point where she was able to enjoy any of them. Between her busy schedule of taking summer courses in Art History at Temple University to earn credits toward her senior year, completing a certificate degree program in Interior Design, and styling hair, Casey barely had time to close her eyes for a good night's sleep. At twenty-one-years-old lying around in bed was still a distant dream.

Casey did, however, make time for other indulgences like shopping, reading, an occasional date, some mild partying and although styling hair was a job; Casey enjoyed it like free time. The freedom of determining her own work schedule made her an entrepreneur and she was very proud of her self-employment. Daemon had converted their basement into a full service salon equip with everything she needed to wash, curl, straighten, perm, style, and braid hair. It financed her weekly shopping trips and her recent addiction to shoes.

Both Catrina and Briannah had chosen to attend universities outside of the state of Pennsylvania leaving her to figure out her way through college life without either of them. Their separation had left her shaken and lost without them for the first year and some of the second but by the third she'd discovered enough about herself to exist happily without them.

Adults, Casey thought to herself. Over the course of their college years, they'd all become adults. Both Catrina and Briannah had graduated only weeks before. Catrina from Howard University with a degree in Institutional Management with a minor in Marketing and Briannah from Savannah Art and Design with a business degree in Sales and Marketing along with an Art degree in Fashion Design.

She could barely hold back her excitement for them to adjust to their new adult lives with jobs, bills and some overdue girl time. Catrina had started working at The Downtown Marriott as a Sales and Marketing Representative; living out her passion for event planning. Briannah was pregnant with her and Tyree's first child and they were engaged to be married.

Life, she thought, really couldn't get any better. Serena had moved to Virginia during her third semester at Temple University after marrying Jonathan Tilghman, an active duty Army man. Though she missed Serena the way a child missed their mother, she was happy for her. Casey smiled as she recalled the whirlwind romance that had Serena falling head deep in love after many years of taking care of both Daemon and her as a single parent.

Casey, sighed as her thoughts turned to Daemon. Happiness was not something she could claim to have achieved with him. They resided in the same residence but lived separate lives. He made a point to stay out of her way, Casey knew. It proved easy to do with him working in his auto mechanic shop and setting up and maintaining various business ventures. His entrepreneurial investments included a music production studio, rental properties left to him by his grandmother, and two food vending trucks. He had plans on opening a full service hair salon within the next year. All that kept him busy and away from her.

Along with all his women, Casey reminded herself.

She turned on the bathroom stereo to play R&B singer, Kelly Price's title track from her "*Mirror Mirror*" album. The song told the story of how she felt for Daemon and his resolve to never touch her or look at her in any way that did not exude that he was a brother figure and nothing more. Her own resolve was just as solid as his but in the end she hoped that his would falter. Casey had no intention of giving up on him.

She adjusted the volume on the stereo so the music would drown out the sound of the water as she slipped into the shower and began singing off key. The song was on replay because it was currently her favorite. When she favored something she didn't let it go easily.

"Case, I would like talk to you when you're out of the shower," Daemon said angrily, pounding on the bathroom door.

There was no answer. He could hear the music blasting and realized that she couldn't hear him. Annoyed, he opened the bathroom door. Immediately, the scent of what had become her signature scent; Lancome's *Miracle* hit his senses causing him to reassess his plan.

"Casey, I'm talking to you," he said, glad that he couldn't make out her body parts through the shower curtain.

Calm down, girl, and get your senses together. "What?" she shouted back when she knew her voice was reliable.

As Daemon turned the stereo off, the shower curtain whipped open, giving him a wide view of what he'd been waiting to see again for years. Her chocolate body had filled out more, her breast had grown at least a cup size in his mind. Both her waist and stomach still flat and trim. Her hips were fuller and had curves for days. They both froze, watching one another. Casey's brown eyed gaze slid down his body and settled on his crotch.

Yeah, he want me, she thought convinced that his erection was due to seeing her butt-ass naked. Seductively, she lifted her eyes to his and smiled before she pulled the curtain closed.

Surely he couldn't take that long look at her long, thick, naked body and not want it. After turning off the water, she stuck her hand out for a towel and was surprised when Daemon grabbed her arm and tugged her from the shower.

She frowned. "What?" she asked breathlessly. Being this close to him had its advantages, she suspected. But having him look at her this way, with disapproval, couldn't be a good thing.

"Get dressed and come down to the office," he ordered pushing a towel at her.

"Hhmp," she huffed with a roll of her eyes. Disappointment swimming in her eyes, Casey snatched her arm away from him and murmured, "You can kiss my ass, Daemon."

At twenty-one she proved to be more of a problem now than she had when she was younger. While he wished that she would hurry up and wrap the towel around her body, his erection did not.

"Enough people have been kissing your ass, Case baby, now get dressed and meet me downstairs," he ordered.

41

He does that so well, she thought. "Whatever," she responded. Angrily, she began to wrap the towel around her body. "I don't need this shit from you today, D. I really don't. Do I have to remind you that I'm not your responsibility?" she inquired with a gleam in her eyes.

Moving her body in what she knew he considered his personal space was a calculated move and one she hoped she'd be rewarded for. She leaned closer and whispered in his ear, "Yeah, you remember."

His hands went to her waist. It haunted him daily that at his whim she could be his, that he could have her, if he wanted her, and to know that he never would.

Laughing, she pulled away and circled around him to get out of the bathroom.

"You are my responsibility," he murmured more to himself than to her. He'd forgotten that once, but he wouldn't again.

"I am not and I won't let you forget it," she shouted back. The slam of her bedroom door was next.

The temptation to go after her was there but he suppressed and tapered it down, like he'd done his earlier anger. She'd gotten him so worked up he'd nearly forgotten why she was receiving a royal summons in the first place. Then again, that would've been hard. She paraded different guys around him at every given opportunity. They hadn't interested him until he happened to overhear what went on with these men. He didn't like it one bit and couldn't wait to spell it out for her in big bold capital letters.

Catrina

The loud shrill of the telephone had twenty-one-year-old Catrina Price jumping nervously from her sleep to grab it off the hook. Her voice husky from sleep, she answered, "Hello?"

"Did I wake you up?" a male voice questioned. She recognized the voice but couldn't identify it in her sleepiness.

"Who's this?" she asked, her mind still filled with haze from the night before.

Clearing her throat, Catrina went to roll over onto her back and found herself pressed against a hard male body. Squeezing her eyes

42

shut, she remembered. David, he'd stopped by the night before to catch a movie and dinner with his brother and Chantel. Somehow they never made it to the movie theater. He ended up staying the night and a very long night it had been, if her memory served her correctly.

She winced, it did. Times like this reminded her of that New Year's Eve party in ninety-eight when she'd decided to speak to him again after two years of ignoring him. Coming to the decision had been anything but easy. The hardest thing being her having to bite back her pride to do it. Since he'd made several attempts over the first year to reconcile their broken relationship she didn't think that he would see it as a problem.

They'd been at Casey's house and she'd been debating over the idea since her last relationship had ended. She sat in a corner watching David and his date fawn all over him. She could tell that he hated it. The woman in her had hated the tingle of jealousy she'd felt.

"I thought you weren't coming," Briannah had said to her friend after having observed her watch David. She had done enough staring in that direction as well since Tyree sat there with David discussing business opportunities.

After continuous trying on his part, Tyree had convinced Briannah that they would be good together.

She'd frowned. "Case is my best friend and I certainly wouldn't miss this party because of him." It had been as if the party around them had stopped despite all of the noise that had been fluttering about.

"Come on, it's been a long ass time. And if it was just about him cheating on you, you would have been just dropped this. He's been asking about you and how you like school."

She'd been right. It had been over two years. "Maybe he should just ask me himself." She took a sip of the Bacardi Breezer she'd been drinking.

Briannah's eyebrows had arched at the news causing her to frown. "So where'd the Cat get this new attitude?"

Catrina had shrugged. "He's good in bed."

"What? Are you the hell crazy?" she asked even as she spied Casey flirting with Daemon. Catrina had laughed.

43

"I'd rather the two of you get back together," Briannah had said, even though she'd been very adamant that they break up. "Not use him for sex, heffa."

"Bri, don't go there with me. Plus, he was good at it."

Briannah had shaken her head. "You know that it's all or nothing with him—"

Why is it always about what he wants? she'd wondered. He wanted her, dammit, and he'd go by her terms.

"Not this time. It'll be my way." She'd be in control.

"I still say that it's a mistake"

"What's a mistake?" Casey had joined the conversation. "What are you two hussies talking about?"

"Your best friend is thinkin' about sleepin' with Dave."

Casey's face had lit up. She always had been the romantic. "Y'all gettin' back together?"

"Sleep with him, Case baby. Not a relationship," Briannah had explained.

Casey had frowned then. Disapproval had been written all over her face. A virgin, Casey believed that you only shared yourself in that intimate way if you loved that person you shared those intimacies with.

"Don't say anything," Catrina had warned.

"I just don't want you stressed out over him again." Casey had stated. Their break-up had cause Catrina to move with her grandmother in New Jersey for Catrina's last year of high school.

"I think I can handle myself," she returned.

Casey had decided to change the subject since her best friend had a hard head. She knew that hard heads made soft behinds. After scanning the room she found where Briannah's eyes were glued, she had her next target.

"So, Briannah I heard that you blacked Nyimah's eye."

"I did."

"I'm going to go talk to Dave," Catrina had announced.

He was there with Tyree discussing his favorite thing. "I'm tellin' you that this company is going to make tons of money. Stock per share is only-" David stopped dead in his tracks when Catrina walked up and began talking.

"Excuse me. Hi, Ty" Then she looked at David and had

swallowed hard. "Can I speak with you for a minute?"

He remained silent, had been in shock from hearing the first words directed to him in over two years.

He'd scratched his head when Catrina added, "In private."

David nodded anyway and had followed her into the kitchen. "I thought that it was time that I stopped being drastic. I just wanted to bury everything that happened before."

Assured that she must have been under the influence of something really powerful he had asked, "Catrina, are you serious?"

Taking his reaction as rejection, Catrina continued to hold her head high. She leaned back on one of the counters. "Yes, I'm serious. I just thought that it would be pointless for us to continue to ignore each other when we have the same circle of friends. Maybe I was wrong," she added when he stared blankly. This is such a mistake, she had been thinking, losing her heart to continue. "Yeah, I can see now that it was," she responded when he remained silent. She made a moved to leave the kitchen, but he grabbed her before she could make her dignified exit.

"No, just give me a minute to process this," he'd told her, bringing her around to stand in front of him. "You just decided that I can be talked to, and you thought that I would just fall into line."

Catrina stepped closer to him and lifted her pleading eyes to his. "That's not all I want."

David took a cautious step back and dropped her arm. "Whoa, I must be the fuck dreamin'."

"David, I need to be honest with you," she had explained. "I'm over what happened between us. And that's why I'm able to come to you with what I have to say now." Her heart had been pounding in her chest as each word fell from her lips.

"And that would be?"

"I thought that we could be friends and that maybe we could sleep together."

She would never get over the look on his face when he said, "You want me to fuck you?"

She had laughed. "Yes. Now that I've said it, I'll let you think about it for a while."

David had grabbed her again. "Naw, stand here. You don't

speak to me for two years and four months, and the first words that you basically say to me are can we fuck?" he had exploded.

At that point she had raised her eyebrows and didn't say anything, because she took heed to his grabbing warning.

She then half listened to him rant about her being stubborn and hardheaded. When she through listening to him, she had told him to sit down and kindly asked him to shut up.

They had in that time discussed how their relationship would be.

It was at this point left open if either of them were following the rules and outline they'd agreed on back then.

"It's Mike," the strong male voice said, disrupting old memoires.

Catrina opened her eyes.

Oh shit, I forgot, she thought. "Hey, Mike, what's up?"

"I thought that you were gon' to come down last night?" he questioned.

"Mike, baby, I forgot. I was up all night with Chantel. She and Chris had a fight last night. She was a wreck," she added.

"How 'bout I shoot up dere and hang out with you for a while before I gotta be to work," he suggested.

Catrina rolled her eyes. "I'm sorry, but I promised Case and Briannah that we would get together and do the girl thing. We haven't been out since my graduation," she explained.

He sighed. "Well, can we hook up later on, den?"

Catrina frowned. "Not sure. We may end up just kicking it."

Mike cleared his throat. "When you gon' just kick it with me?" he asked angrily.

Never. "I'ma call you," she led him on.

"You make sure you do that."

Because it was more like an order than anything, she laughed. "I'll talk to you," she responded before hanging up.

"Damn, that nigga don't give you time to get up?" David growled, opening his eyes.

Catrina sucked her teeth and prepared herself for his surly morning mood. "It really doesn't matter now. I'm up, and he might just stop by, so you have got to go," she informed him, making the attempt to get out of the bed.

David grabbed her arm, and pulled her back. Before she could

46

protest she found herself pinned beneath his hard body. David watched as annoyance flashed in her hazel eyes and found himself stifling a chuckle when Catrina tried to push him off her. Proving to be faster, he took hold of her arms, cuffed them at the wrist, and put them over their heads.

"I keep telling you that I don't like being brushed off." With that said, he began planting kisses along the column of her neck, whispering invitations into her ear.

"Dave," she spoke, her voice as clear as it could have been under the circumstances. "I don't have time to play games with you. Mike could be on his way here in a—"

Continuing his sweet assault, he murmured, "Fuck that nigga." Then placing a kiss on her lips, he looked her straight in the eyes and said, "I'm here, and I'm not leavin' 'til I get ready, so get used to it."

Catrina frowned instantly. She hated when he was territorial. She found it annoying and unreasonable. It would've been different if he had a right to be, she mused. "I don't like the macho shit, so just drop it and get the fuck off me." She bucked beneath him.

David chuckled. "It's like that?" he inquired innocently after letting her arms go. It had to be her decision.

"Yes, it's like that. You're involved with someone else." It was funny that she never forgot it when it suited her own purposes.

"Well, you know what you gotta do, right?"

Frustrated, she wriggled more insistently, because he was still atop of her. "Don't start this shit again."

Just recently he had begun to press her about being in a relationship with him and for that, she wasn't ready. Her heart wasn't ready.

"Tell me that every time I'm inside you, you're not thinking of finding ways to keep me there. That I'm not in your head when I'm nowhere around," he pressed. He kissed her hard before the expected denial came from her lips.

Of their own accord, her legs parted, accepting him there. The words he murmured had her hips arching upward, seeking his. Sex with him always made her weak and vulnerable. At that moment she couldn't think, but moaned as he slid his hands beneath her bottom to lift her to him as he slowly slid into her.

"Tell me that it's not mine, that you're not mine whenever I want you and I'll leave you alone right now," he urged.

Catrina didn't attempt to argue; the truth would not be questioned. If he wanted her in his bed, he had her there. They both knew it.

David's hazel eyes bore in to hers, challenging her. Catrina closed her eyes first, breaking their connection, making him angry. Roughly, he pushed her legs up, his fingers biting into her thighs as he began to take the only thing she seemed to give him freely. The way he saw it, Catrina was his, even if she hadn't realized it yet.

What she did realize was that he was once again pushing for something that she wasn't ready to give. Though she didn't like the motive for his attention, she couldn't help the traitorous spiking of blood running through her veins.

"Dave," she murmured in pleasure.

He stared down at her and kissed her lips. Slowing his pace, he breathlessly whispered, "Don't fight it so hard, bey. Just be with me."

Since she needed to be, Catrina arched upwards and reached for his hands to complete their link. Fingers linked, eyes locked, and hearts beating against one another they both murmured small admissions of wanting.

Casey

It was twenty minutes later when Casey stuck her head through Daemon's office door. The neutral tones of the walls and the dark furniture represented the man. He was calm like the ivory with yellow undertones. His moods were dark like the mahogany color of much of his furniture.

The first few days of constant sun caused his golden skin to tan a shade darker than usual. The fresh haircut complemented his handsome face. She smiled as she thought that he reminded her of a lighter version of Idris Elba; an actor from a BBC soap opera she'd recently started watching.

"I'm going out so don't take up too much of my time," she told him, taking a seat across from his cherry oakwood desk.

Hadn't he calmed down? Daemon questioned himself as he watched her quietly. The sight of her thick, five-eight inch frame barely clothed in something he supposed she thought resembled a normal shirt and capri pants. Something Briannah made for her, he was sure. The top was backless and dipped low in the front to show off the swell of her breast. The pants were simple, black, and form-fitting ending mid-calf being met by the straps of her high-heeled sandals.

Casey cleared her throat. "Are you going to tell me what the hell you want, or are you going to continue giving me an unsolicited critique on my looks?" She crossed her legs and sat straight up, causing her breasts to jut out and smiled. "I have to say that I prefer you to look."

In response, Daemon rubbed his temples. She was pressing her luck. "Case, I'm telling you, all this running round with these different niggas has got to stop," he told her

A smile flirting around her pouty mouth, she asked, "Why are you jealous?"

"No, I'm not. But if you go round here actin' like a whore you'll get labeled as one."

Since being a whore was far from what she was, Casey laughed. "I can do whatever I want to do. And if that means going out with someone who works for you, I will. He wanted to take me out; shit, I wanted to get treated. That's more than I can say for somebody else."

Daemon sucked his teeth. He hadn't expected her to be offended about the whore comment, and she didn't disappoint him.

It frustrated the hell out of him. "Don't make me fuck somebody up, is all I'm saying."

"Here we go with that big brother shit. And we both know that the last thing you would like to be is my brother. In any case, I'm an adult; I contribute to the bills we incur. I hate being your responsibility. Your mom did not leave saying Daemon make sure you take care of Casey."

"She did and you are my damn responsibility. I don't know how many times we gotta go over it. Just as soon as you get it in your head the better things will be."

Casey didn't want to ruin her good mood debating the never ending subject of her relationship with him, when he continually proved to be unmovable; and undeniably stubborn. Daemon's refusal to her advancements did not discourage her. "Whatever, if that's what you tell yourself to help you stay away from me, that's fine, D. I'm not gon' throw myself at you— that's beneath me. You do you and I'll continue to do me."

Daemon frowned and considered that. "These niggas got you thinking pretty high of yourself, huh?" he asked, leaning back in his chair. "How 'bout you tell me about your date with Raheem."

She smiled. "Let's just say it was an experience."

"The date? Or you ending up in his bed afterward?" His jaws clenched in jealousy as he replayed that morning's scene in his mind.

Raheem sure did go a little far in his storytelling, Casey thought.

She knew he expected her to be upset, but she wasn't going to give him the satisfaction. She would play it smart and be cool and distant. "I knew it had to be bad for you to call me down to the big bad office and all."

Frustrated, Daemon's patience snapped. "Casey, I'm tryna be real patient with you when I want to choke the shit out of you. You think that this is a fuckin' joke," he accused, standing up.

With a negligent shrug, she said, "I'm not laughing, D."

"You weren't there when that nigga walked in talkin' bout what y'all did."

Casey could hear traces of hurt in his words, but he hid them well. "Do you have any idea what they were saying about you? In my place of business?"

"I figure the normal stuff people say about their latest conquest."

She's such a pain in the ass, he thought. "What happened at his house?" he demanded to know.

"Nothing. We talked." She turned her face away from his, took a little time studying her manicured nails before lifting her gaze back to his and continued. "Ate and entertained ourselves."

Daemon trapped her in her chair by standing in front of her then caging her in with his arms. "Define entertain."

Casey frowned, a little threatened by his anger. "I don't have to explain anything to you. You'n wanna fuck with me, fine. But I will not have you dictating proper date etiquette to me. So back up," she said, pushing at him.

Daemon caught her arm. "Case, Baby, you don't know what you're playin' at. If you keep it up, you're going to end up getting hurt."

If her eyes could have rolled in the back of her head, they would have, she thought. "Yes, so you keep saying."

"Casey, it's hard to turn you away when I know what it'd be like between us," he admitted letting go and backing away from her.

Composed, Casey stood up. "I'm trying to run slow to let you catch me, but if you don't, someone else will." Casey didn't say anything else just left the office.

Girl's Day Out

At the last minute Casey had suggested they go to the King of Prussia Mall instead of going into Center City to shop and browse the stores along Market and Walnut Streets. It meant she had the urge to spend money.

Noting their friend's black mood, both Catrina and Briannah realized that it had to have something to do with Daemon and figured a way to bring him up since their friend hadn't said a word about him. That was a very rare occurrence.

"So, Case, how was your date last night?" Briannah asked casually.

Casey shrugged. Daemon had in fact affected her mood. "It was okay: I only went out with Raheem to make D jealous," Casey explained.

"So did it work?" Catrina asked.

"Yeah, it did. He barged into the bathroom, mind you while I'm in it and demanded that I meet him in his office. Apparently, Raheem went a little too far when he was telling the other guys what happened. Anyway, y'all, I was butt ass naked and D didn't want me. Every guy I know wants to be with me and I can't even get him to admit that. Let's go in here." She gestured to the store they were passing.

"Tyree told me what dude said and just how upset D was," Briannah said. "He's set on not corrupting you. Maybe you should just be happy that he loves you enough not to take advantage," she added.

Casey shook her head. "Take advantage of me!" she joked loudly causing mall walkers to turn and stare. "I'm not giving up. And I am not the naïve young girl that everybody seems to think I am. I can handle adult relationships; I've had practice."

Catrina laughed as she considered. "You don't have the kind of aloof attitude or the coldness in you to pull something like that off. He'd break your heart into a billion itty, bitty pieces."

Briannah frowned. "And I guess you'd be an authority on aloofness and coldness, wouldn't you, Trina?" she questioned her friend in Casey's defense while trying to decide between a pale yellow Armani Tee and a pastel pink one.

Catrina arched her brow at Briannah's sarcasm. "Yeah, I would be. These niggas don't be worried 'bout me loving them, so I don't be worried 'bout them loving me."

Casey stood in front of her. "I know who you worried 'bout loving your ass," she said with a smirk before she walked away to follow Briannah who was already randomly picking out clothes.

"You can say that again." She tuned in briefly, lifting her face from the rack.

Catrina rolled her eyes and went over to them. "And what is that supposed to mean?"

Casey shot her a look over her shoulder. "Don't act like you'n know who we're talking about, honey."

Catrina bristled. Now was not the time to bring up that man. "Whateva, y'all."

"Yeah, we know it's whateva," Casey laughed. "Y'all been kicking it for a minute, and we know that you ain't sleeping with nobody else. So what's up?" Casey pressed.

"Monogamy is not his strong suit. So let's just cut the convo short. I do not- absolutely do not want to talk about Dave or what I have going with him." She had no idea what it was at this point.

Briannah cleared her throat and Casey just chuckled. "Monogamy isn't your strong suit either, sweetie."

Catrina had to give that one to her and laughed with a shrug. "Weren't we discussing you and D?"

"Yeah, we were," Briannah interjected, mentally calculating the total price of her purchases. "But we gon' have to finish while we eat. I'm hungry as hell," she announced, patting the mound that

52

used to be her very flat stomach. Or at least it had been six and a half months before.

"Yeah, get her slim ass something to eat. You look like a damn stick with a pea stuck in the middle," Catrina laughed with a point to Briannah's stomach.

Offended, Briannah stuck her nose in the air and began walking towards the register. "I'll have y'all know that I gained twenty-five pounds," she huffed, pushing her selections toward the cashier. As long as Tyree thought she still looked good was all that mattered.

They ate at T.G.I. Fridays and watched in awe as Briannah devoured all her food and some of theirs. There, Casey came up with yet another plan to make Daemon jealous, as her friends; Briannah and Catrina agreed to help her.

Chapter Five
It's My Party

Casey

There was no surprise in finding Daemon engrossed in paperwork in his office when she arrived home. She just stood in the doorway and watched him quietly. A smile curved her lips. He was, Casey thought, the perfect person to represent the African American male with his dark head of waves bent in deep concentration as his cinnamon-colored eyes scanned the paperwork neatly stacked in a pile before him.

After realizing that he wasn't going to acknowledge her presence, Casey reluctantly knocked. The dream of him lifting his head and finding her there in a sexy pose shattered.

Without looking up from his work he said, "Wassup?" His voice husky in a way Casey considered extremely sexy.

She shrugged and rolled her eyes. "I just came in to see what you were doing."

This time he did look up. "Working."

"That's funny, D," she allowed.

There was no way he would be able to concentrate on ordering car parts or scheduling labor hours while she was present, but he didn't want to rush her away. "Did you have a nice time?"

"Shopping is therapeutic; you should try it sometime. It may loosen you up a little," she advised to annoy him and added to the annoyance by taking a seat. When she saw that she had, she continued. "Bri's pregnancy is progressing well. The slim hussy gained like twenty something pounds, and she could use about ten more." She laughed.

Daemon frowned and made a gesture towards the papers on his desk. "I know. I really need to get back to work."

"Oh, am I distracting you?" She crossed one leg over the other.

Hell yeah, he thought. "Yeah, you are, but irritating is more like it."

Irritating? I bet. She made a smirk, stood up, and attempted to whisk away any wrinkles in her pants. "You use your term, I'll use mine. I just dropped in to remind you about the get together tonight."

"What get together?"

"I knew you weren't going to remember," she chastised although she'd just planned it an hour or two ago. "I told you about it last week," she lied. "You gon' be here?"

"Yeah, I guess. Who'd you invite?" he interrogated sure that this was another attempt to parade guys in his face.

"You have to be here to find out," she told him, then made the decision to work him for a few minutes. So she sauntered over to his desk and took a seat on the edge.

Taking this interruption as his long overdue break, Daemon figured he'd indulge her with conversation. He sat up and pushed his chair away from his desk just in time to see her tongue dart out her mouth to moisten her lips. He smiled. "You gon' let me get back to my work, or do I have to work around you?" he questioned, contemplating what her reaction would be if he finally took what she so blatantly offered. Daemon doubted that she ever thought that he would and was tempted to just to surprise her.

"I'd rather you worked with me. Right here on your desk if you prefer," she challenged. *Fuck it,* she thought. There was no way that she was going to shy away this time. Even if her desired results didn't come out of her little experiment, she'd get to irritate the hell out of him. "You're thinkin' 'bout it," she teased, scooting her body over on the desk to settle in front of Daemon.

"You're sitting on my work."

Seductively, she tilted to the side and lifted her behind just a little to allow him to retrieve his papers. When he reached for them, Casey leaned down and whispered, "I'd rather be sitting on you. Take a break and let me drive you a little crazy," she requested.

You already are, he said to himself.

"Let me drive you crazy, D," she insisted, leaning toward him provocatively. She raised her hand to brush his golden skin but found her wrist deftly caught in his grasp.

Tempted beyond reason was more like it. What man could ignore this continuously and successfully for any period of time?

Daemon stood up, pushed his chair back, and then tilted Casey's chin, letting his lips descend upon hers.

Finally, Casey, breathed as she closed her eyes. *He's giving in,* she thought reaching up to wrap her arms around his neck as his expert lips devoured hers.

"I really shouldn't," he murmured into her mouth while bringing her lower body into closer contact with his.

"You should," she breathed. *Oh, God, you should.* "Daemon," she whispered when he lowered his forehead to hers.

Daemon took deep breaths for composure as her hips ground themselves seductively against him.

"Casey, we can't..." he began to explain.

Shaking her head in denial and tapering down the hurt that rose inside her at the same time, Casey kissed his lips before pushing him away. "I know, but that doesn't stop me from wanting to. Or you," she told him.

As if he didn't already know that to be true, he sighed and backed away from her.

Her lips were swollen from his kisses and now lacked the seductively smile it wore upon entering. "One day we'll finish this," she assured him.

There was far too much sexual tension between them to think or suggest otherwise. She'd simply bide her time until then.

Daemon didn't respond, ashamed that she'd been able to penetrate his defenses against her. "I'll only end up hurting you, Case baby, and I'm trying my hardest not to. So if you keep this up you'll figure out just what I mean," he warned. "Now go, so I can finish my work." *Or try to.*

Not one to dwell on failure, she found triumph in being able to break his control as she eased off his desk and kissed him playfully on the cheek.

Daemon grabbed her arm. "You just don't know," he mumbled.

Casey chuckled as she walked towards the door and then shot him a look over her shoulder that was designed to bring weaker men to their knees and smiled. "I plan on finding out," she informed him. Then she was gone.

Daemon sank into his chair and pulled it up to his desk and stared at the wall outside his office.

Briannah and Tyree

"Bri, I told you to stop pumping up her heart like that," Tyree told his fiancée as they settled in his SUV.

They were on their way to the get together Case had insisted on giving at the last minute. Under Briannah's influence, Tyree surmised. Whatever they'd cooked up was bound to fail. His friend was entirely too serious in his quest to keep Casey untouched by him.

"She wants him. All I did was tell her to go after him," she defended herself. "Is anything wrong with that?" she wanted to know.

Tyree laughed. "Yes, there is. She's living off the encouragement that she gets from y'all asses. These antics of hers not gon' get her anywhere."

"Oh, yes they will. She's come at him in a very grown up way and he hasn't responded so naturally he'll respond in the way that all men who covet do."

Tyree shook his head at that one. "Playing. I was there this morning when Raheem started that shit 'bout what happened between him and Case." A smile danced around his lips when the memory came. "I think D walked in the door somewhere around him wanting Case to wrap her mile long legs around his waist. And that was all he said-"

"Nothing happened between them. The man was probably just expressing simple wishes where Case is concerned. It's not his fault D can't handle simple conversation," Briannah stated, rubbing her belly where her daughter kicked. "A conversation that he wasn't even included in."

Tyree cleared his throat. "I ain't even tryna hear that shit. I was ready to jump all over boah. How he figure he could say that shit 'bout Case in D's shop?" Tyree shook his head at the thought. "That nigga stupid," he added stopping for a red light. He took advantage of the stop and reached over to put his hands on his baby.

"She gon' be grounded 'til she get out of college," he said and got a kick for it.

Briannah laughed. "You're such a fabulous daddy and all; she'll be a good girl. We probably won't have any trouble."

He looked at her. "That's probably what your mom said."

She sucked her teeth. "Ain't nothing wrong with me."

In agreement with that he nodded and said, "You my baby," and added a quick kiss.

"I know. So what's up with D? He want her or not?"

"He does, but he won't do anything about it."

Not if I can help it, Briannah thought. She wasn't trying to hear any excuses. In her world, if a female wanted a male, and that male wanted that female they made an effort to get together.

"So I was right in helping her," she concluded.

Catrina

The drive from David's Center-City apartment was proving to be an amusement in itself. David's sense of humor kept her laughing. Though, she couldn't quite pinpoint that as the one reason she enjoyed spending time with him, Catrina admitted to herself that she did. She reflected on the amount of time they'd been spending together for the past few months and attempted to push the thought of the happiness it brought to her away. At that present moment they happened to be talking about Casey and Daemon.

"He is not going to be happy 'bout this," David told her.

"I pretty much figured that out already," Catrina responded. She laughed even though the slightest feeling of him holding her hand while rubbing his thumb absentmindedly over her fingers made her nervous.

Be unattached, Catrina coached silently and closed her eyes, determined to relax and enjoy.

"It'll be fun seeing Case baby do her thing," David admitted.

"Yeah, she invited Jermaine to make D jealous. You know how he clings like a puppy dog."

"You sure she not... well, you know?"

Catrina grinned and shook her head. "I'm sure."

"Well, it might just work. Daemon is the jealous type."

"Aren't all men?" she inquired nonchalantly, thinking back to the way he'd acted that very morning.

"I'm not. If I were, you'd be mine to keep," he said, playfully lifting her hand to his lips for a kiss

That had Catrina's eyes snapping open. He was doing it again, she thought. Hadn't she just said that she enjoyed being with him because he didn't expect anything in return? Based on his last jealous tantrum, he was proving her wrong.

"We're talking 'bout D and Case, not us," she managed, snatching her hand from his. "And I do believe that you messed that up on your own."

It was apparent to Catrina that her anger was due more to the irritation she felt for herself, just for wishing that she was his, rather than with him at the moment. Nothing was wrong with it, if she never vocalized those feelings; they were her own to keep and harbor.

What about Shay? Catrina thought of the current girl who was claiming exclusive ownership to him. *How would she feel if she found out about us?*

Not wanting to press, because he knew she would react like a venomous snake trapped in a corner, he said, "So you say. In any case, I'm content with what we have and give me a little credit if I feel confident that I'm the only man making love to you," he said, knowing it would annoy her.

It did.

"Trust me, you're only a substitute."

Taking her hand again, he said, "You scared I could be your Mr. Right?"

"Negro, please," she snorted, shaking him off her.

"Yeah, you know you love me," he teased, slanting his sexy hazel eyes her way.

If only you knew. Catrina shook her head to clear it. "You think. What's up with you and your girl?"

"Nothing. Same thing that's up with you and all your dudes."

David's arrogance annoyed her. He was always certain when it came to other guys' place in her life, they had none. It seemed to him that her heart would always belong to him even if at the present time she was acting stingy with it.

"How'd we get on this?"

He frowned. "You actin' all stank-a-dank 'bout being with me."

"David, you have a girl. You don't need me."

I do, bey, so bad. If you'd only let me show you, he thought.

59

Instead he said, "Why you actin' like this? I thought we were cool."

"Things are cool. We're together tonight and were together last night," *the night before and the one before that*, "but a few days don't mean permanence. There is nothing permanent about us."

She's being snotty, he thought. "Here we go with this shit again," he murmured to himself.

"Yeah, here we go with this shit again," she started. "I'm not your woman, you're not my man, so stop tryna act like it," she fumed, folding her arms over her chest like a stubborn child.

David didn't say a word to that but pulled over and cut the engine to the car.

Catrina closed her eyes and shook her head. *Tantrum number two*, she thought. *This is his last.* If he couldn't accept her terms, then she'd just move on. Their relationship, or lack of was certainly counterproductive, in any case. Catrina took a deep breath, opened her eyes, and found him staring.

"I thought we had all this straight. If you're attempting to fence someone in, you're spending your time with the wrong person. I can't handle a relationship with you, David, not right now. Maybe not ever. So if you can't accept what I want this time around, we'll just go back to the way things were before."

Catrina could practically see the anger rising into his eyes, the fight in him to maintain his calm, cool, and collective personality.

Then she saw it explode.

"When you were ignoring me for two years?"

Catrina turned her nose up. Her pride would not allow her to cry, and she would not allow herself to be subjected to his convictions.

Most of it is his damn fault, ain't it?

Catrina looked out the window and saw an old woman in ratty clothing with a broken umbrella walking toward the car in the beating rain. Why, she wondered, would she prefer to be out there getting soak and wet in the tears of Mother Nature than to be stuck beside him in the close confines of the car?

"Look at me," she heard him say. "Don't I get an explanation?"

Her head whipped around. "Are you serious? You cheated on me. I didn't like it, plain and simple, and that was how I dealt with it."

60

Already, she'd said too much, Catrina knew. If he knew that she had a weakness for him, he'd use it to his advantage, use her vulnerabilities for him to break her. And that was something she wasn't giving anyone the opportunity to do, ever.

David swallowed the lump in his throat and said, "We're older now. Much more mature than either of us was six years ago. I don't know what you want me to say for something that happened such a long time ago. If you weren't over it, maybe you should have thought about it before you got at me." In his anger he made the last sentence sound so cold.

She sighed. "I don't want you to say anything. I'm not asking you for anything, Dave, not your heart, nothing." *You talk a good game, girl.*

"What if that's not enough for me?" He questioned, though he had agreed minutes before that he was content with their status.

It wasn't a question, she noted.

David's fingers were tense on the wheel now. He didn't for one second pretend to understand the game she seemed to be playing. One minute she claimed not to want anything he was offering and the next she was cuddled next to him in sleep. Just how indecisive could one woman be, he wondered. It worried him to have her talk this way when he wanted everything she was opposed to.

"Like I said, if you want that, you're with the wrong person," she told him directly.

"Bey," he said. Taking her face between his hands, David looked into her eyes. "Whatever it is that's holding you back from me, you might as well let it go. I want you. That's what I know."

He waited for her to let it, to speak about what he felt only she had a right to speak on. He wanted to hear the words from her mouth.

Catrina pulled her face away, determined not to be swayed by his calm touch or sincere words. The fact that he kept using their pet name for each other didn't make it any easier. He did it on purpose because he knew it agitated her, Catrina suspected.

"People get their feelings hurt when you make false promises. That's what I know."

"True enough," he agreed. "You're just scared though, bey. You're letting things that happened in our past rule what could

61

happen between us in the future."

Catrina shook her head. If she was so mature now, how come he made her feel as if she was confused about being in love?

"A lot of stuff happened in our past, Dave. You were my first everything." She laughed. "And you basically taught me a lesson....one that I'm not likely to forget."

"I'm serious about this. About us," he stated as a matter of fact.

Because she could see he was, she would remain distant. It seemed so easy for him to speak of reclaiming old love, and so hard for her to trust his words. "So you say," she murmured.

Progress, he thought as he watched her deal with the words he'd just given her. A smile appeared. Things would change. They had to. She was the one thing he wouldn't give up. So they'd do things her way. For now, he declared mentally. Time wasn't on his side. His personal and professional lives had never been so close to colliding until now.

Suddenly, Atlanta began to feel so far away. He had the choice of telling her about it, but talked himself out of it. David was well aware of how she thought. There'd be nothing to fight over. She wouldn't have given him the time of day after coming home had she known he would be moving come the end of July.

Resigned, David started the car and without a word to her pulled the car away from the curb.

In the silence, Catrina felt terrified. Just thinking about the 'what ifs' of this situation was bound to hurt. She trusted him, but yet was scared to entrust her heart to him.

Casey

The food, the mood, and the stage were set to bring Daemon to his knees. Candles burned to give the room a dim but yet an illuminated intimate feel. The voice of Philadelphia's own Neo-Soul artist Musiq Soulchild drifted from the surround sound system. Dressed casually in a pair of tight light blue designer jeans and an A/X tank top, Casey couldn't help but feel underdressed compared to the brown-skinned Indian looking female that clung to Daemon. Not that he seemed to notice anyone besides Karen with her short skirt that left nothing to anyone's imagination.

Deciding that Karen was entirely too comfortable in Daemon's personal space, Casey moved over to the stereo. She figured that the place could use music that was a little more upbeat. She was about to change it when *Love* began to play.

She stood there with her finger on the skip button as she dreamed of the love that the dreamy vocals spoke of and her eyes drifted to Daemon's one last time.

"You okay?" Jermaine, one of her many guy friends asked in his southern drawl. When he wrapped his arms around her waist, Casey allowed herself to lean into him. "Yeah, so what are we going to do tonight?" she asked him.

"Go back to my place, snuggle up under the covers, and watch a movie. And then I hold you until the sun comes up," he whispered.

"Sounds like a plan to me," she murmured, placing her hands over his.

She closed her eyes and took a deep breath. Why she couldn't just fall for a guy like him instead of having this heart wrenching feeling for Daemon was beyond her. Jermaine was the type of guy any smart girl would want. He was prime catch— nice, respectful, well educated, an athlete, and handsome— the type that had mamas watching out for gold diggers.

It was too bad she was using him. She felt bad about it. In the end, she'd find him a nice girl, Casey absolved.

Surprised, Jermaine asked, "Really?"

She turned her face up to his. "As long as holding me is all you have in mind," she answered.

"That's all I wanna do, cause it's all you wanna do." Jermaine turned her around to face him and smiled when her arms went around his neck.

Good answer. He is so damn sweet.

"Don't y'all think it's time to eat?" Daemon asked from behind them. Watching Casey kiss the guy was pushing him past his patience level.

Casey looked over at him. "We got three different kinds of wing dings, brought to y'all by Ms. Perfect herself. Hook Trina up with some business," Casey announced, walking back towards the kitchen.

Both Catrina and Briannah were about to follow when they

watched Daemon go in after her. Briannah sighed disappointed that she wouldn't be able to pick at the food before everyone else. Nosy as she was, that didn't last long when she thought about what might have been going on in the kitchen.

"And just what was all that about?" Daemon questioned, closing in on her.

"Nigga, cool out. My naïve self could mistake this for jealousy," she joked, not even turning to face him. Casey felt him behind her, caged in by his arms. "You're crowding me," she murmured. *Stay please.*

Fitting his hands against her waist, he said, "That's supposed to make me back away?"

Enjoying the rubbing of her stomach, Casey all but moaned, "No, but the fact that you have a female waiting in the other room for you should."

"Case, I keep telling you not to push my buttons," he warned angrily. All he could see in his mind was Casey wrapped around the guy. He didn't like the boiling feeling in his gut.

Casey stopped what she was doing. "Let me get this straight." She savored in his fingers massaging her stomach and lower back. "You get to cuddle with what's her name, but the minute I get comfortable with some guy, I have to put up with your shit?" She heard his sigh. "Why you fighting so hard?" she whispered.

"I'on know?" he admitted softly.

"I'm not gon' give up. When I want something, I get it."

Daemon tightened his grip. "I'on know, Casey. You asking for more than I've given anybody." It was true, since Tamika, there hadn't been one woman he'd dedicated himself to.

Casey turned in his arms and looked up at him. "I'm not asking you for anything that you're not capable of giving. I love you and I'd be less than a woman if I settled for a man who didn't love me back."

Daemon understood the seriousness of her statement. "I'm not gon' lie, Casey, I wanna be your first, and I want you in my bed but I just don't know about the rest."

Casey shrugged. "One doesn't come without the other."

He already knew that. "Yeah, I know."

This was more than he'd ever admitted to before, so she took it as progress for now. Relishing in joy, she pressed a light kiss to his lips.

"No wonder I can't get nothing to eat," Briannah said finally, after having spied for a while. "I knew I'd find the two of you in here actin' up."

Daemon turned. "You were just hungry." He sent her an easy smile. "I guess I'll go," he said when Briannah started to laugh at the color that rose in his cheeks.

Casey joined in. "Think about what I said," she told him.

Daemon nodded and left them alone.

Chapter Six
Making Moves

Catrina

It was a beautiful day. The local forecast predicted eighty degree weather with no chance of rain. The sun was already shining, the birds were chirping, and all Catrina wanted to do was pull the covers over her head.

"Aunt Trinnnna?" Cinyah, her cousin Chantel and Chris' daughter's soft voice called from the other side of her bedroom door. The knock was very small and light.

"Come in," Catrina told her.

"Aunt Trina," she said, opening the door. "My mommy said to wake you up."

Disoriented, Catrina glanced at her alarm clock. It was quarter past eleven and had already gone off at seven to wake David up for work. "Aren't you supposed to be at school?" she asked the six-year-old.

Cinyah nodded. "I'm 'posed to be gettin' glasses today," she pouted, reluctant about the thought of having to wear them.

"Aww, baby, Mommy'll make sure that they're cute glasses," Catrina assured the child.

Poor baby, Catrina thought.

Cinyah had every Johnson family trait Catrina could think of: the light skin, their height, the mild hazel eyes, and the poor eyesight.

"Tell her I'll be down in a minute. And don't run."

Of course, she did anyway.

Sleepily, Catrina dragged her hand over her face. The morning was half gone already, she sighed and stretched. At least she had a couple hours before she had to be to work. Due to the mini vacation of the bride of the wedding she'd been planning for the last year, Catrina figured she'd earned the days of freedom granted by the

66

bride and groom to be. She also planned on enjoying it.

"Catrina! What the hell are you doing up there?" Her mother's voice shouted.

Catima Price was climbing the stairs by the time Catrina made it to her door.

"Ma, what are you doing here?"

Her mother never made unannounced visits. It was one of the reasons she didn't mind renting from her parents.

"We're supposed to be going to lunch today," Catima reminded her daughter.

Damn, that's right. "I'm so sorry, Ma. I forgot. I was up really late last night. The anniversary party from last night was a mess."

Catima narrowed her eyes. "That's fine, we can always go tomorrow, or whenever you can fit me into your busy schedule."

Catrina chuckled. "God, Ma, you know that I'd love to go to lunch with you. Could you try to make me feel anymore guilty?"

Catima smiled, and she withdrew a cigarette from her purse and was about to light it when she saw Catrina shaking her head.

"Not in here. I thought that you were trying to quit," Catrina said taking the cigarette from between her mother's fingers and disposing of it in her waste basket.

"I was, but your damn brother is working my nerves. All these girls he got calling the house and then he acting like he wants to start messing up in school."

Catrina frowned. Her sixteen-year-old brother, Terrance, was beginning to be lured away from the detailed path of her parents by the flash and excitement of the street life.

"What'd Daddy say?" Catrina asked.

Catima huffed in response. "You know your daddy. Got the boy in all these programs trying keep him focused, but Terry not trying hear that." Catima flagged it off. She knew how to deal with him.

"Ma, y'all spoil him so much. Stop giving him when he ain't acting right. Daddy shouldn't let him drive his car. You want me to talk to him?" Catrina was sure that she'd be able to straighten him out. She had in the past, she would be able to again.

Catrina moved around the room gathering her clothes as her mother continued to fill her in on her brother, thirteen-year-old sister, and the other current events in her family. Catrina shared her excitement and apprehensions regarding the wedding she'd all but planned down to the last detail. She dreamily shared her plans, and goals for Perfect Perceptions; the event management company she'd started during college.

Catima listened to her daughter because her own dreams for Catrina were great. She had watched Catrina immerse herself in school, work, internships, certification programs, and all the additional planning jobs to build her resume to make the framed business license hanging next to her college degree credible.

Twenty minutes after going into the bathroom, Catrina emerged wearing a trim beige business suit with matching Nine West sling back shoes.

Catima smiled. "Damn, I did teach you how to dress, didn't I?" she commented proudly. Catrina laughed and made her way to the telephone as it rang.

"Hello?" she answered.

"Bey? Are my glasses there?" David asked. He was having trouble going through his finance report without them.

She smiled, looked over at her dresser and said, "Yeah, they here."

"I'ma see if I can swing by and pick them up."

"No, you don't have come get them, me and my mom are coming down there to have lunch at McCormicks, so I can drop them off for you." Catrina smiled at the thought of all the numbers on his computer screen blurring together. David's current position at a downtown money management firm allowed him to follow through with his life's quest to produce and save as much money as he could. "How 'bout you meet us there and have lunch," she suggested on impulse.

"I'm on deadline to complete the expense reports from last month. But we can get together for a late dinner at my place." The intimacy of his tone suggested more.

Disappointed, she said, "I'm closing all week, so I guess whenever."

"Naw, I'ma see you tonight. I'll pick you up from work," he offered.

Catrina looked over at her mother. Catima's face remained

68

expressionless.

"Ma, you mind driving us?"

Catima arched her brow. "No," she answered.

"A'ight, don't be late, 'cause I'll leave with somebody else," she played.

"If you know what I'm trying get into tonight you not gon' leave 'til I get there."

Catrina laughed at that. "Is that a promise?"

Enjoying their afternoon play, David leaned back and twirled the telephone cord around his finger. It wasn't often that he could get her in this agreeable mood. After the other day, they needed this. "How's this for a promise. I'ma make you lose it."

She had no doubt that he would and turned away from her mother. "You know I'm with that."

"You gon' cook for me?" he inquired.

Catrina frowned at that idea, cooking after a long day of work would be the last time on her mind. "In your dreams," she told him.

"Yeah, and you naked. I want you to do that thing-"

As flush crept up her cheeks, she said, "My mom here and you are really going at it. All I'm gonna to say is, back it up."

"Oh, I'ma let you do that too, bey."

Chuckling, she said, "Bye, Dave" and clicked him off the phone.

When she turned around her mother was all in her face. "Really?"

Rolling her eyes, Catrina said, "Please don't start, Ma."

She would do the exact opposite, Catima thought. "Y'all are still with this back and forth shit. I don't see why you digging this hole for yourself."

Catrina felt her head. "Oh my God, I'm getting a headache. My personal business is my own. When and if I need your advice, I'll ask for it, Ma."

Catima narrowed her eyes. "No you didn't just say that. Not when you come crying to me about what that man doing and what he not doing with you, girl. Six years, and y'all still don't have claim on one another. What is wrong with you? You giving him every damn thing for free and not asking for nothing in return. You know what happen when you don't ask for nothing, right?" She didn't wait for an answer. "You don't get shit."

This could go on for hours, Catrina thought. David had always been a big issue between them. Her mother had been against them reestablishing their "relationship." At least she had been up until recently. Now her tune was changing to; 'when y'all gon' get together, or she'd want to know why they were sleeping together instead of dating. These were issues Catrina refused to acknowledge needed answers.

To ease her mind and heart at the thought of her mother thinking she was a complete whore, Catrina attempted to justify that they spent a multitude of time with one another, doing a variety of different things. Catrina, just didn't consider it dating. She had realized that David was her best friend. "Ma, I don't want to discuss it. I know what I'm doing," she told her mother which is the absolute opposite of how she felt.

"You know I love you, and I only want see you happy. So if being with him, however you're with him, makes you happy, then I'll deal with it."

"Thanks."

Catima sighed. "I know you love the damn boy anyway so y'all—"

"Ma, drop it. Dag." Catrina frowned. "I don't know who said I love him," she muttered.

Catima smiled. "I'm your momma; I know these things." She pulled her daughter into her arms for a hug.

Casey

Busy on the telephone, Casey talked the business of interior design with Briannah's grandmother, Nadia, who was a very good friend to the interior designer Casey wanted to apprentice with. She'd had an interview with the interior genius a week before and had yet to hear back from her. Casey had been sure that she'd at least have favor since the designer belonged to the same sorority, but even that hadn't worked. So she used what she had and called in for a favor of her own. And as usual Nadia had been able to pull a few strings and get her a second interview.

"So tomorrow I just take my portfolio down to her and let her look it over?" Casey paused while Miss Nadia spoke.

"Alright, now you make sure that you have your best work to show to her."

Casey smiled. "Yes, I understand that my work has to speak for itself. You've seen it Miss Nadia, you know I have potential to be great; otherwise, you wouldn't have put in a good word for me..."

"Well hopefully we can turn all that potential into a very rewarding career. Staging is something very new and fresh in the designing crowd, and you have the ability to do that. She'll be impressed with you."

"Thank you very much and I'll be sure to drop by the shop to see you," she told Nadia.

"You and the girls should stop by one day and we'll all have lunch. Love you sweetie, tell that young man I said Hi."

"Love you too. And I'll tell him."

That went well, Casey reflected. Briannah's grandmother and Catrina's aunt Chanel were both valuable resources when it came to the networking opportunities. She was finding that the saying, it's not what you know but who you know, was actually true. With the help of Chanel she'd been able to do a co-op at a prestigious designing firm in L.A. the previous summer. It had been an experience, and now she was ready for another one.

Looking down at her work, she sighed. "Time to get to work," she murmured. Minutes passed as she engrossed herself in her designs, choosing plans that contributed to her skill and scrapping ones that she considered had flaws. "Okay, so this, this, and this one, oh and this one too," she picked. Then she fell silent. She'd had her portfolio ready for days, so maybe it would be a mistake to change it at this late of a date. She frowned at it and then went with her initial instinct to make a few minor changes.

It was the light tapping on her door an hour later that had her glancing over at her clock. Time had passed so quickly.

"Come in," she called softly.

Daemon opened the door. "I wanted to see if you wanted to go catch something to eat with me. Nothing fancy. I was just gon' shoot up to Poor Tony's, and I thought it'd give us a chance to talk," he said, lingering in the doorway.

The first few days of constant sun caused his golden skin to tan a shade darker than usual. The fresh haircut complemented his handsome face. She smiled as she thought that he reminded her of a light skinned version of Idris Elba; an actor from a BBC soap opera she'd started watching.

Casey felt like dancing the gig. Hadn't she been telling everybody how it would happen for them soon? Now he was asking her out on a date. She frowned, she wouldn't call Poor Tony's the proper place for a first date, but they did have bomb ass baked macaroni and cheese as far as she was concerned.

Daemon laughed because she only responded to his question by nodding her head.

"You ready?" he asked.

"Just let me throw on some clothes."

"What you have on now is fine, Case. It's only Poor Tony's."

Casey thought about the small soul-food restaurant near Clearfield Street and mentally agreed that her sorority T-shirt, jeans, and Gucci flip flops would have to do.

They were silent as Daemon drove, only music played, filling Daemon's GMC Yukon Denali with the melodies of a love gone sour. This quiet gave Casey time to perfect what she'd always knew she wanted to say but never thought she'd have the opportunity to.

"I need to stop on the Ave. real quick. Is that cool?" Daemon asked as he pulled over on the corner 17th and Susquehanna Avenue.

Casey rolled her eyes, there was no point in asking her, they were already there. She hoped that whatever the stop was, that it did not take a long time.

"Go ahead," she told him. Then she watched as he crossed the street, shook hands with two guys standing in front of the bar before going inside.

Casey folded her arms over her chest and took in her surroundings. Susquehanna Avenue had changed drastically over the last couple years. Though the neighborhood itself was prime real estate for upcoming developers attempting to make room for the increasing student body at Temple University, the residents and its businesses had suffered.

The crab shack which was run by a woman and her two daughters for years had not opened for the crab and seafood season. The building that used to be both a check cashing place, and cleaners had been knocked down and was currently under construction as an apartment building. The church that used to be on the corner had closed and was now abandoned like much of that side of the street except for the Chinese Store.

The deli which everyone in the neighborhood called the Double El, had been there and was owned by the same couple her entire life Casey reflected. She hoped that it would never go anywhere due to the mass reconstruction of the neighborhood.

The neighborhood drug dealers and tough guys loitered the street in groups. They could be found either sitting in front of the empty and abandoned houses or crouched and huddled around a game of dice. It had been their habit for as long as she could remember. The same guys she noted but they were much older now.

Casey could still recall the summer nights she, Catrina and Briannah had spent strolling down the Ave. after a basketball game on 16th St hoping to get noticed by the older and popular guys. The memory brought a smile to her lips. There had been so many guys who hadn't talked to her because she was Tommy's niece and considered her something like a little sister to Daemon. Growing up, she'd hated that.

She hoped that this dinner had nothing to do with sisterly feelings and then she began to second guess the reasons he wanted to have dinner with her.

She sat back, closed her eyes and said a quiet prayer that it didn't.

Tex's bar still stood on the corner of Chadwich St as it had for years. The men and women lingering out in front of it could be found there day in and day out. It had been rumored that her mother had spent an ample amount of her time there. It got under her skin that her father could be one of those men who stood out there day in and day out.

Casey shook the unwanted thoughts away. Wasn't she over her selfish mother and faceless father?

Casey mustered up a half smile when Daemon returned to join her in the car

"Sorry, 'bout that. You cool?" He asked sensing her mild annoyance.

"I'm good, just hungry," She answered.

73

Once they arrived at Poor Tony's, Casey ordered Barbeque chicken wings, baked macaroni and cheese, and candied yams. Daemon ordered chicken breast, collard greens with macaroni and cheese. They decided to eat their food in the restaurant.

The place was small and cramped. The lights were dim and it smelled of all things barbeque. There was four two-tops tables set with cheap salt and pepper shakers on top of them. The tables were accompanied by two metal foldup chairs on either side.

Isn't he going to say something? Casey wondered as she watched him plow through his food with great appreciation for the cooks. Casey was only pinching at her food, too nervous to eat. She decided to lighten the mood and stuck her fork into his plate scooping up some of his greens to get his attention.

Daemon looked up just as she put a forkful of greens into her mouth. "You know I hate that," he told her.

Casey smiled and shrugged. "I couldn't help myself they looked so good," she told him licking her lips. "And they taste good too."

"You too much," he responded with a laugh. "I thought about what you said," he added. Then there was a slight pause as he wiped his lips with a paper napkin.

As the silence prolonged, Casey arched a brow and said, "And?"

"And I'm willing to try."

He said it so simple. Must think it's that easy. After all this time there was no way she was going to make it easy for him.

Casey licked her lips and smiled. "Try what, Daemon?" she questioned.

Daemon chuckled. "Why you being so difficult?"

Sucking her teeth, she said, "Funny for you to be asking me that question."

Daemon cleared his throat. She had a point. In the past five and a half years she had made enough moves to entice him and any other man that happened to get into her path. It shouldn't be difficult to state exactly what he'd decided he wanted.

The night of Casey's get together had put things into perspective for him. He'd ended up in bed alone with his thoughts wondering to her and what she was doing. In the days following, Daemon had decided that his feelings for her were real and worth exploring.

"I want to try this relationship thing with you. I want to try and make you my girl," he replied smoothly.

This is crazy. Casey blushed, but was able to keep a straight face when she said, "That's good, Daemon, cause I want to try and make you my man."

They were both all smiles. "It wasn't that hard, now was it?" Casey murmured.

God, I have him. Daemon Hicks is mine!

He nodded and made sure that his eyes were level with hers. "I wouldn't know what to do if you found someone else. It scares me that I need you. That I depend on your presence," he admitted.

Casey shook her head. "It shouldn't scare you. I've known it all my life. I've had a crush on you since I was ten." Casey reached for his hand. "And I've loved you since I was old enough to handle that type of emotion." She smiled and relaxed a little when his hand went into her hair. "You have to be sure that this is what you want."

"I want this, Case. I want you. I'on know how long it's been. But for a while, it's only been you. I fight it so hard 'cause I'm scared to hurt you. I love you and that is the last thing I want to do."

"You wanna try and that's enough for right now. Actually that's so much for right now." She stood up in a rush of excitement and surprised herself by kissing him across the table.

When the kiss was over and her heart was settled, Casey smiled. As an afterthought, she figured that she wasn't even pissed that their first date was in a place where a meal cost less than ten dollars.

Later when she reflected on their evening, she made a mental note to let him know that he owed her a dinner at her favorite upscale restaurant. That night she fell asleep dreaming about her future with him.

Chapter Seven
Dazed and Confused

Catrina

Why is he here when he's not supposed to be? I come home and find him in my bed and smile. Instead of kicking his ass out, I cuddle in beside him and relish in his warmth. His house, my house, it's too much, too fast. Just what am I doing with him? Catrina shook her head to clear it, figuring that 8 a.m. was entirely too early in the morning to be thinking so hard. *Shit, how'd I let this happen? This is only supposed to be 'whenever I need it dick.'*

Deciding that she wouldn't be able to think clearly with him beside her, Catrina slipped out of bed, slid into her robe, and left the room. Going down the stairs, she could hear Chantel and her family moving around in the dining room. Cinyah was talking excitedly about the much anticipated party in her first grade class. Chris was sitting at the head of the table indulging his child by listening and Chantel, well, she was scanning over a revised copy of a contract for her newest model.

It was very rare for Catrina to be up before nine, so Chantel said, "Good morning. What are you doing up so early?"

"Good morning, Aunt Trina," Cinyah spoke.

Catrina yawned then shrugged. "Morning. I don't know."

"Dave woke?" Chris asked her.

Catrina sucked her teeth. "He still asleep. He don't have be to work until one." The doorbell rang. "I'll get it," she offered patting her scarf covered head.

All six feet and three inches of Mike was standing on the other side of the screen when she opened the front door.

Instantly, her heart jumped into her throat.

She rolled her eyes to cover her fear. He'd always had the problem of showing up uninvited more recently than in the past. The last time he'd had the nerve to question her about why he'd seen her with David one day, she had flipped out on him requesting that he not question her every move. He'd apologized and that had been that.

"Mike," she gasped. "What are you doing here?"

"I thought I'd stop by and see you before I headed off to work. Wassup? Can I come in?" he asked, putting his hand on the screen door handle. He discovered that it was locked when he turned it. His handsome face scrunched up.

"Mike, you can't just show up at my house anytime you feel like it. You should have called first." Hesitantly, she looked back towards the stairs. It was probably best to deal with him outside, since she knew that he would get undoubtedly loud.

"You got some otha nigga in 'nere or something?" he asked when she stepped out the house.

Although she was nervous, she boldly said, "Maybe I do." Catrina figured she had to be that way because Mike would continue to pop up where ever and whenever he felt like it.

"What? You'n fuck wit' me no more?"

She could see the change in his demeanor, the angry vein in the middle of his forehead showed up. As far as she could detect, he was past the point of being upset. "I like you, Mike, but I have some other things going on right now, and you're obviously looking for more than I'm ready to give."

Pissed, Mike stared at her. "You try and kick that shit to some otha dude. All you gotta do is be straight wit' me. If you'n wanna fuck wit' me no more, you need to say it. All the shit I been doin' for you."

Catrina frowned and shook her head. Stingy niggas always threw up what they did for you in your face. If the truth be told he'd only given her two hundred dollars, which she could throw back in his face right now, if she had it in her pocket instead of upstairs in a purse.

"You ain't do shit for me. I can give you your couple dollars back if you want them."

"I'on want dat shit. I was tryna look out. I know what it is, though. You think a nigga stupid. I know why you got otha shit to deal wit'; you still fuckin' wit' Dave. I know y'all ain't just friends like you tried to kick to me the otha day. People been seeing you

77

wit' him."

"Dave don't got shit to do with me messing with you. And I am still messing with him."

Mike shook his head and began to point. "You's a stupid bitch. That nigga got a girl and you still gon' let him dog the hell out you like he did the last time. Girls do like men who treat them like shit over somebody that wanna do right for them."

Even though David didn't treat her specifically like shit, Catrina found truth in that statement. Hadn't she herself made plenty of decisions like that?

"I'm a bitch though? 'Cause I no longer want to fuck with you?" she nodded. How did she expect him to react to rejection? "That's cool, 'cause you entitled to think however you want to think. Now get the fuck off my steps," she told him nastily.

Later in the day, Catrina was still mulling over the words Mike had shouted at her. *The nerve of niggas these days.* Catrina thought. How many times had a guy called her bitch after she'd ended whatever they'd been building together?

Too many...

So many that she'd just stopped counting. Contemplating quietly, she shrugged as she made her way up the front steps of Briannah and Tyree's house. Catrina knocked and waited until the door opened and was surprised when she was greeted by her sorority sister, Alieas. She also happened to be Tyree's cousin.

"Don't speak to me," Alieas joked. "You been home since graduation, and you did not even call me."

The gloom that had begun to fill her heart was suddenly replaced by momentary happiness. Catrina smiled and opened her arms.

"You know I love you, girl."

Alieas laughed as she embraced Catrina and said, "Fakin' and shit. Now, come on in here and tell me what you been up to."

"Nothing. Something must be up with your ass though," Catrina said, stepping into the house. "Look at you, getting skinny on me."

"Trying to," Alieas responded. "Down sixty pounds with exactly sixty-three more pounds to go." Alieas was a beautiful brown-skinned young lady with wide bright brown eyes. At five feet nine inches she was slightly over two hundred pounds and considered a big girl. She was curvy and thick in the hips and behind. Even though she was classified as a big girl, Alieas knew that the big was in every part of her body it needed to be.

Catrina smiled. "Well you look good but you lose any more, you going to look like a crackhead. Your neck getting real slim. Your collarbone makes you look a lil' hungry. Don't turn into a bobble head."

Alieas sucked her teeth as her hand instantly went to her collarbone to check. "Please, I'll be the biggest crackhead I know. And everybody who loses a lot of weight has that awkward transition and bobble head stage."

Catrina laughed as expected. "You stupid and it doesn't look bad. You look damn good. What you are doing here?"

"Bri is hooking me up with some outfits. And you know I had to see the baby's room, you seen it yet?"

"Yeah, Tyree had it done for her since Bri came home from school," Catrina said. "She was crying and shit. The theme is cute though. Pearls work for both of them and the colors are very subtle and cute in pastels. It's nice as hell."

Alieas smiled. As far as she was concerned Tyree was on point with every aspect of this baby's birth. He had his hand in everything and was constantly offering opinions on Briannah's upcoming surprise baby shower.

"You know your best friend and Lonah bought that baby this huge ass elephant, right?" Alieas questioned.

Catrina cracked a smile. "Yeah, I saw. Bri will laugh and thinks it's cute. Oh, and I need to talk to you about the planning for the shower."

"What ya'll talking about," Briannah inquired as she made her way down the steps. She was carrying the fabrics that Catrina had picked out the week before and Alieas's three shirts.

"You," Alieas stated as Briannah handed her the shirts. "Damn, these sharp as hell. I should be able to fit them by the end of the summer."

Both Briannah and Catrina laughed. "You can't fit them now?" Catrina questioned staring at the shirts.

Alieas tilted her head and considered. "No, these are incentive."

Catrina nodded. "Do that, girl," she encouraged.

They all laughed. "I saw Tony last week when I was having lunch with my mom," Catrina said to Alieas

The light of laughter died in Alieas's eyes as she frowned. "We not together no more," she informed Catrina.

That nigga. "What happened?"

Alieas flagged it off. The breakup with her longtime boyfriend was still very new to her and hurt like hell. She'd been sure after all they'd been through that he'd want to settle down and get married, and it turned out that he wanted the exact opposite. Alieas wanted to cry but had already determined that she wouldn't shed another tear for him.

"Y'all I'm fucked up," Alieas said. " I'm washing his clothes, and I find this number. I asked him 'bout it, and he start going off on me like I did something wrong. Then all I know, he start talking 'bout, 'I can't do this no more, and I'm not ready,' and all this other shit. I'm crying and shit, actin' like a bitch begging that nigga to think it over like he was some type of prize. I couldn't think and the shit that makes me mad as hell is that I still love his ass."

Catrina sighed. "That's the worst part of it," she comforted with words and then a hug. "Fuck that nigga."

"I did," she pouted with a sniff. "I'm sorry, y'all."

Briannah smiled. "Don't be sorry to us. You should make his ass sorry."

"I already fucked up his car and bleached all his shit that he left at my house."

Catrina chuckled. "I'm so proud, I did teach you something."

"She love moving around," Briannah murmured as her hand went to her stomach.

Both Alieas and Catrina reached to touch her belly.

Catrina smiled even though there was aching pain settling in her heart. "I'm so jealous I missed this," she thought aloud.

"It is a beautiful thing. And if you ever get the urge to play Mommy, I'ma have a couple round here that you can borrow."

Catrina shook her head. "I'm cool."

Wanting to lock her feelings for Tony back in, Alieas decided to bother Catrina. "I heard that Dave was at your graduation, and that y'all been with each other since."

Well, Catrina figured, had come over to talk about him to Briannah; there was no reason that she still shouldn't. Briannah always gave sound advice. And so did Alieas, when it had nothing to do with her own life.

"We're not together." Catrina said with a sigh. "I'm so confused."

"I'on know why, all the shit that man been doing for you, girl. You better grab his ass," Alieas told her.
Briannah looked at Alieas.

"What's wrong?" she asked Catrina.

Catrina shrugged as she began to pull out a wrapped blueberry muffin from her purse. "I want him but he got me scared as hell this time."

"And you wanna run," Briannah guessed.

That was exactly what she wanted to do, she realized as she unwrapped the muffin. "Yes. He could really fuck me up this time around, if he lying. And I just don't know, we been cool for a minute just doing our own thing. That's fine with me."

"If that's all you want then it should be cool."

Catrina bit into the bottom of the muffin and closed her eyes to savor the warmth of it in her mouth. "It's not, though," she said when her foodgasm was over. "He is stating that he'd like to be in a relationship with me when he still has a girl. I can see myself getting stupid 'bout his ass. Shit, I've been stupid bout his ass. Am stupid right now for messing with him. Actions speak a lot louder than words, and his are telling me the exact opposite of what he's saying."

"You tell him all this?" Alieas asked.

"No. Right now I'm actin' like I don't care. Like I'm not even interested."

The front door opened and in walked the subject of their conversation, along with Tyree and his four-year-old son.

Smiling, Briannah went to meet Tyree with a kiss.

Catrina grinned in admiration. They had such a beautiful relationship. As a couple, they complimented and balanced one another out. Briannah was the same complexion as her own tone of honey. She was attractive with soft features, brown eyes, and thin lips. Her light brown hair was long and streaked with blond highlights. She was of average height but thin. In her third trimester of pregnancy Briannah skin shined like she was constantly glowing. Tyree could have been the walking definition of tall, dark, and handsome. He wore is hair in a fresh set of braids. The dark hair above his lips connected to form a trim goatee. His eye were the memorizing color of chocolate. He was long and lean and at least a half of foot taller than Briannah. *Their daughter is going to be beautiful*, Catrina thought.

"Hey, boo," Tyree said, catching his fiancée around the waist. "You should be sitting down," he told her, pulling her to the sofa. While everyone spoke to one another, Briannah observed her friend eye David as she munched on the blueberry muffin. *She loves him,* Briannah discovered with a grin.

"Hey, cousin," Tyree said, reaching to tug Alieas's hair.

"Hey," she responded with a smile.

"Sup Lieas?" David spoke and then turned his attention to Catrina. "Are you about to leave?" David asked her.

She shook her head. "I just got here. Bri is making some clothes for me," she told him.

David looked at Briannah. "Don't have her looking all naked either," he said.

"If that's what I want," Catrina said to Briannah.

David was shaking his head when he said, "Bey, don't do that to me. All these men are going to be looking at you." Then he pulled her to him, nuzzled her neck a little, making her laugh.

"Get off," she ordered. It embarrassed her to play like a couple in front of others.

"Let me get some of this muffin," he stated reaching, deftly removing it from her hand.

Just as he was about to sink his teeth into the muffin she glared at him. "Now you know," Catrina warned. She only had the top left and was not willing to share. It was the best part.

He squinted his eyes back at her in consideration. "I'ma eat the small piece on the bottom from right here," he returned in compromise before he broke the piece off.

"Ummm, look at y'all. Must be nice," Alieas picked.

She'd known David her entire life, since he was Tyree's best friend. She never seen him happier than he was when he was with

Catrina.

She'd known Catrina since they were teens and had really gotten to know her during their college years. Seeing Catrina with David, she noticed a light in Catrina's eyes that she hadn't seen when Catrina was with another man. She'd also seen guys come and go in Catrina's life and how easy it was for Catrina to dismiss them. Though at some point David had indeed needed to be dismissed Catrina had not discarded him. She may have herself fooled into thinking that what was going on between them would go nowhere, but Alieas was certain that Catrina didn't have others fooled. She couldn't be happier for her friend.

Chapter Eight
A New Day

Casey

Ending a relationship that you had no intention of ever starting turned out to be harder than she'd expected, Casey realized as she let herself into the dark house. Because of her, Jermaine's feelings had been unnecessarily hurt. Casey hadn't figured that it was that serious. They had only been casually seeing one another for two months. She assumed that he was also seeing other girls, but today she'd found out that he hadn't. From what he had said, he'd wanted to ask her to become exclusive with him. But, she'd beat him to it, telling him that she couldn't date anymore.

When he had asked what he did, she tried to assure him that it had nothing to do with him and everything to do with how she felt about someone else. The funny thing about it, now that she thought of it, was that she hadn't needed to tell him who the other guy was. He immediately guessed that it was Daemon. He sensed it from how he'd seen her look at Daemon and how Daemon had looked at her whenever she wasn't paying attention.

"Long day?" Daemon asked out of the darkness, startlingly Casey.

It had been one. Besides running into Jermaine, she'd taken Nadia out for lunch to thank her for getting her the interview with her new boss, Yevette Carter, the week before and Yevette had accompanied them. It had also been Casey's first day as her assistant. The woman was eccentric, which reflected through all her designs and even in her everyday life. Lunch had been an experience since Yevette and Nadia had known one another for years. She was the godmother of Nadia's twin granddaughters. Casey laughed; she had come to think of Yevette as a very colorful, animated character during that lunch.

"Yeah, I'm so tired," she said it with a smile. "I had a good day, though."

"So your first day was cool? How was Mrs. Carter?" he asked, taking her key and shoulder bag from her hands. She had been so nervous about meeting the designer again that he'd given her a speech on how good she was and tried to assure her that all would go well.

Casey nodded as he took her hand, after putting her bag on the coffee table.

"My boss is so funny. She had me cracking up all day. And I swear she is sharp as hell. She had on this sharp ass Dolce and Gabanna cream linen pant suit. I'm going to get Bri to copy it for me. Anyway, she's been married for twenty-one years, has three children, and she my number," she exclaimed. "How 'bout that?" She had been very excited to find that out.

Daemon smiled. "Sounds like you like her." He pulled her towards the kitchen.

"That's good. Tell me a little bit more over dinner," he told her when they entered.

The table was set intimately for two with candles burning, creating a flickering glow.

"You cooked?" she asked.

"Something like that." He smiled and pulled out her chair. "Sit down."

"I sure will." She sat, and he pushed her chair in. "Thank you," she murmured, catching his hand in hers.

Daemon leaned down and kissed her.

God, no man has ever cooked for me before.

"Just enjoy," he said when the kiss ended. He moved to the stove and took out two plates from the oven. "I thought about you today," he was telling her as he set the food before her. "And I said, 'what could I do to surprise her?' Are you surprised?" he inquired when he sat across from her.

"Yes, very. This isn't like you." She eyed him considerably.

He shrugged. "I know, but this is something I overheard you mention like two years ago, when you were on the phone with one of your friends." He cleared his throat and put his hand to his heart. "I would love for a man to cook for me," he imitated her with his best impression. "Candlelight, flowers, music, me and him..."

Casey laughed. She wasn't sure what time that was, because there had been so many times she'd been on the phone with a friend explaining what she wanted from a man. The important thing was he remembered.

"I do not sound like that," she told him, shaking her head.

Daemon grinned. "Yes, you do. But it's cool; I like it," he told her.

It was a surprise for him to find out that he enjoyed making her smile. This was all still very new to him. He hadn't been in, or even attempted to be in, a serious relationship for over five years. He'd only been in love once and that had been for less than a second when the girl, up and transferred to another college. That had been the one and only heartbreak that turned him into a dog. There hadn't been anybody he'd cared about, except for Casey in all that time.

Casey stared at him and wondered what he was thinking about as he ate his food. Occasionally, he'd stare at her for a second, ask a question, wait for her response, respond, and then go back to eating.

Casey knew she was ready. That this was the right moment to do what she'd dreamt about doing her entire life. He was also ready for her, she thought. This had been six years in the making. And tonight he's set the stage for something she was sure he had no idea was going to happen.

Casey stood up as he began clearing the table, grabbed his hand leaned into him and said, "You know, D, I didn't need a home-cooked meal, but I'm grateful." She pressed a light kiss to his cheek. "You made a dream come true and you have no idea how that makes me feel." She took the plate from him and setting it back down on the table. She kissed him again, this time on the other cheek, trying her hand at quiet seduction. "How it makes me wanna make you feel," she continued, placing her hands on his chest, and pressing her body into his.

"Casey..."

She sighed. "I know we talked about waiting, Daemon, but I don't want to wait. I've been waiting forever," she murmured, watching him intently.

He was tempted but held back. "I don't want to move too fast for you," he told her.

Casey laughed and took his hand. She began walking out the

kitchen. "I've been ready for a while," she let him know, starting up the stairs. "I was waiting for you." She noticed that she was no longer pulling him along, that it was more like he was walking with her.

"You sure?" he inquired, when they reached the door to his bedroom.

Casey turned the knob, opened the door, and stepped inside. "You on the wrong side of the door," she told him.

Daemon stepped into the room and took her by the waist. He sighed heavily, like he was giving up. "I'll stop, if you ask me to."

Always the gentleman, she thought, shaking her head. "I won't. Now stop trying to make me nervous." She blushed.

She loved him and yearned to tell him as he kissed her in a way that only could be a prerequisite to love making. Yet, she was afraid to involve those emotions until she felt he was ready to reciprocate them. She knew he loved her; it just wasn't as intense and consuming as hers.

"Don't tell me you're afraid to put the hammer to use," she purred playfully into his ear.

Daemon laughed as expected, took her hand and guided it along his slacks until they rested on his erection. "I'on think he'll have any problem getting down to business, do you?" he asked arrogantly.

She swallowed. *Holy shit,* she thought as her hands explored their way past his waistband and into his boxers. *I didn't think it was this big,* her thoughts continued. "Can you say Mandingo?"

Casey didn't know she'd said it aloud until she heard him chuckle and say, "You think you can spell it?"

Flushed with red cheeks, she buried her face into his chest. She laughed even as butterflies began to swim in her stomach. Was she supposed to tell him that she was nervous as hell now? Could he tell that she was scared to death of what they were about to do?

As if reading her mind, he whispered, "It'll be okay."

Shyly, she looked up at him. Her eyes for the first time that night were innocent and trusting. Daemon knew that he was complicating their relationship by not giving her the words she deserved when she was offering herself to him in a way she'd never offered herself to anybody else before. Though, he had yet to realize how deep his love went. He did understand that he loved her and owed her something.

"It means a lot to me, Casey, letting me be your first. I've fought so hard against you for so long when I want you like I can't remember wanting anything. You mean so much to me and I don't want to hurt you so, I'll try not."

Casey softy kissed his lips to silence him. "Shhh," she murmured, her hands going to work on the buttons of his shirt. "Just be with me. I know you can't make promises to me about not hurting me, 'cause maybe you will, even if it's not intentional."

Time seemed to freeze as they slowly peeled away each other's clothing piece by piece. Daemon surprised Casey by picking her up and carrying her to his bed. Casey watched him, mesmerized by all that was going on inside her as he went to his stereo and turned on a compilation of what she considered R&B singer R Kelly's greatest loving making songs, then to his dresser to where he pulled a few condoms from the drawer. She swallowed a lump as she watched him encase himself, protecting them both. Casey smiled at his thoughtfulness and was happy that he'd thought of it before she'd asked him about it. Her heart began to pound double time in her chest.

She assured herself that what she felt was natural as he replaced the larger light with a smaller, dimmer one and laid his body beside hers. Casey moaned as he quietly began to explore her body with his hands and lips. Her eyes closed as the sensation of his touch filled all her senses.

Oh, God was all she could think as he played with her breast and took the rigid brown nipple into his mouth and massaged the other.

Oh, God was all she could murmur when he kissed his way down her stomach and legs, only to spread her thighs to taste her.

Oh, God was all she could shout when her world burst into a thousand pieces from his lips and tongue work. She gasped and rode the wave for a minute.

Daemon didn't give her time to fall from the cloud she was on before he settled between her thighs. He kissed her lips. "Just relax, Casey," he murmured against her lips when her body tensed at his slight intrusion.

She was trying to relax, and nodded as she attempted to loosen up just a little and whimpered at his next down stroke. She closed her eyes tight and bit down on her bottom lip against the pain of it.

"Ahhh," she moaned, clenching her thighs around him. Her leg was shaking from her withholding and tensing.

Steady and go slow, he warned himself. To her he said, "Case baby, relax and let me in."

Slowly, Daemon lifted one of her legs higher so he could administer more of his lengthy shaft into her. When he was buried securely in her, he stopped. Casey's eyes fluttered open when she realized that there was only a little of the initial pain there and that he wasn't moving.

"You okay?" he asked her, dropping a kiss to her lips. Breaking down barriers had never been so difficult before, he thought as he felt her hands roam down his back, less frightened than they'd felt before.

"Yeah," she answered huskily. She turned her face into his neck and lightly kissed him there. "You feel so good," she told him.

Daemon had been holding back until that point and slowly gripped her hips and began his dance. He moved in and out slowly at first allowing her the time to catch the rhythm. When she began to stir beneath him, he dragged her hips higher to deepen his strokes. He whispered things he'd thought about doing and planned on doing for the rest of the evening.

Casey did a combination of a moan and a hmmm both in appreciation for current treatment and in anticipation of what was to come. Her hand began to get slick with his perspiration as she kneaded his backside. By the end she was practically begging for him to release her from what she felt.

When he did, she screamed his name and tightened her grip on him. Daemon continued his work until he reached his goal. For a minute he laid there on top of her depleted of all energy.

Hours later when the silence was so thick that you could count the breaths of the person beside you, Daemon lay awake and placed his hand on Casey's hip. Her body already so responsive to his curled into his and ended up with Casey's head resting on his chest and their legs tangled. While she sleepily dreamed of a future, Daemon cautiously analyzed the now and how he would handle what was next. There was no pretending that he'd be able to sleep alone in his bed again when it seemed as if she now belonged. No denying that he'd just enjoy having her in his arms until the sun came up.

"I have no clue know what I'm going to do with you, Case baby," he murmured into the darkness of the room.

Chapter Nine
Losing It

Casey

Waking up with a man's arms around her wasn't a new thing for Casey. Those mornings included her virginity; it was something she was so happily missing today. She sighed as she replayed the events of the night before. He had filled the bathtub up and taken a bath with her, then had given her a massage and debated with her about how flexible she was. She chuckled; she didn't think that she could move.

After trying to prove him wrong, every muscle in her body had to have been used the night before, because they all ached and cried for warm water.

I'm not a virgin anymore, and he is still beside me. Casey wanted to stay beside him until the end of time.

When Daemon stirred beside her and pulled her body closer to his own, the morning after butterflies began doing their job. Flustered, Casey sighed. She was sure that she would be past nervous reactions, but it was apparent that she wasn't. There had to be a thousand things racing through her mind at this point.

I hope he isn't feeling guilty; I'd be crushed, then I'd kill him. I wonder what I'm supposed to say. 'Thank you, Daemon, for devirginizing me?' She didn't think she could say that with a straight face. Casey giggled to herself even as she thought about it. She decided to play it casual and go off of his vibe. But not too casual, a girl doesn't lose her virginity every day.

"Umm," she purred when Daemon dropped a kiss to the base of her neck.

"Good morning," Daemon murmured sleepily.

Smiling, she turned to him and said, "I thought that you were asleep."

"I bet. And you were contemplating how to handle this

morning. I can hear the gears working in your head. What do I say? How do I act?" Ain't that right?" he questioned, rolling them over.

Casey tried her best not to laugh when she began her speech. "Daemon," she started, running her hands down his sculpted back, "I would like to thank you for devirginizing me with as less pain as possible." She burst out laughing. She couldn't finish.

Daemon laughed along with her.

Casey frowned. "Was I okay, though?" she asked quietly.

"Worked me like a pro," Daemon answered with a smile.

Casey's eyes widened. "What?"

He kissed her. "I'm only playing, Case, but I can teach you to work it like a pro, if you want me to," he informed her.

Casey rolled her eyes. "You must have lost your mind," she told him, even though the idea of being a freak tempted her.

Daemon licked his lips, then hers. "No, but I'm definitely interested in making you lose yours." He began nibbling on her bottom lip.

While she wanted to scream something corny like, '*Make me lose it, Daddy!!*' she thought, *This is real,* and told him, "Well, I'm definitely interested in you trying." Then she thought of how sore she felt down there. "On second thought, how 'bout you make me lose it later, I don't think I can... I'm kind of sore," she told him.

"We sorry we made you sore," he teased, kissing the hollow of her neck. "We'll see if we can make you feel a lil' better," he added, rolling off her.

"Where are you going?" she questioned him.

"To run some bath water."

Beside her head, the phone began to ring.

"Hello?" she answered as Daemon went into the adjoining bathroom.

"Can I speak to D?" The voice was female.

Casey frowned. "Who's this?" she questioned.

"Karen. Is he dere?"

"Hold on." She got up, wrapped the sheet around her, and carried the phone in the bathroom. He was adding bubble bath to the water when she handed the phone to him and said, "It's for you." Casey folded her arms over her chest and stood there.

"Sup?" he asked unaware of who was on the phone.

"Where you been at? What have you been up to?" Casey could hear her talking.

He looked at Casey and then started talking. "How you been?"

Really? He gon' carry on a conversation while I'm standing right here? Casey didn't say anything when she left him alone in the bathroom.

A minute later she heard him say, "I'ma get back at you a lil' bit later."

Casey kept her mouth shut when he came back into the room.

Daemon had expected her to say something but when her silence continued, he shrugged and said, "You mad 'cause she called? She ain't know."

Frowning, Casey put her hands on her hips. "And you sure didn't tell her ass either."

Now it was his turn to be silent.

So, Casey started talking. "You're going to get back at her later? Are you fucking kidding me?"

"It's not that serious, Casey," he told her.

His attitude is all wrong for this. He way too cool, Casey thought. She nodded her head. "We not that serious that you couldn't tell her not to fuckin' call here 'cause you're involved with me?"

Daemon shook his head. Here comes the relationship shit, he thought. When was the last time he ever had to answer questions? For the longest time he'd answered only to himself. Now he had Casey and a reason to answer any questions she threw at him.

Daemon dropped the phone onto the bed, and then he tried to assure her by saying, "It's not even like that."

Her eyes narrowed as she began pointing in the air. "You used to fuck with her." Casey shrugged. "How is it then?"

"If you're going to trip, we might as well not even discuss it."

Casey frowned and took a step towards him. "What?"

"I'm not for this stupid arguing bullshit. The nice thing to say was, 'I'ma get back at you. That don't mean I am."

She laughed. "You not for the bullshit? If one of my dudes would have called here this morning, and I said that, you wouldn't be trippin'? That's what you sayin', though ain't it?"

Daemon didn't say anything in his own defense, because he

knew he would have flipped out. Not after he'd just spent the night making love to her was she going to talk to some nigga on the phone.

"I haven't talked to her in like two weeks."

Casey lifted her arms out at her sides. "I don't give a hell when you talked to her. You could have told her that we're together now. And you did not do it! All I want to know is if you plan on getting back at her while we together. You might as well let me know now," she demanded.

Daemon looked at her in disbelief. "I'm going to cheat on you now?"

She shrugged, it felt childish but she couldn't help it and added, "Are you?"

That made him angry. Here she was accusing him of something he hadn't thought of doing. Something he had no intention of doing but had feared that at some point he would.

"You are really being extra'," he told her. "And I need you to calm down, if you think you going continue a conversation with me."

Did this nigga just say what I think? After he fucked me all night, he gon' say think I'ma talk to him? "I'm not interested in talking to you then," she told him. She refused to, when he had this type of attitude.

Daemon looked at her. He knew that she had a very bad temper, and he figured that he was testing it. She'd probably expected him to react differently to the situation. He'd tried, but then she started yelling and he wasn't going to permit anyone to yell at him. Yelling was a 'no-no'. And if Casey thought that she was, she had another thing coming to her.

"Casey, you need to get that attitude together."

She sucked her teeth at that. "I have a freakin' attitude, because you didn't tell her. What are you not understanding about that?"

He laughed at her. "If she call here again, I'll tell her. Okay? Is that fine with you?" He made an attempt to reconcile the problem. When Casey rolled her eyes, he added, "Make sure you do the same thing with your dudes." Then he went into the bathroom and slammed the door.

Casey stood there stunned. She'd never had a door slammed in her face before. First time for everything, she figured. She looked at the door and wondered how pissed Daemon was.

The land line telephone rang again just as she was about to knock on the bathroom door and she answered.

"It sure is nice to know that you haven't dropped off the face of the earth," Catrina told her.

She smiled a little and said, "Nag, nag, nag. What are you doing?"

At that present moment she was in David's bed with Cinyah and Yah curled beside her. "Laying here waiting for these kids to wake up so I can feed them."

"Who letting you watch they babies?" Casey questioned.

Catrina frowned. She wasn't supposed to be watching anybody, but when she arrived at David's after work, the kids had been there. "Dave is watching Nyah and Yah. He's in the shower, so if they wake up, I'ma fix them a bowl of cereal. We got to get together for lunch today. I really need to talk to you," Catrina said deciding, that it was time to get up.

"Me too. Me and D had an argument. The girl Karen called this morning, and we had just got finished boo loving, and he starts talking to her, and then he told her he was going to get back at her later. I flipped out on him. And now he pissed. He practically slammed the bathroom door in my face."

Catrina scratched her scarf and squinted her eyes as if that would make her understand more clearly. "Wait a minute, wait one minute. Define 'boo loving."

Casey sighed. "I told you I had something to tell you."

Catrina's jaw dropped and would have hit the floor if I were possible at the implication that Casey had lost her virginity. Casey was supposed to talk to her when she felt she was ready so she could answer any questions she'd had.

"I'm coming over when I drop these kids off."

She should have known Catrina would assume the mother role. "Okay, but tell me what to do about D. I kind of blew the entire thing out of proportion," she continued to explain in detail what had happened between herself and Daemon that morning.

Catrina cleared her throat before saying what she wanted. Her best friend was stubborn and would probably frown at her

95

suggestion, but she gave her opinion anyway. "Kind of apologize, but not apologize," she added before Casey could say anything. "You did blow it out of proportion. Was he supposed to call every girl he talk to and tell them not to call him no more? Be real, that's not gon' happen. I'm sure you didn't call all the guys you talking to."

"The point is that he told her he was gon' get back at her."

Catrina sucked her teeth. "That don't mean that he is, Case. It's just something to say," she told her.

Casey huffed. "That's what he said. I hate apologizing," she fumed.

"Hold on," Catrina told Case when she heard David call her from the bathroom. "What?" she answered.

"C'mere for a minute," he said.

"I'ma call you back," she told Casey and put the phone down before she went to see what David wanted.

He bet not ask me to cook him nothin' to eat for breakfast either, she thought as she stepped into the steam-filled room. "What?" she asked, folding her arms over her chest.

The shower door cracked a little, and David's head peeked out. He smiled upon seeing her. "Take a shower with me," he invited.
Catrina frowned. "I don't think so, David," she responded, even as the thought of tangling with him in the wet, and becoming one beneath the spray of the water, appealed to her. "Stop," she murmured when he attempted to grab her. "The kids are asleep," she reminded him.

David made another grab at her and was successful this time. "All the more reason to do it now," he enticed. "Come on, bey, take a shower with me."

The sprinkles of water were bouncing off his body and onto her pajamas. "Come on, now I'm getting wet."

He grinned at that. "I like when you wet."

Catrina shook her head. "My nightgown is getting wet," she clarified.

David could see that she was warming to the idea. "Well, we'll just have to work on the other. Now you either get them wet or you take them off," he warned his wet hands going to the hem of her silk nightgown.

She had yet to agree to anything when David began to slowly pull the hem up her thighs. "What about my hair?" she asked him when he did away with the gown.

"I'll get it done for you. Now stop actin' like you don't want me to love you down," he joked.

Catrina laughed as he helped her step into a shower that was big enough for four. "If I slip, I'ma kill you," she warned playfully.

When was the last time I took a shower with a man aside from Dave? she mused as David began massaging soap into her skin. She closed her eyes and let herself be taken away. He was the only man who'd ever made her feel this way. He could make her want even though she'd trained herself against him. It had always been him. Every guy she'd had sexual relation with had been compared to this man, and none of them had matched. Well, maybe a select few, but even then she had found herself thinking of him.

This is crazy, she thought with her head leaning back on his shoulder as he caressed her breast with his hands, then they traveled down to the valley between her slick thighs. On a sigh of pleasure, she arched her back against his chest while he whispered the things he wanted to do to her in her ear.

Crying out, she sagged against him, her energy depleted. That had always been a skill of his. After a second, Catrina realized that she was now pressed against the shower wall, sprinkles of water dancing around on her chest.

David lifted her and waited until she locked her long legs around his waist before he entered her.

Catrina moaned, arching her back, fingers digging into his shoulder as he slowly worked himself in and out of her. Her sighs and whispers of encouragement enticed him to put in the best work he ever had.

David bent his knees and drove upward in a determined stroke, causing Catrina to cry out in pleasure. She began going crazy for something to touch. First her fingers kneaded his back muscles, then grabbed his bald head and held on to it. Her body began to make huge demands on his.

David groaned when he felt her muscles tighten around him. She ready now, he thought knowing when he achieved this response she was on the brink. She continued to make the noise that he loved to hear.   Times like this, David knew that he could get her to go along with just about anything he said.

"Say my name," he murmured breathlessly against her ear. He began to pull lightly at her ear with his teeth. "Say my name," he pleaded again.

Catrina bit her bottom lip, set against responding, but on the next stroke his name slipped fluidly from her lips.

Chapter Ten
News to Them

Guy Talk

Tyree shook his head at his best friend. David was further gone over Catrina than he'd assumed. Being his best friend he knew that David held feelings for her; he hadn't realized until today how deep they went. The man was faced with making a business decision that would change his life, and he was debating what to do because of a woman.

One hand he had Catrina and all the confusion they created together. On the other he had a new position as Junior VP of a new branch his firm was opening in Atlanta. After having been nominated by his current branch's senior VP, David had undergone the application process, been selected and without regard for anything except his career, had accepted the job. That was a month before Catrina had come home, and now it was a month and a half after. He had yet to murmur a word about the job to her.

"You have got your priorities fucked up," Tyree told him and looked to Daemon to co-sign.

David rubbed a hand over his baldhead. "I know what I'm doing," he murmured. "In two years I could be heading up that branch. Niggas like me don't get opportunities like that on the regular."

"You know you going. Just tell her. Lying is what got y'all into the mess y'all in right now."

David shook his head. Nothing was ever that simple with Catrina. "I am. I just haven't found the right time."

Daemon laughed. "Dave you going to search for an apartment next week. When do you think the right time will present itself? This shit is gon' blow up in your face, man"

That was one thing he was afraid of. "I just don't understand her. I been telling her for weeks that I want to be with her and she just been putting me off like I'm talking out my ass."

Daemon stared at his friend. "That's because you are. You're moving to another goddamn state and she doesn't know shit about it. You haven't opened your damn mouth. You just now told Shay that you not fuckin' with her no more. Trina's biggest problem with you is the fact that you talk before you act. How you expect her to respond?"

Tyree nodded in agreement. "That's about right."

The situation wouldn't have become so sticky, if she'd just went along with the idea of them getting together. The last thing he wanted to do was keep this from her. He had because he figured that they would've established a solid relationship before he let her know his plans.

They all knew that Catrina wouldn't have given him her time. She may have been with him, but she wouldn't have limited herself to him exclusively like she was doing now.

"I love her. I can't see my life without her, y'all."

"So you want to marry her?" Daemon asked and didn't bother to mask the surprise on his face.

David nodded and shrugged. "Yes, I would like to marry her."

Tyree smiled. He had no idea what the world was coming to. First Daemon was sleeping with Casey and now David wanted to marry Catrina. "That's a big step," Tyree informed his friend.

"I've loved her since I was eighteen. It's been years in the making."

Daemon stood up. "Let me get this man a drink," he said pulling out a bottle of water from the refrigerator. He shrugged and cracked a smile. "It's too early for liquor," he explained.

He set the bottle in front of David and grabbed two more for himself and Tyree. "You do plan on telling her before you ask her, right?"

"Of course."

Since this was news to him, Tyree asked, "So when is all of this going to happen?"

David smiled. "Don't have much time.."

"Exactly what we have been telling your ass. So what did you tell Shay today at lunch?"

"I told her that I was moving to Atlanta and that I couldn't see her anymore. She started talking 'bout how she wants to move down there with me and shit. I haven't seen or talked to the girl for more than two weeks. I figured she knew it was over, until she called me."

Tyree frowned and said, "You know that girl naïve as hell."

"Dumb as hell," Daemon corrected.

They all got a chuckle out of that one. "Anyway, she was trippin' in the restaurant so I just left her ass there."

Daemon shook his head. "You's a funny nigga."

Tyree was laughing too. "She gon' fuck something of yours up. She a young girl too. Got all them young girl friends and them young girl tendencies. You better watch your car."

David frowned and considered the possible of Shay lashing out. "She ain't the hell crazy." He took a gulp of his water and thought on it a minute more. "Hardly crazy," he said dismissively. "I'll get Zah to beat her ass."

Tyree frowned and shook his head. "You're not getting my lil' sister involved in your mess. Shit, Zah might kick your ass. She at that stage when all men are dogs."

The nagging fear began to rise. "I heard Alieas fucked up Tony's Camry."

Daemon laughed, remembering how banged up the car had been when the tow truck had brought it into the shop. "Did she ever. All the windows, two tires, and she keyed it."

Tyree laughed. "My cousin did not do that shit."

Daemon looked over at Tyree. "Yes the fuck she did."

David felt afraid. His Lexus was only six-months old. "If she do something to my car."

"Stop bitchin'," Tyree laughed.

"Y'all know how much I love my fuckin' car," David stressed.

Chapter Eleven
No Laughing Matter

Casey

Every student taking summer classes must have been at the Paley Library that day, Casey imagined as she settled down at a computer. She'd already moved twice; once because the white guy she sat down next to kept digging in his nose, that completely disgusted her and then because a woman sat down beside her smelled like she hadn't washed her coochie in two years. Casey wanted to throw up. She felt like asking the woman if she could smell herself because, if she couldn't, Casey sure could.

"That's a nasty bitch," Casey murmured to herself as she typed in her password. She shook her head to clear it. She had a paper to write and studying to do. It was her habit to sign on to AOL instant messenger to see who was online and check her e-mail account with Hotmail before she did any work.

What was the use of having the junk mail filter if it never filtered out the junk mail? Casey wondered. She hated having to sift through all the mess to locate her important mail. Most of the time, she got frustrated and just deleted anything that didn't look important. It had only been two days since she'd last checked it, and it had one hundred-thirty new messages.

Casey laughed then glanced down at her watch, she realized that she had only one hour to type her paper before she had to leave to meet Catrina for lunch. She pulled out the notes she'd scribbled down during class and began typing away.

Within that hour she was able to create a sensible flow of words that would resemble a paper for her room restoration class. Casey frowned; she'd have to come back tomorrow to finish it.

She logged off the computer, packed up her stuff, and walked towards the exit. Casey almost lost her breath when a person ran right into her and almost knocked her down. She rolled her eyes and said, "Dickhead." as a hand closed over her arm to prevent her from falling.

"You okay?" Jermaine asked her.

Casey shook her head. "Yeah, I'm fine. I just wish people would watch where they're going," she said, raising her voice. "Thanks," she said to him.

"No problem. How you been doing, Casey?" he questioned, not quite ready to let her go.

"Good. How are you?"

"I'm cool," he responded in his practiced Philly speech which hinted at his southern drawl.

"Jermaine, I'm really sorry. I didn't think that anything would happen between D and I."

He frowned and flagged it off. "Don't worry 'bout all that. He's the love of your life. I understand. But if he ever treat you wrong, you know where to find me." He kissed her forehead.

As he let go of her and began to walk away, Casey said, "Can we at least be friends? I really did enjoy your company, Jermaine, and I don't want to lose that."

"I don't think your boyfriend would like that," Jermaine told her.

Casey smiled, despite the fact his refusal hurt. She completely understood his position. "No, he probably wouldn't, but I would," she answered.

"I'll think about it," he told her.

Casey had to refrain from letting her jaw drop to the ground. Instead she nodded her head and said, "I'ma see you around."

Lunch Date

Casey met Catrina for lunch at the Downtown Philadelphia Marathon Grille. They were seated at a booth by the windows which they had views of both Chestnut and Broad Streets. The sidewalks were crowded with shoppers and workers browsing the shopping area during their lunch breaks. The city streets were alive and vibrant with activity during the daytime hours. They giggled a little over a street beggar who had been doing his rendition of the moonwalk in front of the restaurant until the security guard requested that he moonwalk right past the restaurant's windows.

Casey was bursting to tell Catrina how Jermaine had treated her. She did so over salads and strawberry daiquiri's. Catrina laughed and laughed. "How you expect him to act after you told him you used him to make D jealous?"

She frowned at her friend. "Think about it, though. I wanted to ask him if he knew who he was talking to. Shit, he don't know who I am."

Catrina shook her head. "You are a trip. Now fill me in on you and D."

"Let me tell you 'bout how D tried to walk out on me again this morning. He said something smart to me like make sure you tell all your niggas to stop calling my house. I laughed at him. So hard, in his face. He was still mad at me 'cause he stubborn as hell, and I was just like, 'if you gon' be getting back at your female friends then my guy friends can call here.' Oh, he did not like that. He ain't say shit to me and tried to leave like I was going to let him. He had already slammed the bathroom door in my face and he thought I was going let him walk out on me too."

Catrina smiled. "Casey, you need to be telling me why you not a virgin no more. Why didn't you tell me you were thinking 'bout sleeping with him?" she asked.

Casey's eyes lit up and a huge smile crossed her lips. "Oh, my God, it was so sweet. He cooked dinner for me. You know how I'm always like, 'I'd love for a man to cook for me.' He heard me say that before and surprised me with what I'd described. Us sleeping together was unplanned; it just felt like the time was right." Casey closed her eyes. "I swear, I think I shocked him when I started getting fresh with him. He didn't expect it, and I did good."

Catrina sat back and listened as Casey shared the details of her entry into the world of love making. She still found it hard to believe that Case baby wasn't a virgin anymore. Miss I'm only gone give it to the man I love or Daemon, whichever one comes first. In this case Daemon proved to be both.

"You finally got what you wanted, Casey. I'm so happy for you."

Catrina was relieved that Casey still had the fresh air of

innocence about her. "Start as you plan to go on," her mother always said.

Casey had started out saying that all she wanted was true love, and then had focused her attention on Daemon, unlike herself who'd been attracted to the flash and cash of the street life. Catrina had wanted a boyfriend who drove, had a job or managed to make that money. How he made his money had not been a huge concern back then. Any guy vying for her attention had to look good, have a nice body, no kids and some extra money. She had wanted a boyfriend that would make all her girlfriends envious. Somewhere mixed with all the wants she had hoped to find love as well. Somehow David managed to be all that she had been looking for back then.

If she were honest, she'd admit that he was everything she wanted now.

David had been the first guy to take her to the movies, and to a nice restaurant. He had opened her eyes to more than what she saw on the urban streets of Philadelphia. He had helped her obtain her intense appreciation for literature and art in a way that her parents had been unable to.

Casey saw the sadness lurking in her friend's eyes despite the smile she showed. "Trina, what's wrong?"

Catrina shrugged and picked at her Chicken Caesar salad . "I was just thinkin' 'bout how different we are. You didn't settle for the first boy that offered you the moon and stars and in the end you got exactly what you wanted, exactly what you deserve."

Casey reached for Catrina's hand and searched her face. "What happened?" Concern apparent in her eyes.

"Is it supposed to hurt when you love somebody?" It felt childish to ask the question of Casey but she was her best friend. "He's been my only serious relationship my entire life and I've had sex with so many guys who didn't belong to me, Casey. And I've always wanted him…"

"Trina, you really haven't given yourself an opportunity to be with anybody else. Aside from the two years you weren't speaking to him, you've been involved with him sexually for five years."

Catrina nodded and sniffed. "I know. And I didn't see it until this year that I was subconsciously ruining any attempt at future relationships. It was like I'd get a potential man, and he'd just call to

105

see how I was doing, and that was it, I'm back to fuckin' with him. I didn't have a dude at school 'cause they all thought I already had a boyfriend 'cause his ass was always there."

Casey could see where the conversation was heading. "Are you saying you want to be in a committed relationship with him? It's not that hard."

There was nothing left to do but answer. "Yes."

Casey smiled and tightened her grip on Catrina's hand. "You sure?"

"He's my best friend and I love him for that alone. I don't want him to be with anyone else and I don't want to be with anyone else. But I'm in love with him and for some reason it makes me confused."

Casey hurt because Catrina did. "You know that he loves you," Casey assured. Two of her favorite people were finally on the same page. "You're probably confused because you still have unresolved feelings about what happened between the two of you."

Casey knew things that both of them were hiding from one another but understood that it was not her place to tell either's. But as a friend, she would make Catrina aware that her being honest was just as important to their relationship as it would be for him to be honest. "I wish you both would just be honest about your feelings and what's going on in your lives."

Casey hoped that somewhere along the lines David's friends were telling him the same thing. And because this was all she could give her, Casey held Catrina's hand. "Just talk to him and listen to what he has to say."

"I will."

Because she had other and more important things to obsess over other than David, she yawned.

"I need to have a clear head this week, and this whole thing with him is fuckin' up my concentration. I have to be on point with this wedding."

Casey could agree with that. Catrina's company; Perfect Perceptions Event Management had its largest test this week: Its first wedding. This was the make or break it for her in the business. Event management was a word of mouth type business and one bad event could ruin her reputation before she'd even been able to establish her name in the industry. She'd been making great sacrifices to keep her daytime position as a sales manager at the downtown Marriott Hotel and to establish a name in the city for her own company.

"Girl, you got this wedding in the bag. When have you done anything that hasn't been on point?"

Catrina smiled. She'd never done anything that hadn't been on point. All her events went off perfectly. "It's scary 'cause it's the first time. I worked really hard on this and I want it to reflect that. Thanks for all your help with it. And the help for the wedding day," Catrina told her.

Casey flagged. It was nothing for her to be Catrina's assistant for the day. "Please when you rich and famous just know you planning my wedding for free."

"Of course," Catrina agreed. Her mind wondered back to David. "Shit, I been dreaming 'bout getting married and having kids with that nigga. What the hell am I doing?" she murmured.

"Finally realizing that you can't control everything," Casey answered.

Chapter Twelve
Never Dreamed

Catrina

It wasn't sadness to be exact, Catrina figured examining her feelings as she rushed to get to the elevator from across the parking lot. A week had passed, and her feelings for David were still unresolved and sitting heavy on her heart. Yet, she found herself at his place. It was, she admitted the only place she wanted to be.

The wedding was less than twenty-four hours away and she couldn't get over the pounding of her headache.

In her opinion the mother-of–the-bride had consumed entirely too much alcohol. The woman had been able to control her liquor, Catrina recalled. Her action wasn't what could be described as wild but her inconsistent chatter had really gotten on Catrina's reserved nerve.

During the rehearsal dinner the bride's parents constantly argued about everything. It was a wonder to Catrina that they were still married.

The bride had also gotten a little tipsy and cried all over Catrina's brand new Prada linen suit jacket as she thanked her for understanding her vision for her wedding. The ache at her temple eased a wee bit at the thought of the praise as the doors to the elevator slid open.

Catrina was looking forward to having David give her one of his famous back rubs. She yearned to cuddle in the crook of his arm. She needed rest and knew that she would find none without him.

After getting off the elevator at his floor, Catrina slid the key that David had given her for convenience the week before into his door and stepped into his darkened living room. Her eyebrows rose as she heard the soft music that filled the room.

"Dave, where you been at?" a feminine voice asked from the bedroom.

Catrina saw David's current girlfriend, Shay come through the bedroom door in a skimpy nightie made of white silk and lace.

Shay stopped dead in her tracks and stared at Catrina. She folded her arms over her chest and sucked her teeth. "What the fuck are you doing coming here this late?" she questioned Catrina.

The headache grew so she had to squint. "I was looking for Dave, but since he's not here, I guess you are too," she responded coolly.

Time to go, she concluded. Shay had every right to respond the way Catrina figured she was about to; Catrina just didn't see herself standing there listening to her.

Shay let out an angry huff of air. She wasn't stupid. She had known about David and Catrina for weeks now. In addition to seeing a picture of the two of them snuggled up to one another in a picture booth at Six Flags Great Adventure, she'd heard rumors in the neighborhood that they were getting back together. At one point she'd questioned David about his relationship with Catrina and he'd told her that they were friends.

No further explanations had been given.

It had been a task to get David to meet her at the restaurant earlier that day after he'd been declining her calls for a week straight. Shay had hoped that being in his apartment when he got home would help change his mind about breaking up with her.

It irked Shay's nerve to discover that Catrina had a key when she had to slyly steal hers. "Bitch, don't play no games wit' me. Why are you here and how the hell did you get in?" She began cracking her knuckles.

Catrina smiled and let out a disgusted laugh. Not only did she have a headache the size of the Grand Canyon, she also had an angry girlfriend who seemed to be ready to fight.

"You think this funny?" Shay demanded.

"Yes, I do. You act like you wanna box me, and you can't beat me, so don't try."

Shay shook her head. This was not the late night scene she'd envisioned after David left her at the restaurant earlier.

"I can't stand bitches like you. You had him already and you didn't want him and now you think you can just take what's mine. I don't think so. So if you want him you gon' have to fight for him."

109

Catrina frowned. Now she was sure that Shay was out of her mind. She said, "Shay, I'm not about to fight you over no dick that's going to be mine, anyway." and turned away from her.

"You don't even respect yourself."

That had Catrina turning back around.

When Shay was sure she had Catrina's attention she said, "Doesn't it matter that he's with someone who loves him?"

I love him. "You 'bout to fight over a nigga that is cheating on you. Don't be stupid, girl. I don't have time for this bullshit."

"You in my man's house," Shay pointed out.

Catrina frowned. She had no time to assess the hurt she felt in her heart. "I'm leaving."

Just then Shay stood close to her face. "No you not. You think you the fuck tough, that you gon' take my man, and I'ma be cool," Shay said, grabbing Catrina by the arm.

Catrina looked down where her arm was captured. "Girl, you better get your hands off me," she said with a tug. "I've been with *your* man for years, and regardless if he's with you or any other bitch I can get him, if I want him." Catrina began walking away from her.

Shay used all the power in her to push Catrina from behind.

This bitch put her hands on me again. Catrina's reflexes had her jumping all over Shay in less than two seconds. Shay winced in pain as Catrina's fist connected with her cheek. She backed away, trying to hold fast to the principle of not fighting over men. It quickly went away when Shay pushed her again.

Catrina grabbed a handful of the girl's hair and began to tug at it mercilessly. She didn't use her fist, because she considered Shay easy to take down. In Catrina's opinion, Shay didn't look like the fist-fight type.

After a minute, Catrina freed her hold on the girl and said, "This is not worth it."

"I bet he ain't tell you that I'm moving to Atlanta with him next month," Shay blurted out when she saw that Catrina was going to leave.

"What?" Catrina muttered. *Who's moving to Atlanta?*

Shay was positive that her news would crush Catrina. Now she had an advantage over her in this fight even if it wasn't true. Catrina wouldn't know until she asked David about it anyway.

110

"You heard me. When he move down nere, we gettin' an apartment together."

"What the hell are you talking about?" Catrina questioned, not following the girl's side trip. "Who the fuck moving to Atlanta?" Shay smiled at the simple blank expression on Catrina's face.

Oh, this is even better. She doesn't even know about Atlanta. And this bitch think she know everything, Shay thought.

Amused to find that Catrina had been clearly left in the dark about David's plans to move, Shay figured she'd be the one to tell Catrina what David had not.

Shay told her about his job offer, and how he'd accepted it, and viciously added that he'd asked her to move down there with him. Then added, "Yeah, he your man all right. All this time he been fuckin' you, he ain't bother to tell you that he was moving." When she saw the confusion crowding in Catrina's eyes, she said, "I'on even wanna fight you no more now. Just to have you look like a dumb bitch is enough for me."

Casey

Glancing at the clock to confirm it was almost 3 am one more time before she climbed into bed, Casey huffed and picked up the stack of mail that she'd neglected to look at before. There were credit card bills, a letter from Serena, a couple pieces of junk mail, and the last was addressed to Daemon.

The handwriting was very feminine from what she could tell, but the return address was a company that she'd never heard of in California.

Casey shrugged as she put the mail aside and turned out the light. Just as she sank down into the bed the phone beside her rang.

"Hello?"

"Can I speak to D?" the female voice questioned.

Casey looked over at the bedside clock. It was three o'clock in the damn morning.

"Who is this?" she returned.

"Excuse me?"

Casey laughed despite the fact that she was very heated. "I said who is this?" she repeated.

"Casey? Is that you?"

Frowning, Casey tried to catch the voice. It was obviously someone she knew, or at least was familiar with. "It's me. But who are you, and do you have any idea what time it is?" she asked still unsure.

"Tamika. Daemon and I used to go together a couple of years ago. I'm sure you remember."

Casey sat up in the bed. She would never forget Tamika. Daemon had been in love with her from the time they got together until months after she'd left him to go to another school all the way across the country. Casey could remember the two years of their relationship as the worst years of her teenage life. She had wanted Daemon and couldn't stand Tamika because at the time she'd had him. She disliked her even more because Tamika had realized Casey's crush on Daemon and decided that she would flaunt it in Casey's face at every given opportunity.

"Yeah, sure I do. How are you?"

"Good I guess. Do you think it would be possible for me to get Daemon's contact number? I need to talk to him."

At three in the morning? "I don't think that would be a good idea."

"I see someone still has a childhood crush, isn't that cute? Or does he have a girlfriend now and you're worried that I'll get him into trouble?"

Casey laughed. "Girl, that California sun must have really been going to your head." It took all that she had in her not to give Tamika a piece of her mind and let her know that she was the current woman in Daemon's life. "Yes, he does have a girlfriend and the next time you wanna call here at three in the morning, remember that."

"I'll just call him in the morning," Tamika replied.

"Goodnight," Casey told her clicking off the phone before Tamika had a chance to respond.

The phone still in her hand began to ring. She hurried up and answered.

"Hello?"

"Casey?"

Casey frowned. "Who else would it be? And where you at?"

"At the front door." Daemon was opening the door as they spoke. "Were you asleep?" If she was mad at him for coming home at this late hour, he would soon find out.

"I was but Tamika called here."

"Who?"

"Tamika. As in your old girlfriend Tamika. What she want?"

Casey was getting up from her bed to open her bedroom door.

He questioned cautiously as he went up the stairs in four quick steps. "I don't know. What she say?"

Daemon closed his phone when he saw that Casey was standing in her doorway with a frown on her face.

"Do you know what time it is?" she questioned him as he tried to drop a light kiss on her cheek. Casey quickly turned her face away.

"You mad 'cause it's late? Sorry, Ma, but we was just kicking it," he explained backing her into the door frame. He was on the brink of wrapping his arms around her very exposed body when she pushed him away.

"I'm mad 'cause some hoe is calling my house at three in the morning."

Daemon stepped into her room, stood up straight, and squared his shoulders. "She is not a hoe, Case. I don't know why she called here."

Is he defending her? Casey folded her arms over her chest. "Do I look like I'm the fuck stupid to you?"

Daemon shook his head. "Not stupid. You look delicious, good enough to eat," he told her as he sat at the foot of her bed. She was wearing a pair of Victoria's Secret boy shorts and a black tank top undershirt.

Casey held up her hands. "Please, I am not fucking you 'til you tell me why she calling here."

Daemon stood up and spread his arms wide. "Babe, I don't know. I haven't talked to that girl in like two months."

"Two months?" she repeated as if she had a mouthful of salt. "So why you act like you had no idea who she was when I said that she called?"

Then he realized that he'd never once told Casey that he'd spoken to, and had seen Tamika, on several occasions since their breakup years before.

"Before you flip out and shit."

Casey held up her hand. "Wait, You never told me that y'all talked. I was under the impression that you hadn't spoken to her since y'all broke up."

"It is not that serious, Case. And to be honest there really wasn't any reason to. She don't have nothing to do with you or us. We've kept in touch over the years and that's it. Nothing more nothing less," he told her.

Casey stuck her bottom lip out in a pout. "Why you always get so defensive when I'm talking to you?" she asked him.

Daemon glared over at her. "Casey, you talk at people. Grown men don't like being talked at and since you've known me your whole life, I would think that you would know that by now."

Casey knew him all right... the nasty attitude and all. "I don't talk at you, D. I just get so wound up, because this isn't just some regular chick. When y'all were together, I was damn near invisible. You used to be in love with her. She is the only girl you've ever loved. I couldn't stand her ass," she told him as she sat in the empty space beside him and laid her head on his shoulder.

"Not the only girl. I love you, and you don't have to worry about her."

The head that lay rested on his shoulder slowly lifted and her eyes met his. "You love me?"

Daemon licked his bottom lip and a smile appeared. "Yeah."

Forgetting about Tamika and anything having to do with any other women, Casey eyed him. "Like in love with me love me, or love me like we've known each other all our lives love?" She had told herself that she would never press him into telling her that he loved her. That she would wait for him to do what came naturally. Faced with him doing exactly that, she couldn't wait for it to fall from his lips. Casey actually felt like snatching the words from his throat. But like the lady Ms. Serena had raised her to be, she sat patiently with her innocent brown eyes trained on his.

Daemon chuckled and gently touched her face. "Like in love with you, love you," he declared. "I've been in love with you for a very long time, Casey." He felt a weight lifted from his heart.

Everything forgotten, she leaned her lips closer to his. "It took you long enough," she told him with a smile. She closed her lips over his answer. "Say it again," she breathed.

"I love you," he murmured nipping her lips.

Casey inhaled the words like oxygen. *He loves me!*

Right now Casey imaged Daemon figured that she would want to be loved tenderly. That she'd want him to lay her back and do the many things to her body that in days she'd learned to love.

Any other moment she probably would have allowed him to, but she's claimed this as her moment to do as she pleased her opportunity to take the lead. Tonight she would show him what his love did for her. Even as he kissed her she let her left hand slip into his boxers. "I think he's in love with me too," she purred into his ear as his penis became erect with her massage.

Daemon breathed. "Of course he is," he murmured.

Casey chuckled and nipped at his bottom lip. She used her free hand to lift the back of his undershirt up. Breaking away, Casey then stood in front of him. "Take it off," she told him. Her voice was husky with the demand as she assisted him in pulling the shirt over his head.

Daemon smiled up at her. He recognized the look in her eyes and knew that she was about to unleash her freak on him.

Licking his bottom lip, he laughingly asked, "You gon' be in charge?"

Casey cocked her head to the side and eyed him. Then with a sultry smile forming, she told him, "I am in charge."

Excitement tingled up his spine as she leaned over him. His voice was thick with lust as he laughed and said, "Oh, shit, Mami."

"Stop," Casey murmured knowing that she'd lose her nerve to embarrassment if he continued to tease her. "Move back," she ordered with a nudge of her shoulder.

"I'm gon' like this," he said, following her instructions.

"Yes, you are," she agreed, crawling up his body. When they were face to face and Casey was braced atop his body, Daemon leaned up to kiss her. She settled firmly, pressing her hips into his.

"You have on too many clothes," he reminded her with a playful slap on her barely clothed behind.

Casey thought of the black beater and lace boy short thongs she had on as Daemon traced the edges of her underwear and thought that he was right.

"I fuckin' love these panties," he told her.

"You doin' a lot of loving tonight," she told him with a kiss to his neck.

"Ummm," he palmed both her cheeks and light ground himself into her. "You don't know the half of it. I'ma hit this from the back."

Casey licked his left nipple and then looked up at him. "You know I like that."

Daemon used one hand to grab a handful of her hair. "What else you like?"

One long finger touched his lips. "Shhh, this is my show."

With that said Casey dropped a light kiss to his lips and then went to work on the rest of his body. Kisses were placed to each of his shoulders, and she continued by licking a line down the middle of his chest and dipped into his belly button to tease it with her tongue. Driving him crazy was her goal.

Daemon was a man who prided himself on control over every situation in his life and tonight she would test his strength when it came to letting someone else handle business.

Anticipation increased his arousal as Casey would soon find out, Daemon suspected as she kissed his hip and hooked her hands in his boxers. She made a move to pull them from him just as Daemon lifted his hips to do the same.

Casey licked her lips at the sight of his enlarged penis. "Ummm," she hummed. "Now I'm in love." She held his shaft between hands as she eyed it as if she wanted to swallow it whole. Well, she did want to.

"Tell him about it," Daemon suggested, closing his eyes.
There was a very throaty laugh. "Oh, I'm about to," she answered and took him into her mouth.

"Shit, Casey," he hissed, playing in her hair as she worked her mouth up and down his length while her hand slipped down to massage his balls. She spent ten minutes sucking and jerking before she released him from her mouth to lightly blow on the head.

Daemon sighed as she began to lap at his penis like a lollipop. After a while she began to alternate the laps with beating it against her tongue, which had him in minutes trying to find his way back

116

into her mouth. The grip on her hair tightened as they worked together with him pumping his hips and her taking him as deep into her throat as she could.

He rubbed her face. "You're doing such a good job, mami. Umm, hmm...You know what it do to me," he moaned.

The first time he'd said that she had found herself embarrassed, but now it seemed to drive her to do even better. Casey smiled as she felt the first tingle of a spasm begin and increased her pace when his leg muscles tensed.

"Wait," he gasped out as she continued to suck at him. "Casey, let me just..." He grabbed her by the arm.

"Unt uhn." Casey showed a little resistance, because for the first time she was really enjoying sucking his dick. She really anticipated what would come out of it.

Daemon was ready to bust, and he desperately wanted to bury himself inside her before he did so. In his mind, he calculated the time it would take for him to recoup, if he let her have her way and decided against it. He pulled away from Casey, who was pouting, until he positioned himself behind her and gripped her hips only to pull them into him.

Casey sent a curious glance over her shoulders only to have him push her upper body onto the bed.

Quickly he pulled the lace boy shorts over her behind and down her thighs. It would take too long for him to take them completely off, he suspected, and assumed correctly when he heard Casey pleading in desperate anticipation of what was to come.

Casey strained back in invitation, but Daemon stilled her with a firm hand to her back.

"You had your turn. Now, I'm in charge," he told her as he entered her waiting body.

Casey moaned at his demanding back strokes.

Daemon let his head roll back as he continued the motion that connected his body with hers. A hand slapped soft skin.

"Now throw that shit back like you want me to have it," he instructed.

Casey did as she was told. Excitement driving each movement back. She found that she loved when he hit it from the back.

He lost control, just went wild with putting it in. The reigns of control were shifted from him to her and then back to him. She knew that in the end that the reserved Daemon Hicks would be making all types of demands on her body. Demands that she would gladly meet head on.

Casey worked her body with his until she heard the magic words that meant he was about to kill it and give them both what they so gladly worked for.

"Hold still." Then there was the quieting hand at the base of her back. "Arch your back and don't move," he told her.

With that said he did exactly as Casey knew he would. Daemon pumped and Casey moaned into the pillow. She closed her eyes against the pleasure of what she was feeling.

"Ahh, shit, D," Casey cried as she neared her climax.

"Ummm hmm." was all he said.

A shriek escaped her throat just as he went in for the stroke that did it all. Shivering, Casey remained on all fours as Daemon quickly withdrew and shot his load on her behind.

Out of breath, she looked over her shoulder to find him wiping himself off with a T-shirt and then taking the same shirt to wipe away the semen he'd left on her. Casey smiled and let out a shaky breath.

"Always the gentleman." She chuckled as he collapsed on top of her. "God, at least let me get up to get this off me," she murmured into the mattress.

Daemon rolled onto his back, allowing her to move her body over his. "And you wanted to start a fight."

Casey kissed the base of his neck. "Tell me that I'll always feel like this."

The plea was almost silent and let Daemon know that the innocent Casey was back. "If I had my way, we'd never have to get out of bed."

She snuggled closer, put a hand over his heart, felt it beat, and said, "Tell me you love me."

Tipping her face up to his so that they were eye to eye, Daemon did as she asked. "I love you, Casey in a way I've never loved another."

Casey accepted his admission into her heart. "I love you too. Now, you think you can wash my back."

Daemon smiled. "I can do a lot more than that."

Later, after a quick shower and quiet words, they lay wrapped together arms and legs intertwined with Casey's head resting on Daemon's shoulder as she slept. Yet, it wasn't Casey who he was thinking of. Tamika and the reason she'd been calling close to three in the morning was. He'd have to call her in the morning to see what was going on.

"Hmm, you still up?" Casey questioned sleepily as she snuggled in closer.

Daemon kissed her forehead. "Yeah."

Casey could feel the worry of his heart beneath her ear. "What you are thinking 'bout?" she asked as she felt the pace of his heart quicken at her voice.

"Nothing really. How about you?"

"Just you."

Chapter Thirteen
All Cried Out

Catrina

The angry storm of tears should have stopped by now but they hadn't ceased in the time it took for her to leave David's apartment and make it to her spot where she now sat being comforted by her mother.

Eight hours had passed since her run in with Shay and she was still reeling from the hurt the girl's words had caused. Blindly trying to run from her conscience, which also kept dealing her blows, she went home to her parent's house to seek solace from all the terror love caused.

Home, Catrina mused as she curled onto the cream sofa, still sniffing tears in her mother's lap. It wasn't the structure or the foundation of the building as much as it was the family who occupied it.

Silently as her tears began to recede and her heart stopped racing with both fear and hurt, Catrina watched as her father, Terrance, adjusted his tie.

Terrance looked at his eldest daughter and frowned. He hated seeing her this way, because as her father, there was nothing he could do to stop the pain she felt. He shook his head as his better judgment came into play. Catrina was a grown woman of twenty-one, and as she'd reminded him on numerous occasions, she did as she pleased.

Understanding that she would break her wings a few more times before she began to fly steadily, Terrance decided to just let her do her thing. If he were against it, she would anyway.

If she was set on learning from her mistakes, that was how she learned, he reasoned.

"Cat," he began. When she was a small child, he'd called her Kitten. "your mother and I have talked to you about this relationship with him, and you insist on being with him. You're grown, and we've come to the conclusion that nothing we say will change the fact that you love him."

Catrina lifted her head from her mother's lap.

"Yes, I said it," Terrance responded when his daughter's wide eyes met his.

"He's moving to Atlanta in less than a month, and I knew nothing about it. I've spent practically every hour of my free time with this man for the last couple months and he didn't find it necessary to inform me that he's moving to another state," she whined.

Catima could see that her husband was nearing the end of his rope, and that in itself surprised her. Terrance had spoiled, and continued in her adulthood to spoil Catrina ruinously.

Catima said, "Catrina, you haven't even spoken to him about it. How do you know that any of this is true?"

"'Cause she thought she was throwing something in my face when she said it. It came out too easy to be a lie," she concluded.

"Look at me," Catima ordered. "You defined your relationship with that man. No attachments."

"It was never like that between us," she stressed. "We've been friends for so long."

Terrance saw this all as nonsense. "You need to get yourself together so you can go and talk to him," he told his daughter. Despite their earlier differences David had proved himself to Terrance a year ago when he had come to him and told Terrance how he felt for his daughter and had tried to assure him that as a father, Terrance had absolutely nothing to worry about. It had been that talk that had changed the opinion of his daughter's childhood love/unborn baby daddy. "You're the one who doesn't want to be in a committed relationship with him. This is what you deal with when you make these types of decisions."

They were painting him as a saint. Like they hadn't heard what she'd been saying the entire time. "Y'all make it sound like it's okay that he ain't tell me. Like y'all taking his side in this."

"There are no damn sides, girl," Terrance shouted at her. "Catrina, if you love him you need to talk to him. It's as simple as that."

Catrina rubbed her eyes. "He's moving to Atlanta," she yelled. "He did not tell me."

She didn't know what hurt more; the fact that she'd finally admitted to herself that she loved him, or that her fears were already beginning to come true before she even got a chance to tell him.

David awoke as the alarm clock beside him blared noisily. Grunting in response, he rolled over and was surprised to feel nothing there beside him. Rubbing his eyes, he sat up and curiously scanned Catrina's bedroom for traces of her. When he thought about it, he couldn't remember Catrina climbing into the bed the night before.

After yawning and stretching, David rose from the bed and scratched his bald head. Anger began to pump through his veins like blood.

If she wasn't at home in her own bed, just whose bed was she in? He wondered. Rationalizing reasons began to swarm through his mind. It was easier to make rationalizations than to think of her with another man. Maybe she worked late. No, she's having that big wedding today. Rationalizing did not help one bit he concluded as his blood pressure began to boil.

Catrina's not showing up at home or attempting to contact him left him feeling out of sorts. It was the lack of communication that he believed as the type of Catrina behavior that scared him. Her moods were unpredictable.

Where the fuck is she and who she with? He thought.

"Hey, Chantel," he called when he walked into the hallway.

Chantel's scarf covered head popped out the crack of her door. She yawned and covered her mouth. "Wassup?"

"You know where Trina is?" he asked angrily.

The door widened, and Chantel slapped a hand to her face. "What did you do?" she accused him.

David watched as she folded her arms over her chest. "I ain't do anything. You haven't talked to her?"

Chantel shook her head and said, "Nope."

"She be playing way too many games," he replied, not able to think clearly.

Chantel shrugged. The past few days Catrina had been on an

emotional roller coaster due to her feelings for the man standing in front of her; she was probably just cooling her heels, Chantel figured. She also hoped that Catrina was doing it alone.

"You know how she is. You should call her on her cell."

"Yeah," he muttered with the thought of why he hadn't already tried calling her in his mind. "Where's my brother?" he asked, turning away.

"Downstairs. And Dave?" she said, bringing him to a halt at the top of the stairs. "She has a big day today, it's probably not what you're thinking."

It better not be what I'm thinking. He thought

David made his way down to the kitchen where he found Chris buttering a couple slices of toast. "What's up?" Chris asked.

"Not sure yet. Make me some," he told him, picking up the cordless phone.

David looked so angry poking at the number pad, Chris smiled and asked, "Why you so mad?"

David held up a finger as he waited impatiently for an answer.

"Hello?"

Hearing a masculine voice answer Catrina's phone sent him into a huge fit of anger. "Who is this?" he demanded. "Where is Catrina?"

Catrina was still sitting beside her mother when her father passed her the phone.

Clearing her throat, Catrina answered.

"Where you at?" David questioned her.

Catrina frowned and didn't look at her caller display on her cell phone as she questioned him in return.. "Why? Where are you?"

"I'm at your house, and who was that nigga answering your phone?"

Silence was her answer. "I really need to talk to you," he told her.

Catrina nodded. She could at least agree with that. There was an abundance of four letter words she wanted to say to him. And liar would be the first one. "Fine," she murmured, trying her hand at keeping calm. It wasn't easy to be tight lipped about how she felt. "What are you doing at my house?"

"I couldn't find my house keys, so I came over here last night. I
123

guess I should have checked your plans, seeing how you're with another nigga right now."

"I guess you should have." Her voice was cool enough to put frost on the sun. "I can't talk right now. I can't do this, not today."

That wouldn't do. It steamed him to think that she was with another man at that moment. "No, we do need to talk today."

Catrina went into the kitchen so her parents wouldn't hear what she said to him. "Too damn bad. It's the biggest day of my career, and I do not feel like dealing with bullshit between us."

"Bullshit between us?" he repeated. "You the one that's with someone else."

Tears sprang into her eyes. "I'm not with anyone else right now," she said weakly before cutting their connection.

The phone began to ring as she suspected it would as soon as she set it down on the table. Taking a deep breath, Catrina took a seat and let it ring. The phone rang three more times before she finally answered it.

"Where you at?" he demanded.

Catrina saw no reason to lie to him. Right now, lies would only make things ten times worse. "I'm at my parents. David, today is really big for me, and I can't be anymore fucked up than I am. I need to be focused, and I won't be, if I see you."

As angry as he was, Davis understood what today's wedding meant for her company. "After the wedding then. Bey, I really need to talk to you."

Catrina sighed. "I don't want you to take this the wrong way." Then she considered. "Well, I really don't care how you take it. I don't want you to be there when I get home, so could you just please do me a favor and go before I get there?"

David cleared his throat. "I can do that, if you promise me that we're going to talk about whatever you're upset about."

Catrina nodded. "Okay, I promise that we'll talk."

Chapter Fourteen
The Letter

Daemon

January 11, 2001
Dear Daemon,

I know that things have been a little strained between us since I left. I had so many reasons for doing so. We've discussed those reasons countless times over the past five and a half years. I know that you've forgiven me for breaking your heart, and I'm sorry that I had to. I really did love you. But there were things that I had to do for myself without you. Things that if offered, you weren't ready for. You were adamant about wanting to remain in Philadelphia and at the time, I didn't see any way that I could get you to move.

Okay, this is the coward's way of dealing with an issue, but it is the only alternative I have short of bringing it to your doorstep.

First, I want say that I need you to be as open-minded and understanding as possible. I'm moving back to Philly this summer permanently, and this only concerns you because I have a four year old daughter. You have a four year old daughter.
Karea Deana Hicks
Born: Feb 1, 1996 weighing 7 lbs. and 8 oz.

"Are you the fuck kidding me? She even got your last name. Is she serious?" Tyree questioned Daemon, the letter still in his hand.

Daemon shook his head. "Read this one," he told his friend.

June 1, 2001

As you can see from the previous letter which I never had the heart to send back in January we have a lot to discuss. I didn't know that I was pregnant until after I got to California and couldn't kick what I thought was a stomach virus. I didn't tell you because at first I was going to get an abortion. Then when the time came, I couldn't do it. I didn't realize until that moment that I was carrying my future in my womb. Daemon, she is everything to me and I couldn't fathom what my life would be without her. She is my success. Everything I am is wrapped up in her. I did what I thought was right for us. I had so many concerns with telling you. I didn't know if you were ready. Things would have been very difficult trying to make it work out. We live at opposite ends of the country. I just didn't know how to tell you, and trying to contemplate the changes that would need to be made to accommodate our lives seemed more than impossible. I could write forever on how wrong I was or trying to explain the circumstances that led me to make the choices I'd made, but I won't. I realize that this is a lot for you to take in, but I'll be waiting on your phone call. You may not believe me but I'm willing to do whatever is necessary to prove to you that she is yours. Like I said, I'll be moving back to Philly soon and if I don't hear from you by then, I'll stop by your house, and we can take it from there.

Tamika Johnson

David sucked his teeth. He already had enough on his mind without trying to contemplate what a child would mean for Daemon.

"She is lying," David said. "Have you spoken to her yet?" he asked with a frown.

"I received them today. And not that I think she lying or anything, but I'm still trying to process this," he told them. Both of his friends stared blankly at him. Tyree sucked in a breath.

David chuckled although there was nothing funny about his friend's situation. "You a dickhead. I know you didn't say that you believe her," he tried clarifying.

"I know you'll get a test. No botch walk up to you and say you got a kid and you believe her ass. I raised you way better than that. And you talked to this hoe like a million times since y'all broke up. You even seen her lying ass," Tyree added.

Daemon pushed his chair away from his desk and dragged his hands down his face. Damn, it had been a very long day. He'd spent the better half of his morning reading the letter over and over. He waited for Tamika to call like she'd told Casey she would do the night before but hadn't. He had tried calling her but had hung up, because he didn't know what to say. Based on calculation of the dates Tamika had provided in the letter, the child would be five-years-old. Five years without a father, without him if he was her father. He'd spent his entire life without a father and be damned if his child would do the same. He, just didn't know where to start.

By twelve that afternoon he'd called his friends and arranged to meet with them around six o'clock in the evening to break the news to them and get their reactions. At one p.m. he'd called his mother who had first questioned his belief of the situation and then advised him to have a DNA test done. Serena Hicks had raised him to take care of all of his responsibilities, but that didn't mean taking care of someone else's.

"I'm so damn angry that she would do something like this, Ma," he'd said to her.

"Well, so am I, boy. You think she want money?" she had asked him.

"No, she has a good job. And I don't see her lying about this."

"Daemon Karon Hicks, she is a liar. She's saying that you have a five-year-old daughter who she kept from you. Wake up, boy."

Hearing the impatience in his mother's voice had Daemon sighing. He hadn't expected Serena to be happy about the potential granddaughter. "She want something and we are not about to give it to her until we sure."

"I know, Ma." A knock on his office door reminded him of his one-fifteen appointment. "I have an appointment. I'ma call you later, after I speak with her."

"Okay. Love you, baby. Tell Casey to call me; I have a couple things to go over with her." Their conversation ended with that. He was grateful that the afternoon run to Voyce Record, and meeting with the realtor to check out a couple of locations for his hair salon filled the rest of his day. There had hardly been a free minute for him to think of anything other than business. That was good.

"What the fuck do tell Casey?" he grumbled.

"Keep it to yourself 'til you find out what's up with Tamika. This kid may not even be yours."

Both Daemon and Tyree knew their friend and understood how David thought. His philosophy never proved to yield any positive results. When it came to relationships David was a master at loving and leaving them. He would not be used as a fountain of creditable advice.

"Dave, no offense but you never think clearly about telling a woman the truth," Daemon informed him. "A woman that you love and respect deserves the truth."

David frowned and stood up. The truth, or the lack of it, always got him into trouble when things seemed to matter the most. "Yes, she does deserve the truth but you don't even know what the fuck the truth is, nigga. You don't take this serious, not from no bitch who wrote it in a letter mind you, that you got a fuckin' kid that you know nothing about, and just turn your girl's life upside down." David then stared at Tyree, anxiously waiting for his best friend to co-sign. "Can you tell him, please?"

"If this were any other girl you would be right. But it's Casey. He owes it to her."

Resigned to being alone in this, David shrugged and said, "Do whatever you want. Long as you're smart about it."

"You niggas act like I'ma just claim some kid. Y'all know me better than that," he said to his friends.

David smiled, despite his sour mood. "I was worried."

Tyree chuckled, "Me too, man. You used to love the shit out of that girl."

Daemon sucked his teeth. "That don't mean I'm dumb, nigga. What the hell am I going to do with a five year old? I can't believe that she'd do some whack shit like this."

"You 'bout to be going through it. And you know Tamika still want you, right?" Tyree asked. He had his share of baby momma drama with Nyimah and felt he knew.

Daemon hissed. "Please, I am not about to fuck with her."

"Don't front, nigga. Like three months ago before you decided to start messing with Casey, you was gon' give her a chance. I couldn't stand her ass, but she was throwing that pussy on you and had you whipped," Tyree remembered.

Daemon yawned and cracked his knuckles. "Well, we even, 'cause we couldn't stand Nyimah."

David nodded in agreement. "She wasn't even that pretty." Then he added, "Okay, she was hood cute, but her attitude was trash," when both his friends eyed him.

"Whatever," Tyree said. "The only person any of us liked was

Catrina. Aside from Casey."

"Wasn't today that big wedding?" Daemon questioned. He'd forgotten in the mist of his day.

Tyree said, "Yeah. Briannah was excited as hell this morning."

"Now who whipped?" Daemon commented absently to Tyree. "Weren't you supposed to go to the reception?" he added to David.

She doesn't want me there, David thought, as he rolled his head around and stretched his arms over his head. "My head is fucked up with the thought that she didn't want me there."

There was never a question of who when David used the pronouns she or her. There was only one she and her in his life. Catrina.

"What did you do?" Tyree questioned sure that Catrina's usual drastic approach to these situations were never unfounded.

Utterly confused for the first time in a long time, David shrugged. "I didn't do a damn thing. The night before last we were all boo lovin'."

"Boo lovin' dog?" Daemon asked.
David shook his head. "I hear it a lot. I have no idea what's wrong with her."

Tyree frowned at his friend. "Are you certain you didn't do anything to her?"

"Yes, I'm sure. Y'all think she seeing somebody else?"

"Doubt it," Tyree told him.

David looked over at Tyree. "How you so sure?"

"'Cause, like two weeks ago you said that she wasn't, and Briannah would have told me. She did suggest that I tell you to step up your game or something."

"And you know that's right," Daemon chimed in. "You know she in love with love you, man."

"She was crying and I want to know what happened. I can't take her ignoring me for another year."

They all understood that not speaking to David was a possibility.

"Let's hope it's not that serious," Tyree added.

Chapter Fifteen
What You Say

Casey

"You could have called me to let me know that you were okay," Daemon told her as he pulled back the covers of his bed.

Casey sighed. "I talked to you like twenty times, Daemon. Why were you calling me all day anyway?" she asked him.

Daemon frowned. He'd made those phone calls out of guilt. The news he was ready to drop on her was very heavy. He could barely carry the weight of it himself.

"I was worried," he said, leaning over the bed to grasp her hand.

Casey laughed. "About what? You knew that I was with Trina and Bri."

Daemon looked down at his watch. "It was like nine when you stopped answering my calls. You listen to any of the messages?"

Casey shook her head and squeezed his hand before letting it go. "Aside from a very busy day, Trina was a wreck. She found out that Dave is moving to Atlanta, and to calm her down, we took her to get drunk after the wedding and reception," she explained.

"And you ain't feel the need to call me back?" he questioned.

Casey sucked her teeth. "Did you hear me?"

"Yes, I heard you."

"So you know that I was busy, right?"

"Fuck being busy. It's two o'clock in the morning, Case," Daemon said.

Casey stepped away from the bed. "I think I will sleep in my own room." She began picking up her clothes.

Daemon frowned. "What?"

Casey rolled her eyes and sighed heavily before saying, "You don't fuckin' listen."

Daemon folded his arms over his chest. He had too much of his own issues on his mind to listen but said, "I'm listening," not wanting Catrina's problems with David to interfere with their relationship, especially since he had his own news.

Casey shook her head. "Only because you think that's what I want. Why are you always so closed off when it comes to Trina and Dave."

"'Cause you always get so worked up about their bullshit. You always so damn concerned with what's going between them and how hurt Trina is. She working my boah and you and your friends always actin' like she the victim."

"The victim? What the hell?"

How could he explain that he blamed Catrina for as much as he blamed David when it came to what was lacking in their relationship? They both played games, and he knew that Catrina was not an innocent party. Yet, everybody would vouch for how hurt she was when David cheated on her six years before and gave a wave to how she'd treated David afterwards.

Irritated because his anger actually had nothing to do with Catrina or David, Daemon flagged, "I'm positive that you will take this the wrong way so I'm not even gon' say shit."

"Are you the fuck serious? We have been down since we were kids. What the fuck you got against Trina and how she *"workin"* your boah?" She used air quotes to show her irritation.

Daemon sat down on the edge of the bed. "I not 'bout to get into it with you. You know I got love for Trina. But right now I'm more concerned with my own shit than I am with theirs," he explained.

His own shit? Casey's eyebrows rose slightly. She couldn't control her facial expressions so her lips easily slid into a frown. "What shit?" The question didn't carry the air of confusion, but the demand of authority. She straightened her back and folded her arms over her chest. "Is there something going on?"

Daemon walked over to his dresser and picked up two pieces of paper, walked back to Casey and handed them to her.

"What is this?" Casey questioned as her eyes briefly scanned the sheets and honed in on Tamika's name. "She tryna get back with you?" she concluded before reading the actual words.

"No. You gon' read it or do you want me to tell you?" Daemon offered. Prepared for anything, Daemon took a step closer to Casey. He was prepared but quite unaware of what to expect.

"Why the fuck is she writing you letters then?" She looked from him then back down at the sheet. Afraid of what she'd read, Casey began reading silently then aloud when she reached, "...and the only reason this concerns you is because I have a four-year-old daughter," she then looked directly into his cinnamon-colored eyes. "You have a four-year-old daughter?" she finished.

Casey turned away from Daemon and began pacing the hardwood floor with one hand to her hip and the other holding the two sheets of paper. Millions of thoughts raced through her mind. Not one coherent.

Casey stood still for a moment. It was really no more than ten seconds. "Is she serious?"

Daemon put in hands into the pockets of his pajama bottoms. "From what I understand she is," he responded. This time he stayed where he was, confident that she wouldn't want him crowding her.

"From what you understand?" Attitude was dripping from every word that fell from her lips. "You mean that you ain't call this bitch and see what she talking 'bout?"

Daemon shook his head. "I attempted to call her but I'm still thinking."

Casey scratched her left eyebrow. "Okay and how is it possible that you didn't know that she had a four- no, she's five now. How you ain't know when you just told me last night that you guys have talked and seen each other since y'all broke up?"

Impatient, Daemon removed his hands from his pockets and rubbed them together. "Casey, I didn't know that she had no baby. You know me better than that."

It was true, she knew him better than to keep that type of secret.

This is like some type of nut-ass Lifetime movie, she thought. "Call her."

"Case," he interrupted.

She wasn't having any of that. "I said call her and find out what the hell she is talking about," she told him very firm. She shook her head to rattle her thoughts a little. "We'n got time for this. You believe her?"

That was a very good question and one Daemon wasn't entirely sure he could answer honestly. If he said yes, Casey would question his sanity. If he said no, she would get all womanly on him and tell

132

him that it was a possibility that the child could be his. The safer way to play it was just not give a direct answer, he decided. "We gon' get a test to see."

The pose went from standing straight to hands on both hips. "I asked if you believe her."

"What the fuck you want me to say, Case? If I say I believe, you gon' get mad, if I say I don't believe you gon' be mad," he shouted. "I was completely blindsided. How you think I feel? I've had less than twenty-four hours to take in the fact that I might have a kid I knew absolutely nothing about."

There was no way to object. Daemon in this case was as innocent to it all as the child was. He needed her support. She understood that's what he was asking for without saying the words, there was no need to.

"I'm not going be mad," she paused. "At you anyway. I'm the hell angry with her. You know I don't like this bullshit game irresponsible parents play with their kids. I have zero tolerance for this type of shit. Daemon," she dragged her hands over her face in frustration then clasped them together close to her lips, "you really need to call her. The faster things are out in the open, the quicker we can take care of them. I'ma go to my room so you can have some time."

"Casey," he said. His voice was pleading.

She found that his eyes were as well when she separated her emotions from what this was doing to her and took time to see what it was doing to him.

Daemon went over to her and captured her hands in his and used the joint hands to tip her face up to his. "I need you. As my friend, as the woman I love to stick with me," he told her sincerely.

There had been a time when needing a woman equaled weakness to him, now need ran an equality race with necessity. Casey wasn't just any woman. She was the girl he'd spent his adolescence trying to ignore; his adulthood trying to deny, and the only woman he'd loved with such intensity that he saw a future with her.

Casey sighed as she unwound her hands from his. "I need you too, D. But if this is real— I mean if this is true, it changes everything."

There would be the permanent presence of a vulnerable five-year-old little girl and her mother. The child's mother and her permanent presence. Taking this situation at its worst, which would be him being the child's father, her dreams of being the only woman to bear his children would be ruined.

"Babe, we have to find out if it's true. I'm not gon' stress until I know the truth."

The truth was that he was already stressing but didn't want her to stress along with him.

Chapter Sixteen
Our Friends

Briannah and Tyree

"Boo, do you have any idea what time it is?" Tyree questioned Briannah as he flicked on the sofa-side lamp as soon as the front door was securely shut and locked behind her.

Briannah rolled her eyes and rubbed the ache in her back. "Don't scare me like that," she told her fiancée. Tired, Briannah sat beside him on the sofa. She laughed and put her hand on his leg. "You all sittin' in the dark and shit."

"You okay?"

"Yeah."

His dark chocolate-colored face carried a frown. "I been worried 'bout you all night, Bri."

Briannah smiled. "I told you I was going out with Trina after the wedding."

Tyree looked at his watch. "It's almost three o'clock in the morning."

"Well, we had to drive Trina home. And let me remind you that you just came in the house last night at quarter to three."

"I'm not seven months pregnant. You weren't answering your phone; Trina and Case ain't answer theirs. I was 'bout to start calling hospitals. I thought something happened to you."

Briannah squeezed his thigh. Her man was so protective, and mad as hell apparently. The vein in his neck made an appearance.

"Awww," she cooed as he pulled her into his lap. Smiling, Briannah wound her arms around his neck and kissed it. "Baby, I'm sorry. For some reason me, and Case ain't get no service and Trina was so fucked up that she turned her phone off."

"What happened with Trina?" he asked curiously. Tyree had no doubt that Briannah was going to spill the beans about whatever was troubling Catrina so he, in turn, could tell his best friend.

"The shit is going to hit the fan tomorrow," she began.

Like the male gossip he was, Tyree sat patiently waiting for the next tidbits of information.

"Trina knows about Atlanta, and she is so hurt."

"Whoa!"

"I know."

Tyree leaned back a little to look into Briannah's face. "Bri, I know you did not open up your damn mouth."

"What?"

He sighed. "You know that shit ain't none of your business," he told her.

Briannah's arms fell from around his neck. "Whoa, what you say?" she asked him.

Tyree rolled his eyes. He knew she hated when he chastised her actions. "Nothing, boo." Briannah removed herself from his lap. "That's what I thought," she said.

"You funny," he told her.

"Whatever. She one of my closest friends and I neglected to tell her."

"Well how she find out then?"

"If you would let me get the story out, you would know. Gosh."

He chuckled. "My bad. Go 'head."

In detail Briannah relayed the story to him.

"That's fucked up," was his response. Tyree picked up the phone.

"What you 'bout to do?" Briannah questioned him.

"Call Dave and let him know what's up. He was a lil' fucked up today."

Briannah folded her arms on top of her bulging belly. "No you not. Mind your own damn business."

"Boo, he stressed the fuck out. She told him that they were done, and that she didn't want to talk to him today," he embellished.

"One of my best friends just spent the last three hours crying over that nigga. She stressed the fuck out."

Tyree rubbed his head after replacing the telephone in its cradle and thought about all the things that had come to surface concerning his best friend and Catrina. "They got a lot to talk about."

"Yeah. How your friend keep on disappointing her. I'm

messed up, 'cause I felt guilty for not mentioning it."

"It wasn't your place, and Trina got her secrets."

Briannah sucked her teeth and frowned. "She ain't even got no secrets from that nigga."

"Okay, all right. Don't play dumb with me."

"Whatever, Tyree. He know everything about her. How many niggas she fucked; how many dicks she sucked, everything."

"Yea, okay, boo. That's your girl, and you gon' say whatever to protect her."

"Protect her from what? She ain't scared of shit. What are you talking 'bout?"

"You ain't know that she was pregnant back then?" he challenged.

Those words closed her already open mouth.

Oh shit, Briannah thought.

"That's what I thought," Tyree responded.

Briannah was so taken aback, she didn't know where to begin her questions. "How you know?"

"When you hurting 'bout something, you talk to your friends, right? Well, mine talk to me."

"Dave know about the baby? How he find out?"

"Don't worry about it. She ain't tell him."

Excuse the fuck out of me, Briannah thought. "I know he better not bring that up."

"If she's gonna be kicking the shit to him like I know she going to, he gonna bring it up."

"Tyree, she would really flip out on him."

Normally there were no secrets between the two. It was surprising to Briannah that Tyree had known and not shared the information with her. It was not however, surprising to Tyree that Briannah had known and had not shared the information with him in an attempt to protect her friend.

"I know, Bri. Their situation is fucked up right now. All I know is that I love you," he told her.

A smile spread across her caramel-colored face as she went to him. "I love you too." Quietly, Briannah fit her body into his, the baby pressing into his side. "Seeing our friends so upset just makes me so thankful that I have you," she murmured as he rubbed her stomach. The baby kicked beneath his touch.

"Your friends are gonna need you, Bri," he said close to her ear.

Because his eyes were serious, she asked, "You know something?"

An explosion of air. "D may have a five-year-old daughter by Tamika."

Frowning, Briannah leaned back. "What?"

Tyree laughed and tighten his hold around her. "That's what we said. She wrote him this letter saying that she had a daughter and that the little girl was his. She even had the nerve to give the kid his last name."

I know Case is flipping out, Briannah thought. "You think that's funny?"

He shook his head. "You know the boah always calm and composed. I think this shook him up a little bit. And we think he believe her ass."

"I know he ain't that stupid. What he say she said when he talked to her?" she inquired.

Tyree shrugged. "He hadn't talked to her before he talked to us."

"Niggas." As a female, Briannah could imagine what was going through Casey's mind.
The news warranted an ass whopping for Tamika from all parties involved. "When is he going meet her?"

The inquires she made couldn't be answered.

"Boo, I don't know. I'm just saying that she is definitely going to need you. And Trina is too, cause no matter what happens, he gonna move.

Chapter Seventeen
I Ain't Tell You,
You Ain't Tell Me

Catrina

There was no justified reason for her to feel pissed. Not when she'd told him that she couldn't and wouldn't deal with him, and that for once in their confused relationship, he'd listened. That being true, why did she feel so utterly incomplete after experiencing the greatest career success in her life? Success somehow seemed hallow without him to share it.

Never being one to drown her sorrows in liquor, Catrina had done just that. At least she had tried to, in any case. The alcohol that Casey and Briannah had encouraged her to drink to numb the pain had not done its job. There was still a faint pounding in her head just above her right temple. She had dry tear streaks down her cheeks. The tears had come so easy when she was in the presence of her friends.

The fact that they'd known about David's decision to move to Atlanta hadn't made her any angrier; it actually made her more emotional. As usual they'd been there lending shoulders for her to cry on. They both apologized to Catrina for not sharing their knowledge of David's plans to move before she had discovered it in the way that she had.

How many times had she cried on borrowed shoulders over him? Too many to count, she thought as she twisted the doorknob to her bedroom.

She opened the door and spotted him sitting comfortably on her bed with the television remote in his hand.

He's here. Catrina could have cried at the sight of him. Was there any way to explain the mixed emotions that came along with his unexpected presence? Happiness, hurt, confusion all rolled into one.

Tired with defeat, she gave up, leaned against the back of the door and massaged her right temple.

"What are you doing here?" she choked out.

David sat up and stared at her for a brief second. She looked very tired and rumpled in her white linen pant suit.

"I needed to talk to you earlier, but I wanted to respect your wishes about the wedding even though I really wanted to be there to support you. But, I had to see you."

Catrina shook her head as she stepped out of her high-heeled Nine West shoes. "I really don't want to talk to you right now, David, so I think you need to leave."

David stood up. "I'm not leaving until you tell me what's going on with you. What's all this about?"

Catrina cleared her throat. "You really want to do this?"

"Bey, something is wrong when you tell me that you're not interested in talking to me. Especially when you think I'd leave it at that."

"You don't have a choice."

David frowned at her and began to move around the room. "I don't have a choice? Really? You gon' have to do better than that, bey."

Catrina shrugged and removed her jacket. She contemplated hanging it up, but threw it over the back of a chair instead. "I'm tired. And I really just can't take it anymore."

"Let me know what the problem is straight up."

"Atlanta. You're moving to Atlanta," she answered.

It would take a minute for the shock to pass, she knew. His expression and his silence were signs of his guilt, Catrina assumed. With more patience than she realized she possessed, Catrina sat on the arm of the chair and looked up into his surprised face.

"You mighty quiet now," she said laughingly, but it hurt.

It would be best for him to just explain everything before he questioned her on who supplied her with the information. It wouldn't prove to be difficult, David figured, his choices were limited to two people.

"I was going to discuss it with you." It was a weak attempt at an excuse. One that he understood wasn't good enough before it left his lips. "Bey, I love you."

"Love?" she questioned, jumping up. "What the hell do you

know about love? How can you say that you love me when you're moving to another freaking state in a month, and the woman you 'love' knows nothing about it? It's just like you're nineteen again. Stupid and thinking that I am too."

She was presenting a heavy case against him, he realized. "I don't think that you're stupid, and I'm not behaving as if I'm nineteen. This time I'm loving you as a man loves, and I'm not scared or confused about how I feel."

"So I'm just supposed to fall in line, 'cause you're ready now? Fuck the fact that you obviously don't give a shit about my feelings. That we've been sleeping together for over two months, and I thought it was so much more, and you didn't feel the need to tell me that you got a fucking job in Atlanta. Fuck that you're my best friend, right? Fuck all that, 'cause you say you love me."

Catrina wasn't as skilled as she'd once been at shielding her true emotions against the onslaught of questions.

Despite the language she chose to use, David could see that she was hurting. He reached for her, but she backed away. "Bey..."

"You asked me to trust you and I know that I shouldn't have, 'cause everything always has to be your way. And when shit end up being your way, my feelings always get hurt. Always. I'm so tired of this. Back and forth." She made a hand gesture from her to him and back to herself to emphasize her point. "Always going through the motions, trying not to get my feelings hurt. Not trusting my heart, 'cause it ain't reliable. You have no idea what I've been going through attempting to trust what you say. Trying to trust that you love me, tryna trust that I love you and, the fact that I thought it'd finally be enough."

"Bey, I apologize. I didn't expect for you to find out from somebody else. I just needed time to get things together in my head. I knew that if you knew that I was moving that you wouldn't have given us a chance. I know you, Catrina, and I know that is how you would have handled it."

She smiled at that. A pitiful smile. "You know me," she repeated. "How can you know everything that goes on inside me and not know that all I've ever expected from you was the truth. How could you not respect me enough to give me a choice to something so important in my life?"

David sighed heavily. "I wasn't thinkin' about anything but getting you. About nothing but having you feel the way you felt about me before I messed everything up. I'd give anything to have you trust me with your heart again. I didn't care what the end result was. I didn't care about what I had to do to get you as long as I got you."

Catrina spread her arms out. "And you still don't have me."

"You never make it easy on me. What about what I've been going through? Having to watch you go from one nigga to the next and act like we cool enough for you to do that shit. Fuck me, right? Fuck that I'm always here when you need me."

Catrina frowned and held up her hands. "You are not going to turn this around on me. I was right from the beginning. There is too much stuff between us to ever have anything."

Though he had been trying his best to remain patient, David's annoyance with her was beginning to show. "You keep saying that, and although you apparently think that I'm not capable of loving you, I'm good enough for you to fuck."

Catrina nodded and accepted his words with the hurt of truth. "Maybe I deserve that."

David took a second to massage his left temple. He was about to take the conversation to a place beyond anything they had ever discussed and he wasn't sure what her reaction would be. "Always the victim," he murmured.

Catrina narrowed her eyes and glared at him. She couldn't believe that he had turned the whole situation on her. As if she were the one who had been lying. "What?"

"You haven't been honest about everything between us."

"What is that supposed to mean? I've always been real with you, Dave. I didn't tell you that I loved you, because I wasn't sure how to deal..."

His laughter stopped her. "So you're going to continue to pretend like you don't know what I'm talking about?"

Confused, Catrina stared at him and didn't respond.

He eyed her suspiciously.

"What are you talking 'bout?" *He cannot be talking about what I think he's talking about. He better not be talking about what I'm thinking.*

"The baby. My baby. You ain't tell me you were pregnant."

"Your baby? Riiiiight. I guess you got me," she responded dramatically. She showed no traces of her surprise at his knowing. Inside, her head and heart were pounding.

David folded his arms over is chest. "That's all you're going say?"

Catrina shrugged and shook her head sadly. "My baby was never real to you."

David grabbed both her wrists and pulled her to him. "'Cause you ain't feel the need to tell me. I had a right to know. Things would have been so different had I known."

Catrina resisted the urge to yank her hands free but instead stared defiantly into his eyes and even laughed. "Things would have been different because of the baby. What, you would have stopped cheating and straightened up for our baby?"

"All you had to do was tell me."

"I'm not going to discuss this with you. You don't really wanna hear why I didn't tell you. You already have your mind made up. You wanna make accusations."

David let Trina's wrist go with a little force that had her stumbling back a few steps. He turned his back. "Fuck accusations, Catrina. You know what it's like to have someone you barely even remember walk up and ask about how your kid is? About four or five-years-old, right? I'm thinking, what kid? I mean I have no idea about what dude is talking 'bout. So I asked him, and confusion was written all over his face as he revealed that his girl mentioned way back that me and you were having a baby. I told him that he was mistaken, and that you and I didn't have any kids."

She could imagine how he felt. "And then you didn't ask me about it?"

"Ask you about it? You have any idea how confused I was? No, of course you don't. I got people walking up to me questioning me about a kid I don't have. So guess where my mind goes?"

"You thought I got an abortion."

"You know me, I have to piece everything together. So I'm trying to pinpoint everything. You just all of a sudden stopped talking to me, moved with your grandma to Jersey. You were really just trying to get away from me."

"You thought I got rid of it, didn't you?" It hurt her to think that he thought her capable of something so petty.

"Yes, I did."

"And this is the way you chose to bring it up to me? In the midst of your mess."

"Let me talk for a minute."

"The floor is all yours, David."

"Don't be smart, Trina. So here I am thinking that you got rid of my baby, so I ask Ty what I should do. Of course he like, 'ask her. You want me to ask Bri?' Of course, all your friends would know about the baby. I called your dad, shit. I was sick. And to my surprise he was open to discussing what you weren't. It put my conscience to rest that you didn't get rid of my baby 'cause I was an asshole. Then I found out that you lost it, and it hurt that you wouldn't share that with me."

"How long have you known?"

"Since last year."

There was entirely too much going on. Entirely too much for her to cope with at the moment. Nothing had been resolved. In fact, they had been presented with a new set of problems that needed to be dealt with.

"Last year? This secret shit is becoming redundant. And it's basically no point going over any of this. You got a promotion and didn't tell me; I lost a baby and didn't tell you. I guess we're even."

There was no hint or traces of anger in her voice now. That scared him. Calm Catrina always scared him.

"Even? Now is not the time to shut down on me, bey. When I was a young boah, you were everything to me, and I was scared of how I felt. I needed to be a man, and back then I thought that was proved by how much weight we moved on the block, and how many girls I had on my dick . Fuck, I ain't know what I had 'til I lost it. That's not gonna happen twice, bey. I'm not about to let you kick that not speaking to me shit again."

Confidence was one thing that she'd always admired about him. He barked out orders and never thought to question if they'd be followed. "It's not up to you, Dave."

David stepped in front of her. "If I leave it up to you, I'll be waiting forever."

Catrina attempted to side step him but was brought to a halt by his stopping hands at her waist. "For what?"

Then he was dropping down on bended knee, pulling a small box from his pocket. "For you to marry me," He said opening the ring box.

This doesn't make it right, she felt. With closed eyes and tears she told him, "I love you, Dave but I can't."

Chapter Eighteen
Aftershocks

Casey

Nerves were unraveling with the anticipation of seeing Tamika face-to-face in what had been six years. Manicured nails were bound to be bitten. She'd hate to ruin her cotton candy coat in an impatient fury. The nerve of the woman, Casey fumed as she paced across the living room floor.

Anticipation was cut short with a brief buzz of the doorbell. "I'll get it," Daemon said from the kitchen.

Casey endured one minute of anger, pain, frustration, and twinge of envy as she stood waiting for Tamika and Daemon to make their entrance. The moment Tamika did, Casey remembered why she'd hated her. From head to toe, Tamika was a picture of perfection. She was a black Barbie come to life. Tamika's height matched that of a model's and was just two inches taller than Casey. Her slim-almost willowy frame always made Casey wish that she was just a bit thinner. She had a heart-shaped face topped by a mile of wavy black hair inherited from her Native American roots, and her eyes were... What color were her eyes today? Violet, she'd always worn color contacts. That was something Casey had never been envious of. The make-up was flawless, and her style of dress was well chosen for the day based on the low humidity weather forecast. Irritated, Casey rolled her eyes. As she scanned Tamika, she noticed the little girl hiding behind her mother's leg.

This hoe is scandalous. She was trying to use her child to gain sympathy. What mother is going to bring a young child to meet her "father" when nothing had been discussed between the two?

"Hello, Casey," Tamika spoke first. There was a spark of attitude in her voice.

Casey was thrown off by it. This was a fight that she was not about to walk away from.

"Tamika."

"How about we all sit down," Daemon suggested.

"Karea." She was pulling the girl from behind her leg. "She just has to warm up," she told Daemon. "Say hi, baby," she told her.

It was no question that the little girl was gorgeous. Karea's complexion was somewhere between Daemon's golden brown and Tamika's mahogany, which would put her somewhere close to a medium shade of brown, and the eyes were the same shade of rich cinnamon she saw when she looked into Daemon's.

Casey shrugged off the brief feeling of familiarity. The color of eyes meant nothing, she chastised, hopeful that she was telling herself the truth. The child was also tall and thin and was topped with the same dark wavy hair as her mother.

"Hi, what's your name?" Casey waved in an attempt to make the child feel comfortable.

The child smiled at Casey, responded in a very low gentle voice that said, "Karea Deana Hicks. What's your name?"

"Casey, but everybody calls me Case, and this is D," Casey said introducing him.

Karea looked up in wonder at Daemon. Casey could see the curiosity her eyes and wondered if Tamika had given the little girl any idea of what would be going on around her. From the way Karea was staring, Casey could only think that Tamika had done a job pumping that she would meet her daddy today.

"Does she know who I am?" he asked enthralled with the look of the girl. His heart was pounding in his chest and his breath was arrested by the fact that her eyes were his eyes. It was something unseen by the observing eye, because the rise and the fall of his chest and his voice remained steady.

Tamika shook her head, surprising Casey, who would have bet her life savings that she had.

"I didn't think it would be a good idea until everything got settled. I don't wanna shake up your life, Daemon, and I don't want my little girl to be put in a position of having to meet you when you're not ready to accept the responsibility of all this," she explained. Tamika took a seat on the sofa. Karea followed. "So, no, I didn't tell her that you are who you are."

Casey said, "I thought you said that you knew he was-"

"Mooom," Karea let out as if she were frustrated. Then she

147

began leaning all over her mother. "When we going to Grandma's?"

Patient eyes looked at the five-year-old. "Karea, give Mommy a chance to talk, please."

She huffed and her bottom lip stuck out in a pout. "You said we were gonna go."

"In a minute," Tamika responded.

"Is it okay to talk about this in front of her?" Casey wondered. All the five-year-olds she knew were surprisingly intelligent and caught on to more than grown-ups expected. Both Cinyah and Yah were smart as hell, and nothing ever got past them.

Although Casey was the one who asked the question Tamika looked directly at Daemon and said, "I didn't have any other choice but to bring her. We can go in your office, and she can sit out here with Casey while you and I talk."

Casey frowned. "I ain't even bout to sit out here while-"

Daemon shook his head. "Is it okay for her to sit out here alone? I would like for Case to be there."

Accepting that Daemon was letting her know that Casey had a position in his life, Tamika looked over at him. "I guess. It doesn't make a difference to me, but I don't have time for no insecure girlfriends. I'm not here for no drama or bullshit."

Instantly offended, Casey said, "First of all, I am not insecure and bitch, you are the drama. We don't have time for it," Casey told her pointing from herself to Daemon as she stepped closer to the sofa where Tamika was sitting. "And we don't have time for no bullshit." She pointed at her. "So you better not be lying neither, 'cause then we'll have a problem."

"Karea, go sit on the couch over there and close your ears," Tamika told her daughter with a little push.

The Barbie Doll stood up. Didn't mean much to Casey who knew that Barbie's couldn't fight. "Girl, I'm not worried about you and no adolescent crush."

"Girl? You and your scanky ass lucky that I'm not about to beat you down up in here. Coming up in here like your word is the indisputable truth."

Unwilling to be put in the middle of a cat fight, Daemon said, "Casey," while pulling her back, in fear that she was going to lose her patience with the situation and actually hit Tamika.

It wasn't fear that led her to say, "Look, I know that this is a lot to deal with, and no offense, but this really has nothing to do with you, Casey. This is between me and D." Tamika wasn't inclined to getting into a fist fight with Casey who she suspected had her by at least twenty pounds and some street fights under her belt. Had she known Casey, she wouldn't have suspected her of being a street fighter. Yes, Casey had an abundance of mouth. And yes, she was very loud and vocal about her feelings, but it had never come down to her actually participating in a street fight.

Casey nodded. There was no reason to make this woman believe that she was the hood rat that she always thought of her as. Not to get it wrong she was ready to put her foot in Tamika's ass, but realized that there was a time and place for everything, and now was not that time. Her place was with Daemon. But if, no forget the ifs— there would be no way that she would be in the same situation. But in the event she found herself in a similar one, she wouldn't want a woman who was just a girlfriend interfering in her business.

"You're right. Is it alright if I take Karea to the store while the two of you discuss this?"

Daemon eyed both women. "Look, we're all adults here. You can stay, Case."

Tamika folded her arms over her chest. "You can take her."

Casey nodded her head. "That's okay. You talk and I'll go out. I need to call Trina, anyway." She walked to Daemon and planted a kiss on his lips. Then turned to Karea, who had done as she was told and sat with both of her hands over her ears, and extended her own out to the girl. "Come on, Karea; I'ma take you to the store."

The hands fell and curious eyes went to her mother's as if to ask for permission.

"Go ahead. When you come back we can go to Grandma's," Tamika said in a reassuring tone that only mothers possessed.

The moments of bitterness, disgusts and uneasiness passed when Karea's small hand slid into Casey's and took hold. There was an intense silence as they exited the front door of the house. Casey examined Karea and saw that the child seemed to be in quiet contemplation.

"Are you mad at my mom?" Karea's quiet voice questioned as they walked the pavement.

"No."

Karea stopped and looked up at Casey and tilted her small head to the side and squinted her eyes against the shining sun. "You called her a curse word. And you were in her face."

Casey smiled sweetly, trying to find the exact words to say to the girl. "Sweetie, sometimes grown-ups say things that they don't mean. Doesn't mean we're mad."

Eyes wide, she said, "You looked mad. And my mom, she was mad."

Casey laughed. Children had a way of making you smile although there were no reasons for celebration. She shrugged and pulled the child into a walk. "You're right, we were mad. It's just we have grown-up things going on right now."

"Is he my dad?"

Kids. Smart as hell and nothing ever gets by them even when you talk around the subject they still know. "Why would you ask that?"

"My mom got a picture of him."

That stopped her.

"And his name is like mine. I—I can read."

"Okay. When we get back inside, you can talk to your mommy about it."

I knew that bitch wanted him. I knew it. They were at the corner and almost in the store when Casey's cell phone began to buzz on her hip. With the phone to her ear she said, "Stand right here, Karea. Hello?"

"Case, please tell me that you've spoken to Trina," Chantel said in a quick stream of words.

"Not this morning, why?"

"She had this huge argument with David last night. He asked her to marry him, and she said no and then she left. I called my aunt and uncle; she wasn't there, and she didn't go to work today. She's not answering her cell. I don't know what she doing."

A trickle of sweat made its way down the side of her face and she frowned into the sun. Casey wiped her face so she could concentrate on more than the sun and the current baby momma drama.

"You know her Chantel. She probably just needed time."

150

Chapter Nineteen
Nothing Even Matters

Catrina

She was searching for....
Quiet...
Peace...
Time to herself...

If she could just hold on to any of those longer than ten consecutive minutes, she'd be sane. Yet, Catrina could find none of those, and right now, they were the things that were on the top of her wish list.

Why was it so hard to just let her decision be final? she wondered. Why had saying no been so easy but living with it be so hard? She considered herself to be a smart woman, yet when left in moments of reflection, she felt incredibly stupid. Incredibly weak and lost. Oh, God, so lost.

Why had she told him no?

I told him no, she thought as she buried her head between her knees. The distance she'd put between herself and David by running to her grandmother's home in New Jersey only spanned in miles. At the moment, there was no way that she would be rid of him in her mind.

"You're going to get grass stains on your pants," Catherine told her granddaughter. After watching her grandchild for a half hour Catherine decided that Catrina would be ready to talk to her. Already aware of the reasons Catrina had come to her home, she'd planned to be firm. As a child and an adult Catrina's parents had spoiled her beyond comprehension and to her understanding actually paid attention to her theatrical episodes involving David. "You think that crying is going to solve your issues, girl?" she questioned sternly.

Catrina lifted her head to stare into Catherine's face. It was almost emotionless except for her eyes which seemed angry. "Gram," Catrina replied with the tone that implicated 'don't start'.

Catherine patted Catrina's head. "Don't Gram me. You came to my house."

She was right of course, Catrina reasoned. Crying had never solved any of her problems. Not when she'd lost her baby, not when she'd finally lost David. "I just need to clear my head."

Catherine smiled. "And I'm gonna help you. Come inside and sit like an adult."

A weak smile appeared. There was no doubt that Catherine would help.

Mason jars sat waiting on the coffee table to be filled with Catherine's homemade mixture of iced tea and lemonade in a glass pitcher sweating off its chill waiting to be poured. "I thought you could use something cold," Catherine spoke after a long waiting silence from the yard to the living room. "Your mother hardly ever cried as a girl, and that's all I see you do."

"I don't want to talk about it. I just had to get away and I don't expect that you'll take my side, or even understand what I'm going through. I don't even know what I'm doing."

Catherine sat as she handed a glass of tea to Catrina. She sipped and then sniffled.

"Love isn't easy. I'm not going to take sides because there is no correct one to choose. There are faults in both of you. But you're both adults and need to deal with this as if you are. You make a decision, you stand by it. You don't run from it. You should take control of your love life as you have your career. I don't see people walking all over you in business."

Catrina shook her head. "It is not that easy, Gram. I love him. It sounds stupid but I love him. I just don't see a way to hold on to him."

"Why would you be with him if you didn't think that he could love you the way you deserve to be loved?"

After a sip Catrina answered, "I know that he loves me. It's just all the rest that gets in the way. What's the saying: 'Sometimes love just ain't enough'?" Catrina stood up. Suddenly the room seemed to become very small. "God, Gram. Did you know that Daddy told

152

him about the baby last year? And do you think either one of them said anything to me about it? The whole time I'm saying things like; 'I can't trust you' and 'I'm scared of you,' and—"

"What bothers you the most? That he knew about it and didn't say anything, or that you aren't the one who told him?"

"I know that I should have told him and there isn't much more I can do. You can't take things back, there's no rewind button in life."

"No, there isn't and no you can't. He asked you to marry him, and you said no, right?"

It hurt. There was a lump in her throat that was hard to swallow. "Yes. I said no and he's going to leave." She shrugged again and buried her face in her hands.

PART THREE

Looking pass the past to a new day

Memories both bittersweet and precious all have their place

Been through a lot, but no more than I could face

Endured no more than my heart could take

Nothing that I would think to forsake

I let go of the past

And took in a deep breath

I'm ready to embrace what's next

Whatever comes my way

I'll find a way to cope

As I breathe the fresh air of a new day

My lungs fill with hope

Catrina Price *2009*

Chapter Twenty
All Grown Up

August 2009

Casey

Love had never been simple for her, Casey reflected. She had no memories of her mother or father. She could not recall ever being held tightly by the stranger who'd left her with her grandmother. The death of both her grandmother and uncle had left marks on her young heart. Those factors were enough to damage weaker people, Casey assumed, but her heart didn't allow her to feel as if she were less due to the circumstances of her early life. She'd had an angel in Ms. Serena which she knew made the difference between her and others who didn't have someone to love and cherish them. So all in all, despite her earlier hardship, Casey would have sworn that her life was somewhat a fairytale at the early age of twenty. She felt she had everything once Daemon had finally allowed their love to have a life.

Loving Daemon Hicks had not been simple either. Casey smiled to herself as she traced her fingers down the hand sewn lace of her veil. Now, finally eight years later, the three carat princess cut diamond that weighed heavily on her finger for the past two years was finally going to be joined by a wedding band. In three weeks, she'd be Mrs. Daemon Hicks.

Hadn't she spent her entire youth and snatches of her twenties loving him and nobody else? Loving hard when they were together and carelessly when they were apart. She silently prayed to Jesus Christ for forgiveness for that visit to Appletree Street and the resulting abortion of a child she'd created with another man four years before. The reckless one night had left her life, and heart forever changed.

Then a year later there was a miscarriage and a bout of depression that followed over losing the baby and her guilt of the abortion. At the time, Casey was sure that God was punishing her for years of inattention to her professed faith of Christianity. She felt secure that Daemon loved her through all of that.

There were no secrets between the two. The hardest moment was four years ago she had told him about her pregnancy and confided in him that it wasn't his baby. There was a stressful point when she decided that she'd get rid of it, and he suggested that she keep it. Though at the time Daemon seemed supportive and obliging, Casey knew that he would change. She knew that she wasn't woman enough to accept all the things that would have come with having some other man's baby.

Casey could still remember it as if it happened yesterday.

"I can't keep it," she'd said to her friends as she paced her bedroom back and forth. Even then her support team of Catrina, Briannah, and even Alieas had ached with her through the emotional decision. None of them agreed with her decision to abort the pregnancy, but all were supportive.

Catrina who had been emotional, said, "You can keep it. Stop saying that. You have a good job, you're an adult. You have a man who is willing to take care of and love both of you."

Catrina's opinion was all heart, Casey thought. She understood that Catrina's emotions and personal views on abortion made it difficult for her to agree. At any point before this experience, Casey reflected that her own would have been similar.

"Y'all don't understand," she'd pleaded to them.

Briannah shook her head. She didn't, but it was not her place to judge. "It's your body and your decision, Casey. We all just want you to make the right one," she'd said.

The right one for y'all, Casey had thought.

Alieas could feel the tension in the room and wanted to avoid any words that if spoken would be regretted. "Casey, it's your choice. We love you and want you to do what's right for you." She could remember Alieas coming to her, taking her face between her hands, and looking directly into her eyes. "Just know that this is not something to be taken lightly. Give yourself a lil' more time and pray about it," she had advised.

The tears fell as she pulled her face away. "I have prayed about it and my heart is unchanged. I'm probably going to burn in hell. I just don't have—"

"What if you can't have another baby?" Catrina interrupted.

She had been trying to maintain the role of supportive best friend, but what Casey was doing was against all their beliefs. The thought of Casey's selfish reasons brought tears to her eyes. Life was such a gift. Being able to get pregnant was such a gift. How could she be so careless about it, and expect them to have the same attitude?

Briannah had sent Catrina a cautious look of warning. It took everything in Catrina to look past her personal views.

"I'm just asking, Casey," Catrina had said. "I love you, and this won't change that."

In the end, Casey was still her best friend, and she would be there no matter what. Catrina had gotten up from her seat, went to Casey, and hugged her tightly. Both women rocked for a minute.

That's how Daemon had seen them when he stepped into the doorway. He'd cleared his throat to make his presence known. Casey looked over at him but didn't speak.

"You want me to come back?" he'd asked.

Casey shook her head as she stepped away from Catrina. "No."

"We're going to give y'all some privacy," Briannah had told him.

Catrina nodded and wiped her eyes. "Yea, just call us later."

Daemon waited until they all made their exit before he spoke again. "You told them?"

Casey nodded. "I did, and they don't agree. Not that I thought they would," she had murmured as he pulled her into his embrace.

Casey held on to Daemon as she cried silent tears, occasionally accompanied by a small hiccup. "You don't either. You don't really think I'm right either," she told him.

"Babe, it's not about what I think is right or wrong. Not about what anyone else thinks or wants. You already know what I say. You already know what I want," Daemon had said as he stroked a calming hand over her back.

So unselfish, she'd thought. Casey moved to put a comfortable distance between them. It was a distance that she'd began creating since the moment she'd found out that she was pregnant with another man's child. She'd been faced with all her insecurities building up from that moment.

"You don't want that. How could you be okay with me having another man's baby?"

"What choice do I have?" His voice had been rough with temper but tapered down by patience. "If it weren't for me fucking up, you wouldn't even have been with dude. Please don't say that this is for me," he had told her, capturing her hand in his.

Casey had touched his cheek. His sincerity to her dilemma felt almost gut wrenching. He judged that she was being small and weak, she assumed and had convinced herself that it was the truth. She couldn't see past the fact that they'd have a baby they would have to share with another set of parents for the rest of their lives. That another man's name would appear on the child's birth certificate. She couldn't imagine the split holidays spent away from the child.

"D, I know my reasoning is selfish but, y'all think it's so easy."

Angrily, Daemon had stepped away from Casey. It hurt him that she thought so little of him that he would not accept the child as his own. Had she not done the same for Karea? And to this day treated her no different from if she were their own child? How was he not capable of that same love?

"This is not about what anybody else thinks. You want people to agree with you, and they don't. But they'll be there for you, because they love you and know that even if they don't agree, this isn't easy for you. At this point, take that and stop attempting to seek out approval of other people, because you're not likely to get it."

"So you would raise this man's baby as if he were your own. Be able to look at me for the rest of our lives and not feel some type of way because he's not yours?"

"I want you to know that sometimes love can overcome any barriers that you've come up with in your mind. You love Rea like you gave birth to her. Why do you doubt that I would do the same?"

"This isn't what I dreamed of, D."

"Grow the fuck up, Casey," he sighed. "Life is what happens while you dreaming about shit. Real life not some fuckin' novel you read."

"So you think I'm not being a grown up about it?"

Daemon walked back to her. The last thing he wanted to do was argue with her on the subject. Whatever her decision, he would stand by it. "I'm not trying fight with you, babe. Not about this, not about anything."

After the procedure had been completed and she'd emerged from the recovery room, Daemon had been standing there waiting for her. He'd held her as she cried inconsolable tears in the midst of two strangers signing up for the very same procedure.

During the months to follow, Daemon had held her hand and soothed her hurts. He handled her heart and mind with care as she fought to come back from the dark place she'd ended up.

"You look beautiful, Case," Catrina told her, putting an end to Casey's mental and still emotional trip into the past.

Casey shook her head to ward off those demons.

The classic off white lace cap-sleeve A-line gown with the keyhole back and beaded sash that flowed flawlessly into a cathedral train had been designed specifically for her. Casey had originally seen the dress in a collection at David's Bridal as a trumpet gown, but didn't like the idea of the mermaid design for her figure. With Briannah's help she was able to create a dress that combined the top with its sleek cut and lacey bodice and flare out the skirt so that it would appear fuller, and not as confining as the trumpet, considering she was a bit fuller on her lower half.

Briannah had added platinum and diamond accents to embellish the design and make it her own as much as she had made it Casey's. The attention to detail proved to be absolutely arresting, leaving all onlookers breathless.

She smiled, nodding. "I know, Bri did such a good job. This is even more beautiful than I expected."

"You really do look beautiful, Mom," thirteen-year-old Karea told her.

Casey turned to the child and smiled; the girl who she had once glanced at with apprehension was now one of her greatest joys and most important persons in her life. After the DNA test revealed that Daemon was the child's father, she had eased into their life seamlessly. At first just a day out of the week, and then a weekend a month, summers, and then suddenly she was there forever. Sadly,

Tamika suffered a Sickle Cell crisis that ended her life six years ago, and in the time since, the bond between the woman and child had deepened. "Dad is going to think you're gorgeous," she added.

"He already does and just remember that all dress details are a secret, Rea," Carina told the girl.

Karea nodded. "I know. I only told Shiana. She thinks mom looks like a model," she explained of her best friend.

Casey smiled and let out a burst of laughter. "I guess that's definitely a compliment," she added with a touch of sincerity.

"You funny as hell," Catrina told her absently, glancing at her watch. "I don't know what Briannah is doing. How could she manage to be late for a fitting in her own boutique is beyond me! Rea, go ask Sonya to call and see what's taking your aunt so long."

"Oh, please... Briannah? She could manage to be late for anything, but I already talked to her. She's taking care of something really important," Casey informed Catrina.

Catrina frowned and said, "What could be more important than this? You're in the damn dress already." She took a seat on the plush silk lilac colored couch in the bridal suite of Briannah's very successful downtown boutique.

"I'm the one who got anxious and damn near forced Sonya to help me in it. Briannah will probably kill me, and we came early."

"Early is on time during wedding planning time," Catrina murmured.

"Oh, God stop being the stuffy, proper, counting every second wedding planner, please enjoy. Your best friend is getting married. Be my maid of honor for two hours instead of being my planner," Casey pleaded. *It fits perfectly*, she thought as she swayed from side to side with a blissful hmm.

"I'm both. And let's note, I'm always the planner, or the bride's maid, never the bride," Catrina pitifully responded.

Casey peered at Catrina through the mirror. "Shut up, it's your birthday. We're going to have a good time tonight." Casey could barely contain the excitement she felt due to the upcoming surprise party for Catrina's thirtieth birthday. They had successfully pulled it off without their friend suspecting a thing. As much as Catrina hated being surprised, she loved attention. She could almost imagine Catrina's frown and then quick smile of appreciation at them doing something so special for her.

"Aghhhhhh!" Catrina let out an exaggerated scream. "Thanks for reminding me of another year passing, and I'm still single."

Casey shook her head. "Please, you are not single," she reminded Catrina.

"Oh, okay, I forgot. We're now counting sleeping partnerships as actual relationships these days," Catrina quickly said of her two year off and on relationship with Shawn Dean, a corporate tax attorney. She lived off the theory that you might as well be single, if you weren't with the person you wanted to be with. Which could be countered by Casey's theory of: if you couldn't be with the one you loved, you love the one you're with. Catrina smirked at the thought, and knew that a speech would come, if she didn't stop pouting.

"Girl, please. He got a key. And you know Shawn love you, and if you would stop playing, you could probably have him in the committed relationship you so eagerly seek." Even saying that, Casey already knew Catrina's love wasn't easily given, and to date she had only been in love once.

"He called me this morning, you know. Just to wish me happy birthday," Catrina revealed, not even lifting her head to look at her friend.

Casey turned and would have bent down to her friend, but not in her dress. She instead tilted her head with sympathetic eyes.

Catrina looked up at Casey as she played nervously with her pen. "I don't get it. I just don't get it. After all this time, he seems completely happy in Atlanta with Mi-Chelle and their life but he still flirts with the idea of us being able to be more than friends."

Casey could see the clear confusion in her friend's eyes, the sadness that took over them for a minute before they brightened again. "Well, we are all grown now, and y'all did agree to be friends. Right?"

Catrina nodded. Eight years ago that had been her way to deal with their difficult situation. Years of family events and vacations had eased her ability to be in the same space as him. Sometimes the spaces were more intimate than she'd been willing to admit to her friends.

"That's when he lived in Atlanta and was never coming up here

163

and I had no intention of really having to see him or even talk to him on a regular basis."

Casey tilted her head to the side and contemplated the news she was going to break. They'd made a pact all those years ago that all news was to be shared if it could affect someone's life. "D mentioned something about him moving back here by the end of the year. Something about opening a payday loans firm here."

Catrina straightened up from her lounging position. "I think he said something to me about moving back to Philly in passing," she flagged and stood up. "Whatever, doesn't matter to me none." She shrugged.

"Oh my God, Casey, you look so beautiful," Briannah rushed in looking fresh and bubbly in a yellow pastel bubble dress and a matching yellow orchid hair pin tucked in her swept side ponytail. "I knew that you would." Briannah smiled even as she immediately went into designer mode fussing over the fall of the cathedral veil and dress.

Half distracted, she glanced up at Catrina. "Happy Birthday, boo," she exclaimed. "Since you're the first of us to cross that thirty mark, we taking you out tonight to celebrate. I'ma get that ass so drunk, Shawn will be a happy man by the end of the night," she added when she was sure Karea was out of earshot.

"Whatever. And why you so late?" Catrina questioned. "You know I have a tight schedule today," she added.

Briannah stepped away from Casey long enough to take hold of Catrina's face to place a large kiss on her cheek. "Who cares? Who works on their birthday? I already got all those appointments switched. There will no wedding planning today my friend. Soon as I'm done with this one, we hitting the spa."

Catrina frowned, mentally calculating the damage control she'd had to run to soothe all the egos of her brides who would not get her personal attention today. "You fucked my day up. You know my clients will be disappointed that I will not be in to assist them. They're paying me a lot of money for my services."

"Oh, God, Perfect Perceptions will be servicing them." Briannah turned back to Casey. "When did your best friend become so damn snotty?"

Casey shrugged. "I think somewhere after that first wedding.

She getting all this money now and her head all big because they all want her and nobody else."

"My head has always been big," Catrina let out, giving up on her scheduled work day. "I didn't even bring anything suitable for a pamper day," she murmured as the idea of being pampered settled. Why not get her feet massaged before sliding them into her brand new red bottom shoes by Christian Louboutin? Catrina wondered. She deserved something nice.

"That's okay. Shawn packed a bag for you. It's in my car."

Catrina stared at them both, and sucked her teeth. "Y'all some sneaky bitches. Where are we going first?"

Laughter erupted from both her friends. "See, I told you, she easy," Casey whispered to Briannah.

She was getting married to the man of her dreams, her best friends were making it all possible and she had a hell of a night to look forward to, Casey thought as she pulled them all in for a group hug.

"Wait, don't mess up the dress," Catrina laughingly ordered.

Pampered Princesses

This is just what they all needed, Briannah surmised as she watched her friends relax at the hands of the professional masseuses. She could already feel the stress of being a wife and mother of two children and successful boutique owner slip away with each masterful knead of the masseuse.

"God, Austin" Catrina breathed out. "You are the one man I would pay to have his hands on me," she murmured as the "hands" momentarily massaged away some of her worries about turning thirty.

The group had affectionately named their favorite masseuse "hands" because he used his so very well. Since it was Catrina's birthday, they had paid to have him do her massage.

"You haven't been here in a long time, Trina," he told her. "Case and Briannah be up in here all the time, but not you. They tell me you too busy working," Austin said to her. "Too much work and not enough play, I'm putting in work to get these kinks out. Your boy not banging them out either? Ummm, child, 'cause he fine."

Briannah laughed as she lifted her head from its resting hole. "That's right! Tell her ass that this is therapeutic and should be a part of her monthly schedule. You know she got the money."

"It's not about the money," Casey said when she heard her friend grunt. "She never has the time. She keeps that Blackberry attached to her hip just in case she needs to talk some crazy ass bride into not calling it all off."

Catrina's response was a high-pitched shriek. "I'm not even indulging y'all right now. I'm just going lay here and let the hands work me," she said, turning her face away from them.

They emerged from the room fifteen minutes later feeling loose and almost fluid like.

"I'm ready to get my feet done," Casey said, looking down at her flip flop covered feet. She'd painted over her last polish in order to extend her pedicure an additional four days until this girl's day.

"Me too," Briannah added.

"Well, I got mine done yesterday, and I'm not about to soak them in no water. Now I'm mad that I wasted my twenty-seven dollars yesterday when I could've gotten them done on y'all," Catrina said, looking down at her pearly pink toes. For a free treat she would have been willing to forfeit her weekly trip to her regular nailery at Broad and Susquehanna.

"We're eating after this, right?" Casey asked. Briannah and Catrina both eyed their friend and shook their heads.

Casey hunched her shoulders in defense. "What? Y'all try eating nothing but lettuce and see how hungry y'all be."

Their morning passed lazily into afternoon with talk of Casey's upcoming wedding plans, family, current news events, music, movies, clothes, shoes and handbags. They were joined by Alieas during the pedicure and manicure session. It was surprising to the people outside their circle that age, personal growth, success and economic status hadn't changed them. Not at their root or core, not what they were to one another as childhood friends, nor to the women they had become.

"Remember… God, what is that girl's name? She live right on Huntingdon and Chadwich Street and she hated Lieas's ass. What was it? Tarain, right?" Briannah laughed as she sampled her chipotle salmon.

166

"Yes, she did and you too heffa," Alieas laughed, recalling the troubled girl who now had five children, was on welfare and still lived in the same Philadelphia Housing Authority house she grew up in with her drug dealing boyfriend.

"We stopped by there to see my Aunt Lizzy last week, and she lowered her eyes just as I was about to speak, and kept walking like she didn't know me," Briannah went on to say. "Behind her went her stair-stepping children. All five of them."

"You are mean, Bri," Casey told her.

"What?" she asked surprised. "She the one who always had that I'm the shit attitude and could've kept it up, if she actually went to school and graduated. I never acted like,"

"Oh, please, you were, and still are, the queen of high saditty," Catrina exclaimed as she picked at her unappealing and colorless rice pilaf. "Your food looks so much better than mine," she said, to Briannah, whose salmon looked so tempting with its bright tomatoes and corn served on a bed of rice pilaf and some very green broccoli. Even Casey's chicken salad wrapped in romaine lettuce and Alieas's shrimp Caesar salad looked better than her own tilapia dish. "Let me get some of yours," Catrina said to Briannah already dipping her fork into the salmon.

"That's why I hate eating with you, cause your ass is so spoiled. You always complain when you eat at regular restaurants," Alieas accused, pointing her fork.

"I do not," Catrina whined. "I have to go to the bathroom," she added and excused herself from the table.

"Aww, shit," Casey said in a hushed whisper when Catrina stepped away from the table. "How 'bout she said Dave called her this morning."

Briannah frowned. "Something happened between them. She's not saying but something happened. That's why she so moody."

"Y'all think she will be mad that he will be at the party tonight?" Alieas questioned, sure that her line sister's feelings for him still ran deep. Deeper than she led on, or allowed herself to show them.

Briannah shook her head. She'd agonized back and forth over the very same thought. "At this point, I don't think it's enough to make her have a bad time. She might feel some type of way about it, but she would never complain knowing her pride. It is about her, so I was against it, but her mom and dad said that it was okay to invite him. They paying more than half their money for it and they know their daughter, so it was out of my hands."

"Hate to be y'all hoes tonight," Alieas commented.

Chapter Twenty-One
The Big 3-0

Catrina

Time passed by so quickly, Catrina mused as she sipped on her favorite drink of pineapple juice and Grand Marnier. It seemed like just yesterday she had graduated from college and planned her very first wedding. In the eight years since she'd built a very prominent event management firm, she had employees, and people who depended on her. Professionally, she had everything she'd ever dreamed of, and could honestly say that her reality surpassed her childhood dreams. Even now Perfect Perceptions was being auditioned for a new wedding planning show on a local network set to broadcast in the fall of next year. The audition process was exciting and nerve-wracking at the same time. The filming crew could be found documenting the last details of Casey's upcoming nuptials. The pressure was on, and Perfect Perceptions would finally be where she'd wanted it— in the spotlight.

Three years before her parents had given her the money from the sale of her North Philadelphia home to Temple University developers eager to rent to Temple students. Between that and a few lucrative investments she was able to purchase her Range Rover, put a healthy down payment on her dockside condo, and buy larger space for Perfect Perceptions office spaces.

Catrina considered this success beyond her own dreams, but sadness still managed to creep into her heart when she thought she had no one to share it with. All the women in her life were in love and happy.

Chantel and Chris were married, with two children and had moved to New York. Briannah and Tyree were married and in love with their two children. Casey and Daemon were getting married, and well, Alieas was content being a flirt.

Then there was the lack of children. She was sure she could

spend the rest of her life lavishing gifts on her little cousins, Briannah's children. In the end she was still unfulfilled because they weren't children of her own.

And oh, how she wanted children, but at this point could see the likelihood of that happening slowly pass her by. She wanted to be married, but didn't think Shawn would willingly ask her in the near future. Nor was she certain that she wanted him to.

Sexy Shawn she jokingly called him. He was sweet and attentive, self-confident and sometimes arrogant, aggressive, intelligent and oh so male... all six foot two inches of his chocolate body. Catrina had fallen for him quickly, but pulled back when he seemed to not be interested in anything more than causal dinner dates, movies, museums, and night time pleasures. Every time she felt herself getting comfortable enough to relax and slide into the idea of them, Shawn would find a way to put on the brakes. The hints were subtle; he'd say how he needed to focus on his career and getting himself together. That hadn't stopped him from accepting the key she'd given him to her condo.

Nervous like a teenager she'd went to him and let him know that she'd suspected that she was pregnant, after missing her period. At the time, he seemed unaffected, all but letting her know that he wasn't ready for children.

After going to her Doctor, Catrina had been tested only to be disappointed to find that she wasn't expecting. Then he became the knight in shining armor assuring her that when it was their time, it'd happen. He only reiterated that they'd both have to be ready and looking toward marriage at that point. His fear to seriously commit to their relationship did not give him pause to demand exclusivity from her. Another point long thought by women of men: they may not want you but kept you close enough so that no other man could have you was proven by his actions. What Catrina got out of that was that she was great but Shawn just wasn't ready for marriage, or she just wasn't *"The One."* So three months ago after heartfelt bargaining with herself, Catrina had finally placed them in the going nowhere file.

Then there was David and her ever complicated feelings for him. Nothing she did could erase the memory of him from her heart. The time apart did nothing but nag her. The distance did nothing but mock her. Her memories served as a constant reminder that she could still live with a broken heart, but that it hurt like hell every day.

At times she'd been sure that he had did more loving than hurting, but the amount of hurt was enough, she concluded. It proved to be enough to keep her tucked away in her condo in Philly and away from him and all his eagerness to maintain their friendship. It did nothing to help that social networks made him so accessible.

As lowering as it appeared to her, Catrina had to admit she'd taken advantage and had indulged in some Facebook stalking when she just wanted to see him without his knowledge.

David, on the other hand, made no excuses or secrets that he indulged in the same practices. He'd inbox her on a regular basis, or send her a friendly email under the guise of investment business.

Why does he always get to have everything?

"You okay, babe?" Shawn asked, surprising her with his presence. She'd assumed he was still sleeping from their early evening love making.

She nodded. "Yup, just thinking," she said as he wrapped his arms around her waist and leaned down to kiss the top of her head.

"Must be serious. Anything you'd like to share?" he asked, pulling her to him so that she could lean into him.

"I'm thirty." She laughed, tilting her head back.

"Yes, you're thirty; you still look twenty-something, though," he teased. "You actually look very delicious. I love little black dresses." He played with the hem of her dress.

"You're crazy," she said, pulling herself free. "But it is a nice black dress," she admitted with a confident smile. "I'm sorry 'bout dinner and all, but I didn't know the girls had something special planned."

He shook his head, happy that she still had no idea of what her night held in store. "That's okay. I got the earrings to wow you, because I knew that I wasn't going to be able to party with you. "

The earrings. Damn, I didn't even notice how exquisite they were. "Shawn, they are absolutely my new best friends. Thank you for thinking of me," she praised. "I'm wearing them tonight. and all the girls will be jealous." He had let her know that he and her jeweler had spent countless hours on the design. The platinum set diamond hearts were very detailed but classically romantic. This was the part of him she loved, the man who would purchase extravagant trinkets to please her and add to her jewelry collection.

"I thought about making love to you with just these on tonight, so be ready when you come home."

Catrina's cell phone rang. "Hold on to that thought, Daddy," she said as she answered. "Wassup, where y'all at?" A bright smile appeared. "I'll be down in a second."

Shawn stepped closer to her, wrapping his arms around her waist again. "I really want you to be able to unwind and just have a good time. But no niggas on your ass," he told her.

Catrina tilted her head to the side and eyed him. "For real, Shawn?"

The hold tightened. "I'm serious."

Catrina leaned into him and placed a light kiss to his lips. "I know, babe. And as always, I don't need rules on appropriate behavior," she reminded him sarcastically.

"Sometimes your ass does. You look good, damn good. A couple of these niggas might be on your top. I don't want you to be confused. Now give me a real kiss before you leave."

Protest was already on the tip of her tongue as he went in for a deep kiss that made her weak. There was that slow fluttering in her heart as he continued to build the depth of his kiss. As Shawn took the kiss deeper, Catrina held on to him as she fought to keep a clear head.

"I love you," he murmured.

"I love you too," she told him, unsure if this time he was saying that he was in love with her.

Niggas— we exclusive until he wants to do him. I'm 'bout to party my ass like a rock star.

The Party

"I cannot believe y'all got a limo," Catrina squealed in delight as she cautiously stepped from the car onto the street.

"I'm getting drunk and am not even considering driving," Briannah laughed, joining Catrina on the sidewalk in front of The Bleu Martini.

"Hey, keep it classy," Casey ordered as she all but tripped out of the car.

Catrina bit her cheek to keep from laughing. "I'm with Bri. I wanna get drunk, which brings on my next question… why are we getting drunk here?"

"Shut up and come on. They make the best mixed drinks with top shelf liquor. Then we can go wherever you want," Briannah said.

Catrina peered through the window. "It looks empty. What time they open? Ain't this shit supposed to be lit up blue?" she questioned, leery of going inside.

Catrina was looking forward to heavy partying with lots of dancing and drinks. Then she thought about it. She never showed up at a club before twelve. It seems that though times had changed, lateness was something people still made a practice of.

"It's not empty. Come on," Briannah told her, tugging her arm.

"Ladies," the bouncer spoke. "Y'all look good tonight. IDs please," he requested with masculine authority.

Briannah went first without a word.

"It's my 30th birthday and I'm still getting carded. Woo, hoo." Catrina laughed as she retrieved her driver's license from her wallet and handed it to the bouncer.

"Happy birthday," he said to her and proceeded to check Casey's. "Have a good time, ladies," he told them opening the entrance door. The bouncer watched as three of the finest ladies he'd seen in one group entered the bar. Damn, wish I was partying. Ms. 30 is bad, and I'm sure I could get that. Must be special to somebody, he mused shaking his head. They'd bought the whole bar out for the evening, and this party was "by invitation only." He'd spotted a couple sport players and their wives in the crowd. Yes, she is someone special.

The passing of a familiar face in the crowd brought Catrina to a halt. She stood where she was and scanned the room for a second. By the bar stood her assistant and her boyfriend, and her sister Charine smiling in some guy's face. Chantel and Chris were tucked in each other's arms. Then there were her parents offering waves as she reached them. They were seated three seats away from where her baby sister was getting a number. Catrina's eyes narrowed as she turned to her friends who stood behind her grinning.

"I know that y'all ain't—"

"Our birthday girl has finally arrived!" a voice enhance by a microphone said, even as she recognized that it belonged to Briannah's husband Tyree.

"Surprise," he said, walking toward her with a wide smile.

"So everybody was in on this?" she questioned.

There was apparent surprise in her eyes. "I can't believe you guys did this," she said honestly. She'd specifically instructed them not to make a big deal out of her birthday. And here they were throwing a surprise party for her.

Terrance stood up and took his oldest daughter into his arms. "Happy birthday, baby," he said to her, kissing her forehead.

Stevie Wonder's version of *Happy Birthday* began to pump out the speakers. Party goers all turned their attention to Catrina and began singing to her. She shrugged and smiled.

"Yes, Hap-py Birth-day to me. Happy Birth-day," She began dancing and clapping to the beat.

Two hours into the party Catrina found herself alone in a corner nursing her bruised and possibly sprained ankle. She'd lost her footing while doing the Cuban Shuffle. Her foot went one way, and the platform shoe that contained it went another.

Shawn, who was suddenly there at the end of the Birthday Song, all but carried her to the corner where he made sure she elevated her foot.

Now he think he a doctor instead of a lawyer, Catrina mused as he went off to find her an ice pack.

"So did you plan on hiding over here for the rest of the night?" the voice was deeper than it had been in his youth. More velvety than it had seemed that very same morning.

The silent speech she gave herself before she lifted her face to David served as a voice calmer.

Damn, he looks so good.

Catrina flashed him the same smile that she had as a teen. Her voice was the only thing that would remain steady. Her heart was already pounding. So heavy, she assumed he could hear it.

"And somehow, I always thought that wishes came true on the person's birthday," Catrina said, sarcastically.

What is he doing here?

174

"I guess they do," he spoke as he took in the sight of her.

She was as she'd always been to him— breathtakingly beautiful. Her hair, which he knew still fell below her shoulders, was bundled under a black cropped bob weave cap. Her face was fresh looking and almost unpainted, except for the lilac eye shadow which highlighted her hazel eyes and her gloss-painted lips. The short black dress cupped her breast and was nipped at the waist and tied with a lilac belt looped into huge bow. The dress clung to the hips that she finally grew in to. Success hadn't tamed her wild sense of fashion, he mused.

Everything about her was attention getting. It was a wonder that the thought of her still held his. David assumed that he was prepared to see her again. He felt he was still recuperating from the last time. The realization that there wasn't any amount of preparation he could have gone through to prepare his heart for her hit him. Over the past years, he'd seen her in the company of their mutual friends, enjoyed group vacations, contacted her just to hear her voice, and had indulged in her company privately.

"You look good."

"I didn't know you were coming," she said, the distraction of her ankle was enough to keep her eyes off him.

"Didn't know if you would've wanted me here had it not been a surprise and all," he tested, stepping closer to her.

For a minute David could all but envision himself settling in beside her and taking her foot into his hands to message the pain away.

Catrina looked up at him. "But you still showed up, anyway," she replied quickly.

David shrugged and inched closer yet again. "I needed to see you. You're always so extra polite when you see me and almost whispering when we talk on the phone. You even type polite emails. You're anything but polite."

Catrina shook her head and laughed. "That's probably because I don't want to talk to you."

David leaned over to capture her hands and just held them in his for a minute. He'd never forgotten how they felt, the delicate weight of them in his own larger hands. "Now we both know that's not true," he reminded her.

Irritated by his arrogance, Catrina snatched her hands away. "You continue to overstep. How is Mi-Chelle doing?" She looked past him and caught sight of Briannah. The look she gave must have echoed *get your ass over here,* because Briannah pinched Casey and they started making their way to their friend.

"Don't get all stank on me. Maybe we could go to lunch or dinner. I have some things we need to discuss." he told her.

"Here's your ice, babe," Shawn said, approaching Catrina and David. Though he was talking to Catrina, his eyes were on David. Shawn had no clue who the stranger was, but from Catrina's expression, he was sure that he'd over stayed his welcome. With the tension between Catrina and the man apparent, Shawn addressed the stranger, "What's going on my man?"

Catrina's mouth could have dropped to the floor as she turned her attention to Shawn. The ice pack he placed in her hand damn near fell to the floor. "Thanks, babe." Catrina made the introductions. "This is Dave, Dave this is Shawn."

"Her boyfriend Shawn," Shawn added. The stare he was giving almost seemed challenging to David.

David dismissed Shawn quickly. He'd seen the guy hovering over Catrina for most of the night. David had thought nothing special of him until he saw Catrina gyrate her ass on him during the clean version of "*Occhie Wally*" by Nas.

Noticing that Catrina was the focus of David's attention, Tyree had informed his friend that Catrina's dance partner was her boyfriend, and that by all accounts, they seemed to be happy. Still, David didn't take that to heart. No one would stand in his way of what he wanted. "Nice to meet you, Shawn. I'll let you get back to your party, Trina, and see you later," he said just as Briannah and Casey reached them.

"Hey y'all," he spoke to them as he walked away.

"Who the fuck was he?" Shawn demanded.

"Ummm, Trina, I think it's time to cut the cake," Casey offered.

Chapter Twenty-Two
Some Things Never Change

So What Y'all Think?

"So let me get this straight?" David said to his two best friends. "Y'all invited this nigga to come out with us?" David was surprised to hear that Daemon's Atlantic City trip also included Catrina's boyfriend Shawn as a partying member.

In the time since his move eight years ago, David had made several trips back to Philly. He had maintained his close personal relationship with his two best friends who were as much as brothers to him as Chris. These men, were the same brothers that he had played in school yards with, ran blocks with, stacked money with, built businesses with, and were both now fathers and for the most part, husbands.

The fact that their lives had taken that direction made him pause to define his own. At thirty-three years of age, he had what most boys from the hood dreamed of. Yet, there was the dull ache that he was missing something. Though he already knew what that something was.

David condemned himself on a regular basis that his yearnings for her were simple and weak. How could any sensible man spend years out of his life, no, his entire life wanting a complicated woman who didn't want him back, or didn't love him enough to try? He knew that she casually pretended that she did not maintain a personal relationship with him beyond their mutual friendship. It annoyed him, and along with the annoyance, there was a mild ache of hurt.

Tyree toyed with his keys and sat them down to pick up his glass of water. "Why does it matter? Tyree questioned his friend even though he already knew the answer. "He's cool with us. Been hanging out with us for the last year."

Daemon laughed. "Please stop fucking with him," he said to Tyree, and turned his attention to David. "I don't know why you think that everything is about you. We cool with the man, and I didn't know that I needed to check with you about inviting him. You act just like a fuckin' girl sometimes."

Neither of them mentioned that Catrina was in a serious relationship until Tyree had done so after seeing the pair on the dance floor.

"So neither one of you thought I would have a problem with him when he fucking my girl." *Yes, my girl. My future wife.* The possessiveness in him allowed him to make the claim proudly.

"Some things never change for you. That girl ain't worried about you. It took her a long time, but I think she happy. I think dude make her happy, and because I love her, I'm happy for her. I love you and I just think you should get over it," Daemon said to him. He wasn't about to have David's problems with the Catrina situation disrupt his fun, or thoughts on his upcoming marriage.

Shit, he was getting married in fourteen days to the woman who had taught him about true love. He thought back on the years that had passed since he'd finally let his guard down. There had been the separation over Tamika weeks after they'd found out that Karea was his child. Casey had shouted about him letting Tamika twist her way into their relationship, playing the *"we have a child together"* ticket. He'd loved her more, because she saw through all of it and at first was patient, then irritated that he hadn't.

There was the brief moment when he'd paid more attention to his studio, salons, and properties than he had to her.

Casey was the woman who had become the mother to his child, when she'd lost hers. She was, he summed up, his everything. And in less than a month, Daemon would be pledging his heart to her, to cherish and keep her, and love her through any and every thing that would come along. More reason to love her, he carefully thought.

All the wrongs between them had somehow added to all the things right for them. Daemon had almost died when Casey suggested that they have a two year engagement so that they would be able to pay for their wedding without any loans or other financial assistance. The outside wedding extravaganza was going to cost them over fifty thousand dollars. Now that it was all put together, he couldn't believe that the time had actually passed by so quickly. The fact that they were able to save the money and not touch it had been another wonder.

"What about Mi-Chelle? Are you just going through some type of crisis because we're both gonna be married and you're not?" Tyree interrogated.

There had to be something to his best friend's constant need for his teenage sweetheart. Tyree could have sworn he was past those obsessive feelings. He must have been wrong, and by all accounts, it seemed that Catrina had finally moved on.

"I'm moving back up here; Mi-Chelle is not, at my request. I love her, but not like I love Catrina. I've never been in love with another woman. Never given that part of myself to another woman, because deep down in my heart, it's her... it has to be her. I'm going to marry her," David let on as he pushed away from the table, too comfortable with his friends to act ashamed of his feelings. He continued. "I kept the ring. Mi-Chelle found it and one thing led to another. Before I knew it, she was damn near forcing me to ask her to marry me. I was taken off guard and had no idea why she thought I wanted to get married, and then she confesses that she found the ring."

"Oh, shit. You always breaking hearts. She's nice." Tyree's grin was wide as he pictured Mi-Chelle. Mi-Chelle was fine as hell, had been with David off and on for the past four years and deserved the ring that David kept in his safe.

"What you be doing to these women?" Daemon asked, really wanting to know.

"Y'all niggas playing. I'm serious. Y'all think I got a chance with her or what?"

Tyree shook his head, Daemon just stared. "Hell no," they both let out a laugh, but still managed to say it in unison.

"Whatever, I'll ask her."

"Beyond that. I'ma need you to make sure you clear your calendar next week. We have to damn near do an overhaul on the wedding ceremony site," Daemon informed David.

David scratched the top of his head. "I'm confused. Why y'all getting married outside?"

Daemon had no idea, but what he said was, "It's what my baby wants; that's what she'll get."

"Where is it at again?"

"I don't know what it is. It looks like it used to be part of a house, kind of like a long hallway. The structure is kind of still intact, with a whole bunch of windows. I don't fuckin' know. It's on Strawberry Mansion Drive and Huntingdon or Cumberland, I think. Right across from the Dell, you know where you turn before you get to the bridge?"

David knew the place well; he and Catrina had spent many nights in their youth parked there. He figured he would make a point to drive by it, to see for himself what type of work would need to be done.

Irrational Thoughts

As much as Briannah loved Catrina if she had to listen to Bonnie Raitt's, "*I Can't Make You Love Me*," one more time, she was sure that she was going to scream.

"Are we still apologizing for letting him come?" Briannah quizzed as she scanned the table with horror. Between the song and the manual labor of favor making, she was already suffering. The task was proving to be as tedious as she thought it was going be. Hundreds of assorted miniature chocolates, personalized labels and ribbons, silver bells, and miniature clear heart-shaped blown glass vases were scattered across the table in the production room of Perfect Perceptions.

The current chaos on the table was a vast contrast to the meticulously organized space where their friend created favor after favor for every occasion under the sun. The lilac and violet painted walls displayed black and white photos of the most precious moments of past events managed by Perfect Perceptions. The black wood shelving behind her held a magnitude of wedding books, magazines, and other reference materials. The glass shelving facing her held crystal and glass bowls in a variety of styles, shapes, and colors. Catrina prided herself in centerpiece creation as well as floral designs. The area was a design of contrasting colors and textures.

Casey had captured Catrina's essence perfectly in her choice of decor for her entire office space. As much as she was beginning to despise all things miniature, Briannah mused, doing the favors themselves saved Catrina money, which was just as well as she was planning Casey's wedding for free as her gift.

Briannah attempted to snatch the iPOD control from Catrina's hands only to have her restart the song from the beginning. Briannah laughed and tried again.

Casey laughed and offered, "I'm sure that's a yes." Casey watched with avid interest as Catrina held up the control with one hand and fought off Briannah with the other.

It wasn't that she was upset, Catrina felt. She was more perplexed that his presence had been able to throw her off. But hadn't she always been that way when it came to him?

"I'm not upset," Catrina explained. "I've seen him a lot since-since we broke-up. It's just odd, because I still have feelings for him that extend beyond friendship. Yet, the urge to want nothing more than that maybe the one thing that keeps me sane. I feel like Ally from the movie, *The Notebook*, but without the hope for a happy ending. Who loves someone for that long? I mean, I can't really still be like in love- love with him, right?"

Casey's fingers stilled in the middle of tying a ribbon, and she glanced down to the head of the table. She had to talk herself into the question, but could no longer hold it in. "He calls you more since you went down there for that wedding last year. Did you see him when you went to Atlanta?"

Both Briannah and Casey waited for the answer. Briannah was astonished that Casey had even asked. She had thought to ask the same question a while back, but chose not. If Catrina could leave it alone, then they all could and should seeing how it was not their love lives; it was not their business.

Catrina scrunched up her face and let it go as her decision to be honest with them surfaced. If she couldn't share everything with them, who could she be able to share everything with?

"He's like my Mr. Big y'all," she spilled, making reference to the Sex and the City character and quickly let her forehead touch the table. "I slept with him. I've been out with him on dates. Before Atlanta. It started like three years ago when we all went to Punta Cana. We did it again during the Poconos trip the winter before last." Catrina lifted her head at the gasp and just in time to see Casey's hands go to her mouth. "I know that this is menial and makes no sense but he is the only man I've dated who knows that I never give away the top of my blueberry muffin."

Briannah shook her head and laughed as she asked, "The blueberry muffin? That is too funny." Even though she laughed, Briannah understood that it was the small things that mattered to Catrina.

"In Atlanta we had lunch, went to a couple museums and then dinner that Saturday night, He still knows those spots that make me want to melt. The spots that Shawn hasn't even discovered yet. This shit is in the way. I'm thirty, and I still want him like I did when I was twenty, shit, like I did when I was sixteen." The admission served to shock both her friends.

A bit confused at Catrina's confession and her own blindness to the situation, Briannah dug deeper. "So what happened? And why so secretive about it? You never mentioned it to either one of us."

Frustrated now, Catrina pushed her seat back. "How could I? It sounds stupid that I would let this happen, so to spare myself the pitiful looks from both of you, I just didn't mention it. Any of it. Besides, neither one of you understand what this feels like." She honestly replied.

How could they when Briannah had been with Tyree a total of almost twelve years, and Casey had loved Daemon as for as long as she herself had loved David, or maybe even before then.

Simple contemplation of it left her numb to all things.

"I never should have slept with him. I wasn't dating anyone and the first time was before Shawn. I just wanted to and I did. I don't think either one of us thought of Mi-Chelle. Anyway, he was supposed to drive me to the airport on Monday morning. I missed the plane on Sunday, because I was doing him. He called me the next day instead of showing up at my hotel and said he was gonna be late. I could hear a woman in the background cussing. I assumed it was Mi-Chelle. I just hung up and got a taxi. When he didn't show up before the flight left like he would have had this been a romance novel or movie, I just pushed it along with all the other fucked up stuff between us."

The room suddenly seemed small and stuffy. *That's enough talk of him*, she concluded in her mind.

"Well what did Shawn say about him at the party?" Casey inquired.

Catrina frowned, causing her eyebrows to crease. She'd had to deal with Shawn and all his questions regarding the relationship between her and the stranger at the party. Of course he'd heard of David from Tyree and Daemon but nothing more in relationship to who he had been to Catrina.

On his own, Shawn had come to the conclusion that Catrina had dated David in the past just based on the fact that her two best friends dated his two best friends. She'd at that and point agreed that David had been her teenage boyfriend, revealed information about the baby she miscarried, but spared him the details of their relationship in between.

Instead of the lovemaking Shawn had promised, he ended up sleeping on the couch and she slept alone in her king-size bed.

"Yea that was fun. He went the fuck nuts. Accusations and a whole bunch of stuff about why y'all invite him to a party he helped pay for and more blah, blah, blah. I tuned him out for a minute, and then ended up telling him all about Dave, minus a couple details."

Catrina went to the small refrigerator, grabbed three bottles of water and handed one to both women. "You have way more to be thinking about than me and my mess," Catrina said taking a sip from the bottle. Back in planner mode, Catrina glanced over at Casey and handed her a checklist. "Final count for the reception is due ASAP so I can fax it the Marriot. Then you and D can do the seating charts. The menu is finalized, centerpieces and arrangements approved. Everything with the reception is good. Nita gonna be there to oversee set-up for that. Gonna hit the florist after we finish this. Then on to Denise's for a final cake tasting. Everyone has their dresses. All the guys' tuxes are rented. I do have to say that damn near everything is done."

"I'm so excited about the cake tasting. So leaning towards red velvet. I do have to say that you're the best friend there is to have. I love you. Gimme a kiss." Casey smiled.

"Whatever! Majority of the work is gonna be the ceremony site. The guys are going to be cutting down those tree and branches growing out of the building."

Casey stretched out her arms in a cheer, "Yay! Sweaty men with electric chainsaws."

"We gonna be pulling up weeds, and doing a lot of strenuous

work. I want y'all to mentally prepare for this," Catrina smiled and turned to Briannah. "Especially you," she said to her.

Briannah's frown and pouting mouth did nothing but influence a roll of the eyes from Catrina. "The landscaping crew will be out there all day Friday working on the design that we've finally agreed upon." Hopeful eyes looked up at her friend. The sparkle came when Casey nodded in approval. Catrina clapped. "So, they're gonna mow down the strip from the stairs to what's gonna be covered by the aisle runner. The aisle will be—"

Excited, the vision of her perfect day already swimming in her mind, Casey interrupted Catrina, "Umm, did you tell D that he had to stay out there to make sure vandals don't do anything to my site."

A hearty giggle escaped from Briannah who up to that point was engrossed in the dream vision of the ceremony site that Catrina was weaving with her description. "Oh, shit. I know you don't think that he is staying out there all night long?" she said to Casey.

"Yes, he is," she argued. At least that was what she was going to ask him. She had planted the seed a couple weeks before jokingly, only to be ignored. The chances of him doing it were very slim, but she knew that he would do anything for her. Even if it meant camping out overnight at the ceremony site to protect it from city vandals, spray paints, and bottles.

"Your friend is crazy as hell. I can already see him asking her if she is," Briannah told Catrina.

They all could imagine that conversation, which would probably end with Casey in tears before the agreement came.

"Shit, if you get D to go out there, I'll see if Tyree will do it with him," Briannah added optimistically.

Chapter Twenty-Three
So... that's the past
Wassup with the future?

Catrina and David

How they ended up riding in the same car was beyond her. All Catrina could remember before being pushed into the car with David was the fact that she'd rode to the site with Casey, who was now riding back with Daemon.

With the wedding a week away, they obviously still had time to meddle in the business of others. The unsubtle hint for them to switch came right after Daemon made up a reason to have to go back home, along with Casey. There was no doubt that Casey had shared the information about Catrina and David sleeping together for the past three years. The information seemed to have proved to be a catalyst for Daemon to join Casey in her renewed interest to see David and Catrina together again.

Catrina shrugged to ward off the nervous flutters in the pit of her stomach. The last time they were alone she'd ended up admitting her love for him and sharing a hotel room with him for the weekend.

This moment would be different, though, Catrina was sure. She'd managed it in her youth and was confident that she could hold her ground with him now as an adult with years of experience under her belt.

"They think they slick," David said, sliding behind the wheel of his rented black on black BMW X5 SUV wagon. Because they were blessings for his cause, David inwardly thanked God for the opportunity to finally be alone with her. Not that he planned on seducing her in the secluded area of the car, but to just feel her out. He would test her reserve and push just enough to see if there was still any fire beneath the icy exterior she now reserved only for him.

"You know how Casey is. I don't know why, but she's always had a soft spot for you," Catrina hesitantly explained to him. She quickly chastised herself on the softness and uncertainty of her voice. If she didn't exert extra energy in trying not to relax, Catrina surmised that she would be able to loosen up and become comfortable in his company. Thoughts of him were what kept her too preoccupied to be settled.

"I just told them that I've seen you socially and have slept with you since we broke up. They were kind of shocked. They both seemed to suspect something though because Case asked if I saw you when I went to Atlanta. She was like he calls you more since you came back from there," Catrina remembered.

The notion that she'd been silent about their time together didn't sit well with him. It was odd, he concluded; she shared everything with them.

"Why haven't you told them?" he questioned as he adjusted the volume on the car stereo. He already assumed that driving in the confines of a car would be the best time to talk to her. The chance for escape was on hold for the duration of the ride.

"I knew that they wouldn't approve. Really was no point to, and I, at this point, would rather not talk about it." Catrina closed her eyes, put on her sunglasses, and hoped that he would leave it at that.

And he did for the length of what seemed like an endless playlist of R&B artist Trey Songz beginning with, *All the Ifs* by the time the fifth song, *One Love* streamed into the car from the speakers, David was pulling into a metered spot in front of her building. The fact that he was singing served to annoy her. This was her favorite song, and he was ruining it for her.

Despite herself, Catrina smiled inside. He could sing. While his musical talents were not as established as Trey's, his vocals had the power to make her heart quake. He did so as she waited while he sang through the second verse.

The promise of that "One Love" still eluded her. Catrina remained silent as he continued singing. She reached for the door handle without a word.

"It doesn't bother you that they're getting married in our spot?"

The question caught her off guard, she didn't know why it surprised her that he cared.

"It's not our spot, David. I'm not mad because what I shared there with you was special. What we had was special but in the end it's not like we was gonna ever use it. So when she asked I said it was fine," she responded sadly. She made a motion to signal that she was ready to get out of the car.

David knew the routine and also knew that she was silently telling him that she wasn't going to indulge him with idle conversation. He put a hand on her shoulder to stop her from exiting the car.

"Are you happy?" he questioned, causing her to settle back against the seat. Because the glasses remained, David reached to remove them from her face. "Does he make you happy?" he pressed.

She was looking him in the eyes this time. "Why does it matter to you, David, really? When has my happiness or my feelings ever mattered to you?"

That was just it, they always had, David reflected. Though his past and some present behaviors leaned toward selfishness, his heart had always undoubtedly been hers.

"It has always mattered. Sometimes they were the only thing that did matter. I do love you, have always loved you."

Catrina shook her head. "Just stop. I'll admit we've made some mistakes by sleeping with each other. But people really do survive being friends with people they've had relationships with. There is no difference between now and then, Dave."

"No, there isn't. You loved me then, you love me now," he told her as he glanced over at her.

"Love is a trap word for you. You know I have feelings for you, that I've been in love with you my whole life, and you use that to try and make me weak."

"What about me being weak? You said that you wouldn't marry me, and then stopped talking to me again for the second time in our lives. You wouldn't let me explain, or listen to reason. I accepted that."

"I came to you two months later, and what did I find? You were there with some other bitch, like always," she remembered shrugging. The humiliation of the visit was still fresh in her mind.

"Okay, I was with another woman. How was I supposed to know that you were gonna show up and be stubborn about the situation. You told me you didn't want to marry me."

The idea that she'd said no and meant it had bothered him. It still bothered him. The story was old and very well written.

"Haven't we been over this? I thought we were over this?" she coolly replied.

"I'll never get over you. But if you tell me that you don't love me and that you're happy, I'll take that and just leave it. But you have to tell me." He reached and captured her chin.

This time she didn't protest, or make any attempt to pull away from him. Catrina sighed heavily. "I should be hap—"

The rest of her words were captured by his lips as they skillfully covered hers. Catrina sat motionless as he assaulted her mouth roughly at first, hands in her hair molding her lips to his. The lips then began to softly plunder coaxing her to respond.

"Finally, I love you, just love you," David murmured when Catrina's hand came up to rest on his neck, and her lips responded to his.

There was no way Catrina would have been able to tell how long they'd spent in the car kissing before she stopped him only to inquire, "Would you like to come up?"

Catrina was less aware of his actual answer as he zipped out of the car, was around her side, all but pulling her out of the car and leading her inside the building as if he knew where he was going. She giggled as she tripped into the elevator.

David's body caught the weight of her even as he urged Catrina's body back into the wall kissing her. David could see the clouds of mass confusion crowd her liquid brown stare as she unlocked her front door. The sincerity of her gaze as she backed in the spacious entryway served as an open invitation. David leaned against the door after turning the lock and nodded his head.

My head and emotions are so fucked up; I'll take him any way I can get him.

Still silent, Catrina nodded her head in acceptance and cocked it towards her bedroom and also held her hand out in invitation.

David pushed off the door and intertwined his fingers with her. As she motioned to pull him toward the bedroom, David resisted and brought her fingers to his lips to nibble lightly.

"You know this it, right?" David warned her as his nibbling mouth traveled up her arm, to her shoulder and decided to make a home in the crook of her neck.

Catrina moaned as he lightly bit down on her neck in the spot only he knew existed. Her neck tilted to the side as he explored it at the same time he banded her body to his with their arms behind her back.

The temperature-raising neck kisses brought giggles from Catrina that she couldn't suppress. "Umm," she murmured, pulling her neck back so that David could pay attention to her lips. Catrina's bottom lip escaped from beneath her two front teeth as David stared into her eyes.

He could feel the heat on her; see the urgency of her want in her eyes. They matched his own desire, but he wanted, no needed to take her slow that first time.

As if almost reading his mind, Catrina stepped back, but let her hand and fingers stay intertwined with his, and made her way to her bedroom. She flicked on the track lighting as they brushed past the door. The light served to illuminate the room to a flicker.

The softly painted pastel yellow walls didn't surprise him as he made a quiet assessment of the bedroom. The walls showcased oversized pictures of black art, some African American lovers, some colorful abstracts. There was a huge brown leather chaise catty cornered back in the far left corner. The floor was covered by and oversized cashmere area rug.

The room assessment came to a halt as she began unclasping the large buttons of her designer top to expose her flawless skin and black lace bra.

"Let me do that," David offered.

The lace bra was seductive enough to have him pulling her out of the cropped black wide legged pants to see if the panties matched. His suspicion was confirmed as he slid the fabric down her legs to reveal the matching frilly lace bottoms. He fell to his knees before her.

"Undo these," she instructed motioning for him to remove her shoes.

For the second time, he paid attention to the black and white four inch ice pick heels that she wore, bringing her inches short of his own six foot three inch frame inch frame. The first time he saw those shoes, he wondered what the hell she was doing walking

189

around in them in the dirt and grass. All David could think of now was how they'd be wrapped around him as he put it on her.

"Naw, leave them on," he told her kissing her calf. "Step back," he ordered.

David took in the sight of her when she did. "Ummm," he murmured, looking down at his rock hard penis and then back up into Catrina's smiling face.

"You like it?" she asked, pretending to model the underwear for him, turning and posing so that he could get a better view. She stood in front of him. "You like it, Bey?" she questioned again, her voice husky with desire as she bent over just so that her breast were hovering above his mouth.

"You're so fuckin' beautiful," he roughly said, reaching to pull her face to his for a kiss.

The move brought Catrina to her knees before him. Her hands were relentless as they pulled at the hem of his shirt in an attempt to remove it.

He pushed her hands away as he made quick work disposing of both his shirt, the belt and buttons of his jeans.

Still kneeling, Catrina pulled at the jeans until they were around his knees and braced herself as he took her down on the floor. The softness of her cashmere area rug met her back as she adjusted to feel the weight of him for the first time in over a year. Catrina's body wanted to shout *"Welcome home"* as she enveloped him with arms and legs.

"Unt uhh, Bey. I want it slow," David murmured as he dropped a kiss to her lips, stilling her searching hips with his hands. He kicked his own legs to remove the jeans and boxers from them.

"I want it fast," she hummed. "Right now," she purred, lifting her head for another kiss. "Now, David," she ordered breathlessly as she tugged at her panties.

David lifted up to assist pulling them from her legs and returned between her thighs before she had a chance to miss him.

What is he waiting for?

David shook his head touching his forehead to hers. "Let me show you how I love you," he murmured lifting her to him. Catrina's legs spread wider to allow him the space he needed so she could accept him there. "Let me love you," he murmured again as he

190

began entering her.

Her velvety wetness was like an invitation to heaven.

Catrina closed her eyes against the sensation of the greatest thing she'd ever felt and bit down on her lip in attempt to stifle her pleasure. She moaned a sigh as he filled her with the length of him.

The first stroke was deep and slow. It was followed by a trio of others which brought hushed murmurs and sighs of pleasure from them both.

Long stroke. "I love you," he said.

Long slow stroke followed by two short quick ones and then a deep one. "I love you," he murmured again.

Catrina wrapped her legs around his waist and crossed her ice pick heeled feet at the ankles across his back. "Get it, Bey," she responded, gyrating her hips in return as he sensed her urgency for the need of her release.

"You gon' come on this dick, but not yet," he whispered in her ear. "Now let me get my pussy." Six deep strokes.

"Aaahhh," the cry escaped followed by, "uuummm, give me that dick, Daddy. We missed you so much," she breathed as she massaged his back. "I missed you so much, David," Catrina confessed as she bit at his neck, taking what he gave.

David set the pace but allowed Catrina to do her. Biting, licking, sucking, squeezing, and massaging— all trademark Catrina moves.

Deep stroke, lingered a little, withdrew to the tip, and went back in for another deeper stroke.

She moaned in response.

"You love me?" he asked her as he repeated the motion. He pushed her thighs up a little further so he could touch that spot. "You love me?" He gyrated, touching it again. He could feel her muscles tighten around him as she moaned in pleasure. The response beautiful, still not what he was looking for. "You love me?" he quizzed again and tapped what seemed like the question in Morse Code on her G-Spot.

Catrina could feel the quake erupting from the sole of her feet, up into her legs, causing her thighs to shake and butt to hump and clench just before she let go. "Ahh...ahh. I aaahhh. I love you; I love you," she exclaimed as she arched her back and exposed the line of her neck for him as she shook with ecstasy.

"You good," he breathed at her ear. "That's my girl," he continued to stroke.

Still shaking, Catrina licked her lips and clenched her body around him. "Wait," she moaned trying to get control of herself.

"Naw, Shit, Bey. You feel so good; I fuckin' love you," David let out as he framed her face to kiss her.

Minutes passed as he administered jack hammer strokes molding Catrina's body to his.

David let out a strangled growl as he came and collapsed atop her. He laid there as she stroked his back and head. "You the best, bey," he told her, turning his head to hers after a quick kiss.

When he motioned to withdraw from her, Catrina sighed, "In a minute." She wanted to bask in the sensation of having his body over hers. The feel of him much like the welcoming home she'd joked about.

"I know you fuckin' trippin!" the shout came from the doorway. "If you don't get the fuck up off the floor…"

David didn't move, but Shawn's voice had Catrina scrambling and attempting to push him away.

"Shawn! Oh my, God!" she yelped. A million thoughts ran through her head. "Move," she urged shoving David.

What the hell? Why this type of shit always happen to me?

Catrina quickly thanked God, that Shawn wasn't crazy. Extremely possessive, she acknowledged, but concluded that all men were.

He was still standing in the doorway, possibly contemplating how to handle the situation he'd just walked in on. If he was a killer or crazy, she could be dead. This could be her last thought.

"Get up," she shouted nervously.

Shawn stalked into the room, grasped David's shoulder in an attempt to pull him up and away from Catrina. "Get the fuck up," he shouted. With a dangerous look in his eyes, Shawn shoved at David to get him to his feet.

David managed to pull up his pants before Shawn landed the first blow to his jaw.

Catrina jumped to attention and desperately grasped for something to cover herself with. In the end, she wrapped herself in a cotton sheet as she watched the two men in her life punch at each other.

"Shit," she stumped and seriously thought about breaking down and crying. The adult in her won, and she fought to squeeze between them. She used all her might to push them both back. Because she knew and could predict David's reaction, she chose him to talk. "Come on now." She looked at David with pleading eyes. "I'ma need a minute," she told him turning, her gaze and attention to Shawn.

"What?" David responded angrily, wiping the sweat from his forehead. "You think I'ma leave you in here wit' him?"

"One fuckin' minute, David, damn. Just go," she ordered.

Shawn paced the room as David exited. He noticed that David didn't take anything with him, silently proclaiming that he'd be the one who stayed.

For the first time, he paid attention to Catrina. Her eyes had tears in them. Shawn didn't let that sway him.

"That's what you wanted? To be fucked on the floor like a whore?"

"Shawn, I'm so sorry," she began. The excuses would come. "It just happened," she added, but stayed where she was, her arms wrapped around her body as if providing comfort.

Shawn made a motion to step closer to her, in response, she retreated.

Visions of wrapping his hands around her neck played over in his mind out of rage. He would never hurt her, he concluded, but it would probably feel good to just put his hands around that neck.

"You spent an entire damn night explaining to me and hyping me the fuck up 'bout how there is nothing between the two of you." He took another step. "He used to be my boyfriend and I haven't seen him in years," he mimicked. "All that bullshit."

"It's hard to explain," she stated weakly.

There was hurt beneath the fury. The fact that he cared for her made her hurt. There were no words. There was nothing that she could say or do to right the wrong.

Shawn clapped, no matter how attractive the neck looked or how forceful the urge to choke it, nothing was worth jail time. "You know what? For the first time, you don't have to explain. I'm the fuck outta here," he said, reaching into his pocket, quietly placing the contents onto her dresser.

Catrina swiped at her spilled tears and couldn't bring herself to look at him.

"No point in crying," he told her. "When you grow the fuck up, you going to wish you had made different choices."

Without another word, he left the room. She waited until she heard the apartment door close before she moved. David stood in the doorway as she made her way to the dresser. Catrina assumed that he'd left his set of keys and was right. The key ring contained two house keys and a diamond ring that matched the earrings he'd given her on her birthday.

She eyed the diamond engagement ring, then looked down at her wrist. It was adorned only by the charm bracelet with the heart locket and key charms she was never without.

It was then that Catrina released a storm of tears.

Chapter Twenty-Four
Calling You Daddy

Casey and Daemon

"I don't know. I still think they look good together," Casey said to Daemon as she cuddled up with him on their sofa. After all this time, the idea of them finally being able to be together was all that she could hope for her best friend.

Daemon grunted, but smiled. "Babe, that's because you're romantically naïve."

That being partially true, Casey giggled to herself. She had come a long way from the girl who thought that nothing could ever shake certain beliefs—, that situations could determine certain fates.

Though she was a far cry from the romantic girl she had been as a teen, Casey still believed that true love lasted forever. "I am, but it got me you," she said as a matter of fact.

Daemon playfully slapped her thigh and nodded his head in agreement. "And you would be right."

Casey turned to him and took his face in her hands. "You used to swear you was gonna break my heart. You were so set against being with me," she teased his lips with kisses.

"I did a couple times." He laughed.

"Not by cheating or anything to do with another woman. I want Trina to feel the way I do. I'm done writing my vows," she offered. The smile was enticing, but would not break him. "Would you like to hear them?"

"No wedding talk on date night," Daemon reminded her.

Taking Catrina's advice, they reserved one night a week as date night where talk of all things related to their wedding was prohibited. At times, the mental, emotional, and financial stresses of the planning could cause a couple to forget what the celebration was actually for. The one night gave them an opportunity to just be Daemon and Casey free of all wedding frustrations.

Casey frowned and narrowed her eyes. "Okay but just answer first. Did you finish yours?"

"Yes, babe. And do we really have to watch *The Notebook* again?"

Casey laughed as she sat up and reached for the remote control. "Yes, don't front, you love *The Notebook*."

"It's a cute lil' movie, but we've seen it like a million times," he told her, reaching to pull her back. "I got something better for us to do," he whispered in her ear.

Casey shoved her elbow in his stomach. "No nookie 'til after the wedding, remember?" she sweetly reminded.

Daemon winced. "I don't know who made up that dumb ass rule."

"Whatever, you agreed," she told him pressing the play button to start the movie. "Plus, Rea upstairs."

"You're the one who is going to be loud. Just let me get in that one last time before you become Mrs. Daemon Hicks."

"That does sound interesting," she said biting her bottom lip.

"Stop playin' and let me get that," he invited.

Casey rolled her eyes. "You're so sneaky. We watching this movie and the we're going to eat."

"I wanna eat something all right." he teased.

Casey pushed at him. "Stop being fresh and come on."

"You sure? He hard as a rock." He rubbed himself through his jeans. "Won't you put him down for me?" he teased again.

"Let me get the popcorn," she told him. Casey got up and moved quickly. She could already image herself face down, ass up over the sofa, so she put some distance between them before she ended up that way. "You want a beer?" she called out to him from the kitchen.

"Yup," he answered. She retrieved the beer from the refrigerator.

The cordless phone rang just as she was exiting. She placed the popcorn bowl and two beer bottles on the table to answer it. "Hello?"

"Casey!"

"Wassup, Trina? You know it's date—" she began telling her friend but was stopped by Catrina's sniffling. "You okay?"

Casey listened quietly as her best friend told her of the events that had transpired at her house. "You aren't staying there, are you?" she suspiciously questioned suddenly unsure if Shawn was as stable as he seemed. "You need to come here?" she offered.

"No, I'm going to stay with Dave. Go back to your date. I'ma talk to you in the morning. Love you," Catrina told Casey before ending their connection.

Damn, she thought. *As much as I love Trina, I'm so happy that I have what I do.*

Picking up the popcorn and beers, she headed back into the family room where the man she loved was waiting for her. The news of Catrina's situation died on her lips as she noticed that Daemon had lit candles and turned off the TV, replacing it with the radio.

"You, swear—"

Daemon shook his head and pulled her into the room. "Unt uhn. Sit right here and listen." Daemon sat her down and stood in front of her, looked directly into her eyes, and said, "God has gifted me with the job of taking care of your heart, and I swear to never treat it carelessly, or disregard its needs or wants. I'm here to protect you, and love you through anything and everything, always. I promise to love you with all that I have; with all that I am; with every breath, thought, and deed. I promise to be your best friend, your lover, knowing that you're no less than that to me. You showed me what real love between a man and a woman is, and with God's blessing and guidance, I wanto spend the rest of my life showing you the same in return. I love you more, because you love my child the way you would if you'd had her yourself. The way you would love the ones we'll make. So today, here before our God, our family and friends, I'm declaring that I, Daemon Karon Hicks take you, Casey Aaliyah Moore as my wedded wife for all the days of my life."

Daemon smiled as Casey stood up and rushed into his arms. The flash of tears in her eyes didn't surprise him, but caused him to tighten his hold on her. "I love you, Casey."

"I love you, D," Casey sighed. "I have something to tell you," she said, her head still on his shoulder.

"What? Would you like to say yours now?" He laughed as he patted her back. He'd expected her to be emotional after hearing it.

197

Casey laughed and shook her head. "I was waiting to tell you, but after that, there's no way I can hold it in." She stepped back and looked up into his eyes. Casey took his hands and placed them over her abdomen. "We're gonna have a baby," she laughed, cheerfully.

Originally, her missed period went unnoticed in the midst of all her wedding planning. A routine trip to her doctor's office this week uncovered the unexpected, unplanned but highly enjoyable news of pregnancy. She was ecstatic with joy because the abortion and miscarriage had left her with feelings of uncertainty. Her happiness radiated and transmitted from her to him.

"My baby is in there?" he questioned, and he molded his hands to her stomach. He fell before her to put his ear to her stomach.

Casey's head fell back in excitement as she held his head to her. "Yes, your baby's in there." she confirmed. "I'm eight weeks." She giggled.

Daemon stood up and pulled her face to his for a long kiss. "She's having my baby, what a lovely thing."

Not sure if those were the words to a song, Casey shook her head. "I'm calling you Daddy," she teased.

Daemon picked her up. "You damn sure will," he said as he carried his future wife up the stairs.

No nookie till when? Casey laughed to herself. That's what they were about to celebrate with.

Chapter Twenty-Five
It's now or never

The Rehearsal

Emotions and nerves running high, Catrina paced the now transformed ceremony site. The moment Casey had seen it in childhood she'd declared the location as hers. Even then Catrina had seen its potential to be a place where couples said their "I do's."

It would take a dreamer to see past the weeds and trees all but growing inside and outside of the structure. The broken window frames with cracked wooding and rain beaten bricks all served as a discouragement to the passing eye. The worn down backdrop served as a blank canvas to be designed and cultivated into something breathtakingly special for the dreaming and romantic eye.

Everyone had joked and even gasped at the idea of such a thing. The owners were surprised at the inquiry to rent it as a wedding ceremony venue. In the end, a deal had been made that the rental fee be waived in lieu of the rehab and landscaping. Thanks to Casey, the owners had a new source of revenue.

Catrina had spent some time using that as her defense to strike a deal. Due to the potential earnings and free advertising, Catrina had convinced the owners that they should pay for the renovations, and as long as Casey and Daemon did the majority of the work. The owners would then allow them to use the site free of charge.

For Catrina, the idea of being a part of a reality TV show was another potential stressor. Shit, was a very real stressor as it was her chance at nationwide success. She could already imagine all the new clientele that they'd be blessed with. All her professional aspirations for a much larger version of success could be wrapped up in the outcome of her best friend's wedding. It was the fact that though she had planned it down to the very smallest detail, due to her maid of honor duties, she would not be overseeing the day of the event and was leaving it in the ever capable hands of her sister, Charine, and assistant Anita, that made her nervous. Their perceptions of what counted as perfection would be displayed and although Catrina had faith in their abilities, the last thing she wanted to do was leave it in their hands.

They are just as good as you are. They learned from the best. And they will not let you down, Catrina told herself as she tapped her foot on the newly put together flooring and her hand to the speaker of the megaphone she carried. The thought of it threatened to make Catrina bite her nails, but she'd never ruin a manicure, not even for nerves or reality TV.

One look at her watch told her they had fifteen minutes to go before show time. She briefly scanned the area for all participating members, most importantly, bride and groom. Catrina found them standing in front of where they would be exchanging their vows speaking into the camera. She smiled when Casey excitedly jump onto Daemon back. The camera man, taken off guard, stepped back a little too.

"He said yes, Trina," Casey said, letting out a giggle as she repeated it into the camera.

Catrina shook her head, "Must be love," she murmured. It didn't surprise her that he'd agreed to stay at the ceremony site overnight to allow Casey her beauty rest before her big day.

"Look at you." Daemon motioned to Catrina. "What you plan on doing with that megaphone?" Daemon asked when he noticed that she carried it.

Charine walked up behind her and took it from her hands. Before Catrina could respond she quickly said, "Nothing. I'm the Megaphone Queen 'round here today." Charine placed a smacking kiss on Catrina's check and hugged Casey before she danced off with Catrina's megaphone.

"Ten minutes, Charine," Catrina warned.

Catrina answered a few questions from the interviewer, but maintained a watchful eye on her troops. Credit was given to both Charine and Anita for being able to dramatically round up the wedding rehearsal party participants with the use of the megaphone.

Disappointed, Catrina sucked her teeth. "I really wanted to use it," she admitted to Casey. Her smile brightened. "You ready? Are you nervous?"

Nervous? If the butterflies in her stomach represented nervousness, then the answer was yes. If her heart's steady beat counted for anything, it wasn't nerves, but complete and utter contentment. And today was only practice for the one day that would change all the rest. So no, she wasn't nervous; she'd leave nerves alone until the next day. That's if they decided to show up then.

"Hey, Honey," Briannah walked up and swatted Casey on the behind. "Don't be scared now; you been planning for this since you were like ten."

"Please! Do you know who I am? I ain't never scared!" Casey declared stretching her arms out.

"You crazy," Briannah told her. "You ready, boo?" she asked Catrina.

"Sure, what's my favorite line? Always a bridesmaid, never a bride. Come one, ladies, this might take a minute. I can't wait to get some jerk wings."

With that said, the trio of women joined the rehearsal.

The Rehearsal Dinner

An hour and half later the couple and their wedding party had successfully completed their run through of the wedding ceremony. Casey was relieved that they had decided to barbecue outdoors immediately following the rehearsal. She was, however, a little skeptical about it being less than ten feet away from her site.

"Don't be nervous," Daemon said to her as if he could read her thoughts. He stood beside her, put an arm around her waist, bringing her closer to him. Smiling, he leaned closer to her ear and whispered, "No one but us will ever know that there was even a party here."

Casey laughed and nudged him a little but didn't break their bond. "They better not. We're paying a crew to do the cleanup. If they don't, you and your man friends will be on duty. God, it's gon' be beautiful out here."

"The only thing I'll see is you," Daemon confessed.

Casey smiled and turned to face him. "I'm going to marry you and love you for the rest of our lives."

"Yea, I'm certain those are the terms of the deal," Daemon murmured as he closed the distance between their lips.

The kiss was no different from the million they'd shared over the years, but this kiss made her feel different. This held a promise of their love to come.

"Enough of that kissing," David said as he walked up to them.

"Yea, enough of all that kissing," Briannah added as she joined them.

Casey smiled as she tilted her head to view her friends. "Don't come over here messing us up, we're practicing our kiss."

"Whatever," Catrina let out as she stepped up next to David. "Y'all have been kissing for the last eight years. It doesn't need that much practice."

"I know that's right," Tyree told them, rounding out their group. He smiled as his wife slid her hand into his and brought it to his lips for a kiss.

"We like to kiss anyway," Casey told them, kissing Daemon again. She laughed when her friends whooped and clapped at them making a few barbecue guests turn and stare.

"Last chance, D" David joked.

"That's not funny, man," Tyree told him.

David shook his head, "Casey baby, you know it's a joke."

"Still not funny," Catrina responded with a shake of her head.

David put his arm around her shoulders and brought her close. "So, y'all know she officially about to be my wife now, right?" David announced.

All of them clapped loudly.

"Thank you, Jesus. Now everybody can lead normal lives," Daemon stated dramatically.

"I don't remember saying we all that," Catrina interrupted, shrugging him off.

"Bey, don't try and play me in front of our friends," he said, looking down into her eyes. "We together," he announced again.

This time it went undisputed. "I think this the first time I seen him shut your ass up," Briannah smilingly told her friend.

The announcement didn't need to be made. The discovery of their night together and the news that they'd been caught by Shawn had served as a notice to their friends that they were officially a couple.

"Especially since Shawn had to rough him up so he could get you," Tyree jabbed at his friend.

"Nigga, please. Lawyer boah was 'bout to get this work if he hadn't left. I did say that he had an engagement ring in his pocket right," David added. Even though he'd never want to relive that scene again he thought that if he hadn't been there, Catrina could be wearing Shawn's ring with no thought to ever wearing his.

"I don't even want to talk about it again. I'm so embarrassed by our actions. The look on his face." She could still see it. It had been haunting her for a week.

"I just want to point out that both of you are lucky as hell, because people are crazy. Anything could have happened to y'all," Briannah brought them back to the harsh reality that they were both lucky to be alive.

Their evening had ended with them thanking the Lord that their lives had been spared. The world was a crazy place, and the people in it followed suit.

"You don't have to tell me about it," Catrina agreed.

"So what the fuck is up with y'all?" Tyree inquired. "You thirty-three and Trina thirty."

Casey laughed and clapped her hands together.

"Oh, shit," could be heard from Briannah.

"Thanks, Ty. I know how old I am. But we won't be wearing any matching: *I'm the bride, he's the groom* shirts anytime soon," Catrina smartly replied even as her stomach did flips at the thought.

"What's wrong with our shirts?" Casey questioned as both she and Daemon were wearing the very same shirts Catrina joked about.

Catrina shook her head. "Nothing, I'm just saying that just 'cause we're finally back together doesn't mean we're getting married."

Both Daemon and Tyree looked at their friend. Maybe Catrina was still confused about his plans for their relationship.

"Bey, there's only one place to go when we've been to all the others," David said to her.

Tyree pulled Briannah closer to him, kissed behind her ear, and whispered to her.

Daemon leaned down and said something to Casey that had her

hands going to her mouth.

She has no idea, Casey thought.

All of this went unnoticed by Catrina as she stared at David.

"I guess. You let me know when we get there," she told him.

David pulled her to him. His arms banded themselves around her to keep her from moving. He quietly placed a kiss to her lips, was encouraged to take the kiss depths deeper when she didn't protest.

"Yea, Dave!" Briannah cheered as she watched her friend slide her hands up to settle on the back of David's neck.

"Stop being stubborn and tell our friends that you love me," David coaxed. His handsome face radiating reflecting his happiness.

Catrina obeyed, "I love him." Semi-embarrassed, Catrina buried her face in his shirt to conceal her smile.

David reached for her hand and brought it to his lips.

"Y'all think she got the heart to say no in front of y'all?"

The flips in her stomach began feeling more like cartwheels. "What are you talking about?" She stumbled the words.

David licked his lips and stared at her. "You know what I'm talking about," he told her.

Catrina shook her head. He couldn't possibly be speaking of marriage. "That's crazy, Dave. This is about Casey," she began as she saw him go down on his knee in front of her. "Oh my, God! Get up!" Catrina exclaimed. She pulled away from him, only to be pulled back to him. "This is their time. People are looking over here," she added quietly.

David looked back and smiled as he saw her parents nod their heads at him. He shrugged and laughed. "Let them look."

"It's okay," Casey told her. "This will help make my day so much better," she admitted as she leaned back against Daemon waiting for her best friend to finally have the opportunity to feel what she felt.

"Neither one of us is perfect, but we can create something together that'll be perfect. I love you, and I don't want to spend another minute without knowing that I'll have you for the rest of my life."

Although her heart skipped a beat at the proposal, Catrina's voice was steady when she gave him the truth of what her heart felt.

"I love you and I don't want to spend another minute without knowing that you're mine to keep forever," she returned. She touched her hand to his cheek.

"So, for the record, is that a yes?" he asked

"That was a statement. You didn't ask me yet. And where's my ring?" she joked. Her response tonight would be nothing like the one eight years before.

"Catrina Nicole Price, will you marry me; make and share a home with me, make children with me and share the rest of my days?"

The lump that was lodged in her throat went down as she nodded. "Yes!" she told him excitedly.

David grinned as he pulled her close. Within a moment's time he was sliding the enhanced version of the ring that had waited eight years for her yes onto her finger.

In some deep recess of her mind, clapping could be heard, but Catrina could only hear the pounding of her heart.

David put his hand over hers and put it over her heart. As if it were a command, her heart stilled at his soothing gesture.

Catrina smiled at her friends. "Y'all knew?" she asked them.

"So that's how it's going to be?" the question came from behind them.

Catrina turned to see Mi-Chelle stepping toward them and back to David in time enough to see the smile fade from his face.

David's hand tightened around Catrina's before he let it go. The shock of Mi-Chelle's presence was enough to have him stopping short. It was heart breaking to see the simple pleasure slip from Catrina's eyes as she stood silently sizing Mi-Chelle up.

"I'm sorry, bey," David apologized to Catrina who still stared at Mi-Chelle.

Catrina's response was to step away from him. "I'm not about to spend the rest of my life with this bullshit. I swear to you. So you need to fix this now," she told him.

During their week together David had been honest about his relationship with Mi-Chelle, and the fact they'd ended two months before. At the time, she'd believed him, still had no reason to doubt him, but couldn't help but want to scream. This is what the theme of their love life had been. The weight of the newly placed engagement ring stated their future would be different.

"Let me just talk to her for a minute," David said.

Casey touched Catrina's arm. "Let them talk. Come on. It's not his fault," Casey said to Catrina. Casey half believed what she said, and was mentally praying that Mi-Chelle would remain as calm and composed as she seemed.

It was Briannah who said, "She bet not start no shit." That was because in some womanly part of her, she knew the need to be reckless when it came to the man you loved. She hoped that Mi-Chelle would keep her need to be reckless contained, for she would hate to have to come out of character.

Casey found herself explaining to Catima, Terrance and Serena, what was going on— all of them foreseeing an ugly end to the barbecue. "You mean she came all the way from Atlanta?" Serena questioned.

Casey shrugged. "I guess. I know he better not let her get crazy," she said.

"Oh, thank the Lord that the camera crew left," Catima said. When she glanced at her child, Catima's heart melted. Without a word, she embraced Catrina, attempting to provide her with some support. "It'll be okay," Catima soothed.

Catrina shook her mother off. For the first time in years, she believed that. "I'm not worried," she confidently stated. The statement carried none of the concern that her expression did. At that point, she was inclined to believe he would be able to handle Mi-Chelle.

Catrina glanced at Casey, then at Daemon who stood behind her messaging her shoulders. "I'm really sorry, y'all," she quietly apologized, accepting the responsibility as fully as David.

Daemon didn't respond, wouldn't comment unless the situation escalated. He refused to make a scene, if there was no need for one.

All eyes of the guests were transfixed on David and Mi-Chelle. Somehow the drama free night Casey and Daemon envisioned was now drama filled, thanks to their confused, but in love friends.

This celebration was however not about his friends and was everything about him and the woman he loved. Daemon took the opportunity to refocus his guest's attention back to the reason for the gathering. It would also give David a small sense of privacy.

With a watchful eye, Daemon stared cautiously as David led Mi-Chelle away from the crowd toward the street, hoping they'd cross it.

When they did, Daemon continued. "Casey, and I would like to thank everybody for coming out to help us celebrate our pre-wedding barbecue." He smiled at Casey and held her arm up in the air.

There were claps and shouts of encouragement as Casey kissed Daemon.

"We want all of you to continue to enjoy yourself, but not too much that y'all miss the wedding tomorrow," Casey added with a quick look over at David. She silently prayed that she didn't end up in jail by the end of the night.

Chapter Twenty-Six
First Instincts

Mi-Chelle

This was not the welcoming she'd expected, Mi-Chelle concluded. Not at all what she'd expected. Deciding to come to Philadelphia to attend the wedding had been a hurdle she jumped over when she realized that she wanted her man back. Granted, David had broken up with her two months ago, but she expected him to miss her and be full of regret. Be ready to all but gather her in his arms and express all those feelings. Instead, she'd been confronted with this. She cursed herself, but came to the conclusion that she would not spare herself the embarrassment of expressing her feelings, or having it out with him. It did not matter to her that she'd shown up uninvited and without a word. Considering the events that had just taken place, the woman's intuition that led her was officially unreliable. Apparently, they'd been wrong.

If she was completely honest, Mi-Chelle would have admitted that their relationship had been strained since she'd found the ring she thought was meant for her. The ring that Catrina now wore. Mi-Chelle was confident that David would be in a better mood regarding the status of their relationship, once he saw one of his best friend's preparing to be wed. Shit, she was hoping that when he saw her that he'd take her back.

As always, Mi-Chille's five foot nine inch frame was meticulously dressed and accessorized. She appeared to resemble a J Crew add model dressed in brown platform espadrilles, khaki colored linen pants that outlined her curved bottom perfectly topped with a brown form fitting tank top. She had also accessorized with wooden bangles for her slim wrist and ears, and carried an oversized brown leather Gucci sukey purse on her forearm.

"So you dumped me after four years so you can could up here and do this? So you could be with her?"

Reflecting back, she wouldn't have pushed him so hard; would have been more agreeable about his plans to return to his hometown. Mi-Chelle assumed this was now her fault.

"What the hell are you doing here?" David questioned furiously.

Mi-Chelle swiped beneath her eyes to prevent her tears from falling. "I got invited," she explained.

Technically, she did. Didn't she have the invitation to prove it? "I didn't think that I'd find you here, asking your fucking ex-girlfriend to marry you."

David looked her directly in the eyes. Tears wouldn't stop him. "We broke up. Why would you think that it was okay for you to just show up?"

"I wanted to surprise you. I behaved a lil' out of character and said some things that I didn't mean. Figured we both said some things that we didn't mean. Four years though, David?"

David shrugged. "Mi-Chelle, it would be better for both of us if you just left."

People you had affection for were to be handled with care, he reminded himself. It wasn't that he had no feelings for Mi-Chelle and the four years that she so gladly boasted about; it was obvious that the four years for him had been something entirely different.

She defiantly shifted her weight to one leg, chocked her hip out and placed her hands on top of them. "I'm not leaving 'til you tell me how you could do this to me!"

"You're not listening. You only hear what you want to hear. I'm not doing anything to you. I asked you not to come to Philadelphia."

Though, it was true, Mi-Chelle could care less. "So the fuck what? You break up with me. Give me some bullshit story about how you're not happy when I've spent the last year of my life being this perfect show piece for you. And you up here trying to be with some hood bitch from your past. Are you the fuck crazy?" she yelled.

Didn't he know who she was? There were twenty eligible bachelors lining up to take her out in Atlanta. She'd devoted four years of her life to him. There was no exit strategy for that, after this embarrassment. Nor was it in her make-up to come up with one.

Catrina, Briannah and Casey could hardly be classified as hood

209

bitches. David made a note to let them know what Mi-Chelle actually thought about them. He laughed even though entertainment was the last thing he assumed she'd intended to be.

"That's enough. Now take your ass back home. This is not the place for that. We over, we been over. We already had this conversation. I'm sorry that you're hurt. I am," he stressed.

"And what type of bitch is she anyway? She knew we were together all that time. I don't care if you went together for like two minutes when y'all were teenagers," she ranted more, this time angry enough to get physical. Mi-Chelle used all her might to push him.

Catrina was moving toward them before Casey or Briannah could stop her.

"Catrina, come back," Briannah ordered following.

Shit, she bout to flip out on somebody. Briannah thought with a huff.

"Did, she just push him?" Catrina inquired more to herself than to Briannah, but continued her trek across the lot.

Noticing her approach, Mi-Chelle turned her attention to Catrina. "What the hell you think you're going to do?"

Catrina stepped up, slipped her hand into David's, waited for him to squeeze it before she said, "I'm not going to do anything except ask you to leave. Neither bride or groom is happy with your presence here."

"You better get this hood bitch out my face."

"Bitch? You don't know anything about me. And unless you want me to show you how much of a hood bitch I am when it come to mine, you better step the fuck off," Catrina warned her.

Mi-Chelle held her stomach as she doubled over and feigned laughter. "This is hilarious."

Briannah spoke, "Mi-Chelle, we understand that you're upset, and maybe even a little embarrassed, but this is not the place or time."

Catrina touched Briannah's arm. "Don't worry, I got her," Catrina assured.

Briannah dismissed Trina's objection. "No! You need to leave as you're trespassing on private property."

"What? You fucking her too?" Mi-Chelle demanded to know.

Briannah, Catrina and David all frowned.

"Excuse me?" Briannah responded. "We're trying to avoid an ugly end to the evening."

"I'm sorry, Mi-Chelle, that you had to experience something as distressing as this, but please don't ruin my party and my celebration over something we have nothing to do with," Casey apologized and managed to plead at the same time.

Mi-Chelle looked at Casey, considered her request as it touched her heart. "I'm sorry, Casey. I truly am," she replied, new tears welling. She shook her head, hoping to stop them.

"You ain;t shit, David, I swear!" she furiously yelled as she stepped toward him. She took her palm and mugged it against the side of his face. "I hate you! I hate you!" she screamed at the top of her lungs then spit into his face. The heavy coated mucus landed on his upper lip and nose. Catrina's eyes widened in horror as it hit David's face.

"Bitch!" Catrina yelled. In her opinion spitting in another person's face was the most vicious and disrespectful thing a person could do in a face to face dispute.

"Ugh, that is disgusting." Briannah murmured. She imagined Catrina going ballistic and caught her arm in restraint.

Casey's hand went to her mouth to cover her disdain, "Oh shit."

Mi-Chelle watched a stunned and shocked trio of eyes for a reaction before she turned to walk away in the opposite direction.

She wished she knew which rental car was his; she could imagine throwing a brick through its front window as she laughed off her sadness.

Spiting in his face made her feel good.

Chapter Twenty-Seven
All that matters...

No Wedding Jitters

It served as a credit to both Charine and Anita that they were able to control the bride and her entourage which included their obsessive boss. Catrina was by all accounts more relaxed now than she had been the entire planning process. The fact that she'd enlisted the help of another planner to assist with the day of preparation soothed any concerns or surprises she expected to arise.

"You sure you're not going down to the ballroom to check on the centerpieces, or the setup or anything like that," Charine inquired. Her surprise clearly expressed.

"Of course, I will check it out, but I sent a sample down to the event manager and feel confident in their ability to duplicate it perfectly. If not, heads will roll," Catrina spoke as she raised the champagne flute in a toast to herself.

The reception was being held at the same Marriott Hotel they were staying in, so it was only a matter of going down to check on things before leaving. Professional worries aside, Catrina replayed the evening before just once more and spared a glance at the three-carat cushion cut diamond ring sparkling on her finger. It was breathtakingly beautiful.

"If he takes one more picture of you drinking, everyone is going to think you're a lush and slacking on your job as mega-super planner," Briannah told her.

Catrina sipped. "I hope the cameras don't hear me, but then again I don't care. My best friend is marrying the man she's loved for a lifetime in a few hours. My boo loves me enough for it to just be me forever, and I'm happy as shit! So yes, I'm going to drink."

Drink and dance, she concluded as she swayed to the low hum of Sade's *No Ordinary Love*.

"I think she has had enough," Casey announced as she removed the champagne flute from Catrina's hand. "Come back and get your sister," Casey snickered as Charine exited the hotel suite room.

Catrina's unpainted lips formed a frown. "Umm, I think you need some. Briannah, pour her some."

Briannah smiled and shook her head. "You want some, Casey?"

"No, I'm not drinking today. I want to remember everything," Casey replied.

"She's holding out. I know I plan on getting fucked up then getting fu—"

"Whaoo," Casey interrupted on a laugh. "Somebody is already done."

"You know she crazy as hell. I was so glad that I didn't drink, though. I wanted to be able to remember that look on Tyree's face when he saw me. And there was no haze to take away from that." The memory of Tyree's smile was still fresh in her memory as if it happened yesterday instead of seven years ago. Briannah inhaled deeply and let out the air in a huff as her hand went to her heart. "He still looks at me like that. And I still get that tingle of anticipation, that desperate in love tingle when I'm away from him and see him again."

Catrina's heart softened a degree more. She knew the tingle Briannah spoke of. Had felt the complexity of it for years. "Awww, Briannah is still madly in love with her husband. I love it. That's what it's all about. That is why people get married and vow to share their lives together. This is why I plan weddings."

Casey nodded in agreement. "You're joking, but it is. D looks at me so serious sometimes when he thinks that I'm not looking, then just smiles as he accepts that he loves me a lil' more than he thought humanly possible." The statement was very simply and accurately put. Casey dabbed her eyes. "I'm going to cry. I can't believe that this day is finally here."

Catrina let out a sympathetic smile and a bubble of laughter. Her tone was playful when she said, "You're such a lightweight, Case baby. I told you she was going to ball."

Casey sucked her teeth as she fanned her eyes to keep the tears from falling.

"She's teasing. Just wait 'til her turn. All that tough shit gon' be out the window. She already all mushy over that ring. So go ahead and cry, you still have a while before make-up," Briannah encouraged Casey's tears.   She couldn't wait for Catrina to experience it.   "Thanks. I really love you guys. Our lives would be so different, if we didn't know one another."

"Now you're set on making us cry too. We love you, Casey."

There was no more a perfect time than to share her news with them than now. "We're pregnant. I'm like nine weeks," she shared.

"Shut up!" Catrina exclaimed, "I knew it." She looked at Briannah.   "Didn't I tell you she was, walking round talking 'bout how hungry she is, and your nose is spreading a lil' already.   Aww, my baby is going to have a baby." Catrina folded Casey in her, arms dramatically.

Casey looked around as she freed herself from Catrina. "Shhh, keep your voice down.   Don't want anyone else to know, yet. I should have known y'all would know."

"Ooh, that is so good.   One of y'all can finally join the giving birth club. What D say? I know he's excited," Briannah chimed in.

"He's happy. So very happy," Casey giggled.

"And that's all that matters," Briannah smiled.

"Yea, that's all that matters," Catrina breathed.

The Man Side

Along with barbecues, wedding ceremonies, and receptions, went brunch.   Cheese eggs, grits, home fries, bacon, and waffles were all a man needed to send him into wedded bliss. Their decision to have breakfast at Temple Rainbow was an easy one.   Though none of them physically resided, or made their homes in North Philadelphia, some things were always a constant.   Late Saturday breakfasts had been a part of their teenage, college, and even adult years.   The restaurant had changed, and so had the owners, but they were still patrons.

"Remember that time Ms. Rena came 'round here after she heard that D was selling weed on the block," David reminisced.

"Yea, followed by your moms, and Ty's grandma," Daemon said. "I think she slapped the shit out of all four of us that day. Tommy was kinda shook, 'cause he'd never really been fucked up before in public."

214

"Your mom was straight gangsta back in the day. She used to come get our asses out the dollar parties and all other types of embarrassing shit. I'on know how we got to any money," Tyree joked.

"Come to think about it, we was some nut ass young boahs in our early teens. We got lucky," David added.

"Not all of us. Still seem like yesterday. And I know that if he never would have gotten killed, we'd probably all be dead. But I miss the shit out of him though."

Tommy's death had been their wake-up call to change their paths and come out winners. Sadness lurked in their hearts for the loss of their best friend years later. It had been and forever will be their life altering event. They had never glorified drug dealing but used it as a means to pay their way through college, fuel each of their individual dreams and funded many of their collective endeavors.

"We all miss him, and that's the truth. But that debt been paid in full," Tyree reminded him. The meaning was clear— justice in their eyes had been served.

Daemon considered as he paused before placing a spoonful of home fries in his mouth. "You right about that," he agreed.

David also nodded in agreement. "Damned right he is."

"Casey pregnant," Daemon confided.

David smiled as he swallowed his eggs, waited until he washed them down with some apple juice before saying, "Yea? That's really good for y'all. 'Bout damn time."

"Yea youngin'! A wife and a baby?" Tyree questioned as he touched his heart. "I'm proud of you like you my son," he added jokingly.

"Oh, thanks so much, Dad. I live to make you happy," Daemon played along.

They all laughed.

"Did you ever think back then that this would be happening?" David inquired.

"Hell naw! It was always that attraction to her, but for the longest time I felt like I would be crossing some invisible line."

David smiled to himself as he thought back to all the sessions where he and Tyree bared witness to Daemon talking himself out of

215

getting with Casey. "Please, she kicked dirt all over that line. Stepped across it, damn near was throwing you her goods, and you kept backing her down."

"You sure as hell was up 'til that day she went out with the shop boah. And to ease your heart, Briannah swears only half of it was true."

David laughed into his cup. "He was mad as shit. That was crazy. I seriously thought he was gon' fuck boah up! That's when I knew she had you."

"Yea, it was around that time that the looks got longer, like you were finally considering it but still didn't know how to go about it."

"I gotta give it to Case baby, 'cause she was all over your top, and no matter how you tried to back her down, she never did."

Daemon gave his friends credit for knowing him. "That's why I'm marrying her," he proudly claimed. Then turned his attention to David. "I just want you to know that if Mi-Chelle would have acted any crazier and unsettled Case, me and you was gon' box. Real shit!"

"I'm sorry 'bout that, man. I honestly did not expect no shit like that to go down. I thought I was going to throw up when I saw her standing there. Shit, was more sick when I saw Trina's face," David explained. There were no words to express the pure heartache he experienced when all the joy vanished from Catrina's eyes. "I'm just glad we was able to resolve that without no extra drama," David admitted.

Tyree choked. "You don't think that was drama. She hawk spit in your face. I was sure Trina was 'bout to kick her ass. Then when she accused Bri of sleeping with you, I thought Bri was 'bout to dig in that ass. Yours and hers."

"Again, I'd like to apologize. I was so fuckin' sure Trina was gonna throw that ring in my face."

"You lucky that she didn't, but considering y'all history, I hope she not thinking 'bout it now. And I'm damn sure happy y'all are removed from the singles market, fucking up the hearts of others," Tyree informed.

"You funny as shit but that's so true."

The waitress came up to their table offering refills and any additional help she could provide. Looking at the time, revealing that it was twelve pm and that half their day was gone, they all declined and requested the bill.

"What's next?" David asked mentally prepared to pull out the detailed itinerary Catrina had slipped in his hands the night before with strict instructions to follow to the letter and most importantly, to not be late.

"Barbershop so Mike can hook me up. Trina supposed to be sending over a planner to the hotel to make sure we on schedule. Tell the camera guy we goin' cross the street." Daemon stated.

David paid the bill as they climbed out the booth and said, "Just had your last meal as a single man."

"So, you nervous at all?" Tyree asked.

"Naw, I'm nervous 'bout that, I'm excited! Tonight when we go to bed, she gon' be my wife. And that's all that matters, right?"

Both, Tyree and David nodded. "That's all that matters."

With that said they made their way out of the restaurant to wait at the red traffic signal at the corner of Broad and Susquehanna Avenue. The normal Saturday flow of traffic was heavy on both the sidewalk and the street. Both northbound and southbound trains must have just stopped as people were flooding the corners after coming up from the subway surface. Taxi hacks could be heard soliciting people for rides.

The three were spotted by someone they knew coming out of the Crown Fried Chicken, they stopped and talked, mostly about Daemon's wedding. David glanced down at his watch and smiled, they had made it to the barbershop an entire half hour ahead of schedule.

Chapter Twenty-Eight
Vows

The Checklist

The sun was shining high in the pearlescent blue sky and held a promise of new beginnings. Without a dark cloud in the sky, anyone could easily be reminded of a midsummer garden. The temperature, almost at its peak, reached seventy-four degrees by 4:00 pm. The silent breezes caressing bare cheeks and shoulders made the day absolutely beautiful.

The newly painted building, seemed to be caressed by the ivory drapery that flowed from its top. Vines of lilac and yellow gardenias climbed the eight foot columns topped with vases of calla lilies and purple trimmed orchids. The columns enclosed the podium and highlighted the area that would serve as the marrying space for the couple.

The bare and cracked street had been covered and topped with glossy hardwood flooring to provide a level standing ground. White chairs trimmed with lavender and pale yellow bows were lined across the seating area.

The mowed down forty feet strip of winding grass was covered by an ivory aisle runner lined in yellow and lavender threading. The monogrammed letters of D & C H streamed across to the top as it met the hardwood flooring.

"It's so beautiful out here, Aunt Trina," Karea said. "Mom is going to cry."

Magnificent was the accurate term. "I'm speechless. It looks a hundred times better than it did on that sheet of paper," Catrina spoke aloud but more to herself than to Karea. It took her a couple of minutes to take it all in. Catrina's true calling regained control. "Go get Charine for me, then go check on your grandma so I can make sure she's okay."

Karea hurried off.

Charine appeared less than a minute later, "Here at your disposal, Queen of Planning."

Catrina laughed before saying, "Save it, please. Make sure that the lights are all working. And that the drapery is secure at the top." She looked at her sister. "You need to be writing this down and be quick, guest are starting to arrive. Make sure that those vases are centered."

"I checked everything," Charine interrupted, shaking her head. "Then rechecked everything just 'cause I knew you were going to. Relax, everything is perfect. Absolutely perfect," she repeated, winding her arm through Catrina's.

"It definitely is. You did a wonderful job with this wedding. Thank you so much," Catrina praised.

"You gonna owe me big time after this. I'ma need my own really big wedding with an assistant. With no interference from you," Charine pressed.

"We'll talk about it," Catrina patted Charine's hand.

Of course they would, Charine had all but spent the last three years as an event coordinator for Perfect Perceptions and shared Catrina's dream and passion for it.

"You look gorgeous," David complimented as he approached them. "So do you, Rine," he added.

"Go away, I'm working," Catrina replied with a flirtatious smile. "Charine, don't leave," Catrina pleaded as her sister excused herself. Charine continued to walk away.

"What do you want, David? I need you to assume your best man duties and make sure D and all your man friends are ready."

Dave laughed as he took hold of her hand. "The gay boah you sent over has that under control."

Catrina rolled her eyes. "Daniel is not gay."

"Bey, he is flaming. He's like a kid trapped in a candy store with a bunch of chocolate covered treats," David disagreed.

Catrina flagged him with a laugh. "Whatever! What do you want?"

"I just wanted to make sure you were still going to marry me after last night," David inquired, tilting her chin up so he could look in her eyes.

Catrina held up her hand. "I'm still wearing your ring," she answered.

"I didn't know, was scared that you had too much time to think."
She smiled as she considered his statement. "No, I didn't change my
mind. Didn't even entertain the thought. I do have some choice
words to be said after the wedding, though."

"I'm hoping they include, ohh, yea, Daddy right there," David
playfully added. "You're a clown. Sad part is that you're serious."

"I am. See you when you walk down the aisle." He blew her a
kiss as he walked away.

"You have some explaining to do, Catrina."

Catrina turned to see her cousin Chantel approaching and let out
a girlish squeal. "Chantel, look at you."

"No, look at you. You been keeping secrets! What's up with
that?" Chantel asked.

Catrina captured her cousin in a hug. "I missed you."

"I just saw you two weeks ago and you did not mention
anything about this," Chantel said motioning to David. "We would
have been here last night, but Calea was really fussy. And Ms.
Grown ass Cinyah is trying to work every nerve in my body.
Imagine us at fourteen. But never mind that for right now. It looks
really good out here. Where's Case?"

"She should be on her way here. Where are the kids? I need me
some kisses."

Chantel shook her head. "Unt unh, heffa. What was all that?"

Catrina smiled and held up her hand.

Chantel's eyes widened and her mouth dropped open as she grabbed
Catrina's hand and examined the ring. "Shut the fuck up! When?"

"He asked me last night."

"Oh my God! You going to have to fill me in after. I cannot
believe this. This ring is nice as hell."

"Yea, I'll have to fill you in later. It's all about Casey right
now." Catrina agreed.

The I Do's

At the sound of the first strong cord of "Here Comes the Bride"
all whispers and murmurs commenced and all attention turned to
Casey. She stood nervously as she hooked her arm around

Terrance's arm, who had been in many ways her father as well.

Terrance squeezed her hands and nodded his head to reassure her. He added, "You look beautiful and everyone is waiting on you."

Casey smiled. In the distance, she could make out Daemon standing there, already at attention waiting for her to join him. His eyes already glued to hers as she took her first step.

They remained glued to hers until Terrance replaced his arm with Daemon's. Just at that moment Daemon kissed Casey before stepping up to the pastor.

"Hold on, Daemon, the kiss comes after," the pastor laughed.

More laughter followed as she handed her bouquet to Catrina and laughed at something whispered to her by one of her bridesmaids. Finally settled, the couple stood hand in hand gazing into one another's eyes with secret promises.

"As beautiful as she looks, we're going to require that you look this way for a couple minutes. Then she's all yours." With that said the pastor began with: "Dearly beloved, we are gathered here today to join this man and this woman in Holy Matrimony."

Casey quickly dashed at the tears that streamed down her cheeks. "I've waited my whole life for this."

The wait had ended.

In front of God, all their family and friends Casey and Daemon committed their lives and love to one another for as long as they both shall live. When the pastor pronounced them husband and wife, Daemon was given the go ahead for the kiss. He took his wife in his arms and kissed her as if they were in private. The applause erupted from the crowd as the pastor announced them as Mr. and Mrs. Daemon Hicks.

Hand in hand they walked down the aisle to stand at the edge where their wedding party joined them to create a receiving line. One by one, guests kissed, hugged and well wished the bride and groom.

"You made a beautiful bride... will make an even better wife. Congrats, Casey. You too, Daemon, you make sure you treat her right," Daemon's longtime Neighborhood Watch captain from his old North Philly block said.

Daemon nodded. "I will. Thanks, Mr. Henly."

More hugs followed and almost seemed endless as Casey let out a heavy sigh when finally the last guest walked away.

"You have something better to do?" Catrina inquired.

"As a matter of fact, yes. I would like to..." She laughed and wriggled her brows.

"Ill, that's disgusting. Please not in the dress. And there are fragile ears round here," Catrina reminded them of Karea's presence.

Casey's voice dropped to a whisper. "The dress is coming off."

"Shh. " Daemon told her, laughingly catching her waist. "Don't tell her our plans; she did not put that in our schedule."

"I know that's right and the schedule is tight so pictures are next. The guests are off to the Marriott to have cocktails and some appetizers. No quickies before then."

"That mean we can't fit one in either?" David joked.

"I think we all could use one, my wife looking all good," Tyree joined.

"Negroes please," Catrina interrupted their joint effort. "Not one of these ladies will be lifting up their dresses for y'all before we get to the hotel. I need y'all to focus."

"So that mean you plan on lifting yours up afterwards," David questioned, not missing a beat.

Catrina gave in and laughed. "I might be persuaded to, but later, much, much later."

The Reception

The Marriot Ballroom was picture perfect when Casey and Daemon stepped into it after having been introduced as husband and wife. The wedding party had designed a soul train line and was lined up on both sides waiting for the happy couple to dance down it. Casey and Daemon laughingly two stepped and bopped down the aisle to KC and Jo Jo's, *"All My Life."* They were followed by the wedding party and ended the performance by sitting in the seats behind the main table on a stage.

Within minutes champagne glasses were over flowing and so was conversation. Casey was yearning for a taste of the chocolate covered strawberries she'd passed and been denied during their entrance. She opened her mouth to ask Catrina to get her some just as Daemon appeared with a plate of them large enough for them all.

"Oh, my God, this is why I married you," she joked

"I knew you wanted some.   You kept looking back while the pastor and his wife were talking to you."

"This baby is making me hungry as hell. I damn near wan: to eat everything I see. At least I don't have to worry about trying to fit into my dress anymore. You think you can go get more sweets for your sweet?"

"That baby gonna blow you up. She can't wait to eat reckless," Catrina told Daemon and Casey.

"I'm sensitive about my weight," Casey told her. She looked over her shoulder. "Where's Rea? I haven't seen her in a while."

"She's over there with Nyah and Yah in that corner playing some game," Daemon reassured her.

"I'll check on her," Catrina offered.

"I know you will," Casey agreed when she spied David in that same area.

"Whatever. I'ma go tell the DJ y'all ready for y'all first dance as husband and wife."

The DJ made the announcement and the melodies for Tamika Scott's *Greatest Gift* began as Casey and Daemon made their way to the dance floor.

Daemon bowed in front of her as he took her hand in his. "Mrs. Hicks."

Casey curtsied, and replied with, "Mr. Hicks," as he pulled her to him in an embrace. Casey's body swayed into his as he held her close and they moved to the song.

"You've never looked more beautiful than you do right now."

"And to think if I didn't harass you we wouldn't even be here."

"Oh, we would be here," he assured her. Daemon bent to take her lips with his. "'Cause there's no other place I'd rather be than me here with you and you with me." It was so easy to state the simple truth.

Their friends

"This is such a pretty song for them," Briannah murmured as she leaned her head on Catrina's shoulder

"Yea, look at them. Our baby is married and having a baby."

223

"Well, by the end of next year we might all be married and have babies," Briannah laughed eyeing Catrina.

Catrina frowned even as her heart tripped over the thought. "It's not in the schedule to have a baby next year. But I damn sure will be getting married. You see this ring, girl?"

Briannah rolled her eyes. "Yes, I see the ring; we all see the ring."

"I can't believe this happened. All that time I was so scared of him, of just loving him, and letting all the past stuff go. But when he asked me, all I could think was yes."

"You deserve to be happy. I can't say that I'm not surprised by the turn of events. And that you were keeping secrets about getting busy with him."

"It was so confusing. Our whole relationship has been a huge ball of confusion."

"Dave would be the only thing that Ms. Perfect Catrina has ever been confused about," Alieas joked as she approached.

"Please, I'm not perfect," Catrina admitted.

"No, she only practices perfection," Briannah corrected.

"Is that how it is? Y'all gonna double team me while my best friend is dancing with her husband?"

David and Tyree appeared.

"They related, bey, you know they will always take sides against you. And if you want, you can come over here and be perfect with me," David told her.

"I think I will, bye heffas," she said as she placed her hand in David's awaiting one. "You were eavesdropping?"

"I was interested in finding out when we gonna have our bathroom break."

Catrina shook her head. "We are not having a bathroom break."

"I guess I'll have to wait."

"Umm, they look so good together finally man and wife, right?" Catrina asked.

"No one else would look any better with either of them. Y'all did a wonderful job with all this. You think you gonna get the show?"

"I hope so, and you better be praying. If not, I'm thinking at this point I have everything I ever wanted."

David tightened his hold around her waist, tipped her chin up so that he could look into her eyes. "I love you, Catrina."

"I love you too, David."

Close by on the dance floor Briannah and Tyree danced with one another.

"I can't believe that he finally manned up." Briannah said to Tyree, twirling in his arms as they danced. Their eyes were on each other, but their minds were on their friends.

Tyree kissed Briannah's forehead. He was glad that he had his own wife to be thankful for. "I guess I never understood his love for her all this time but when I think of love and what it means, I would've waited forever for you, and done absolutely any and everything to have you."

Briannah smiled and put her head to his chest. "I'm glad that you know it."

"I'm glad that all our friends get to have it. Get to experience this," he said as he watched Casey and Daemon sway as one on the dance floor.

Briannah turned her attention to them as well. "Be glad she don't have him pressed up against the wall showing her ass up in here. She's having a ball. Ohh," Briannah murmured as she watched Charine walk over to Casey with a mic. "So glad she couldn't drink."

"The Bride and the Groom have something to say," Charine announced.

Casey moved to the center of the dance floor and asked for silence. The music faded as she clasped Daemon's hand. "It's not every day that you get to celebrate the joy of two people committing to one another. Y'all can imagine why I'm so happy right now. But as much as it is about us I wanna pay tribute to our supporting cast for making us possible. They helped keep us grounded while we loved one another. To Catrina, Briannah and Alieas who taught me about friendship while they taught me about love." Casey gestured to her friends. Catrina was snuggled on David's lap. Casey's heart swelled with joy as she saw David's grip tighten and Catrina's slow smile. She was confident that they'd hold on to one another now.

Briannah and Tyree who had been dancing were standing in each other arms. Beside them stood both their children, they represented the family unit she would soon have for herself. Alieas stood off to the far right corner of the ballroom and was leaning up against a wall twirling a straw in her cocktail while dreamily smiling back at her. Casey's smile deepened as Alieas's date surprised her from behind by wrapping his arms securely around her waist. From her observation, Casey could see that Alieas was enjoying him but that she had yet to allow him into her heart.

Casey sincerely hoped that some strong, self-confident, patient man would come along and peel away the hardened layer of cynicism about relationships she had developed over the years. She hoped even more that Alieas would be wise enough to realize it when he did.

"To Dave and Tyree who were like my big brothers and best friends to my husband. Thank you for all that you've been to us, to what you've been to each other. Thank y'all for not talking him out of getting with me. We couldn't have found a better group of friends. So no, it's not every day that we get an opportunity to celebrate love for those who are in love, dreaming about love, and living in love with all the hoopla of wedding ceremonies but we do have the opportunity every day to love like it's our last." She could still remember those days when she was just dreaming. "So love like it's your last chance to love."

Casey turned to her husband who pulled her in for an embrace and a kiss. When she was done, Casey looked out at her friends again. She reveled in their joy as well as she celebrated her own.

Love, no it was not as ordinary as she'd assumed when she was still chasing it, but decided that since she had found it, she was going to hold on to it forever and hoped that they would too.

COMING SOON
SUMMER 2013

HURRICANE

Sharae

I guess you can only be disappointed by someone else's actions if you give them the power to actually disappoint. Maybe my new journey in life will be to harden my heart and not be so naïve to believe every word that comes from a man's mouth. Even if the man happens to sleep next to me every night. Another evening designated for quality time disrupted by work, twenty-nine year old Dr. Sharae Jones thought as she attempted to hold back her tears.

James had spent another night working and disregarding her need for his time. She often attempted to soothe her need and her own loneliness by reminding herself that building his studio and music production company was important to both of them, the home they were building and their future. The thought was easier to bear than the actual acceptance of his constant absence and what it meant to their relationship. He'd sent her a quick text the night before saying that he wasn't going to make it home as expected and that he was sorry. She'd texted him back ok and that she loved him, had even called but he hadn't responded to either.

The lack of response sent her heart into turmoil because they weren't floating on the trusting waters of believing one's word. The constant nights out, vibrating cell phone, the quiet calls taken in other rooms, the fact that he never left his cell phone out anymore and took it with him even when he went into the rest room, or that he sometimes didn't answer his phone when they were together were all signs that something was going on. Signs that all women should wake up and pay attention to, Sharae knew. When she'd brought them to his attention James had sworn up and down that he was working and the calls along with her suspicions had nothing to do with his reality. He'd even gone as far to tell her that if she trusted him she would believe him.

Believe him? She thought. *Hhpmm, not as far as I can see.*

Stressed, Sharae stood from her seated position to look at herself in the bathroom mirror. Through blurry hazel eyes she could see the marred shadows and puffiness beneath them that could tell the tale of a brief crying jag the night before. It did nothing to heal her heart to have found evidence that the baby she'd been hoping for had not been conceived.

Sighing, Sharae turned on the shower faucets, tested the heat of the water with her fingers. She peeled away her nightclothes stepped into the tub. She adjusted the shower curtain so that water wouldn't hit the floor. For a minute, she leaned into the shower wall letting the hot water strip away that layer of disappointment and nighttime worries. It was there that Sharae felt free to let a fresh rush of tears go, sure that the tears like the shower water would be washed down the drain and soon forgotten.

Sharae chastised herself as she washed her body. Strong women did not cry, she challenged her mental but let her mind give way to the rationale that strong women were able to identify a weakness and spend an allotted time mourning over it. When the shower was over, so be it the mourning time. Sharae had learned early in life that time waited for no woman and she did not have any expectations that the rule would change for her. It was the reason she awakened every morning at five am, when more than a third of the people she knew were still cuddled in bed beneath their sheets to hit the gym.

The soft sounds of early morning radio personalities from her favorite station joked carelessly about last night's episode of American Idol. Sharae stepped on the scale she'd placed in front of her dresser as a reminder to weigh herself. She nervously bit her bottom lip in anticipation of seeing the numbers drop since yesterday morning. A confident smile appeared as the number displayed itself. She was one pound down with ten more to go. All the hard work of eating right and working out was paying off. If she didn't get pregnant she'd vacation in the Caribbean this December in a two piece bathing suit, she promised herself.

Sharae closed her eyes for a brief moment. She could already feel the sunlight basking all over her honey toned body. A body that she'd spent the last year perfecting. She'd literally spinned, ran, squatted, and kick boxed her ass off to shed the excess fifty pounds she'd gained in the contentment of her relationship.

At five feet eight inches tall, Sharae carried the majority of her weight in her hips, thighs, and behind. It was a family trait that had been passed down. She had grown up receiving long looks from males who made it known that her body's resemblance to the coke bottle was attention getting. Her light brown-skin was a shade darker than what most people considered redbone but she was easily referred to as light skinned.

Meticulously organized, she removed her sports bra from its designated drawer and then her underwear, sprayed them with some soft fragrance she'd fallen in love with during her youth. She forfeited smoothing lotion over her entire body for applying only to the areas she knew would be seen in her black capri-workout pants and form fitting lilac t-shirt with the words top model stretching across her breast. As she stretched her arms over her head the five silver bangles she wore every day for every occasion danced and clinked around her wrist. She wore simple star-cut 1 carat diamond studs in her ears. Her left hand was adorned only with a thin platinum band that represented her promise to James. One day it would be replaced by an engagement ring and then eventually a wedding band.

She grabbed her favorite everyday bag; the brown Gucci sukey tote, her gym bag and made her way downstairs. She stepped into a pair of retro Nike Bo Jackson cross trainer sneakers at the front door and quickly walked to the back of the house into kitchen to retrieve a half frozen bottle of water.

Finally ready, Sharae stepped out into the brisk August morning air. There was a slight chill to it that carried a cool breeze. It crept up the back of her thighs to her spine, tickled her cheeks, and caused the long black tendrils of hair to dance around her face. Briefly, she looked up into the darkened sky. The weather forecasters were calling for showers and tracking a hurricane heading up the East Coast.

Sharae, could feel it, there was a storm coming.

She hesitated before closing the door as she completed her mental checklist to ensure that her morning haze had not caused her to leave anything. She'd hate to have to go through her day without necessary items or make an unnecessary trip back home once she was in the city.

The iPhone she carried beeped alerting her that she'd received a text message. Once she was settled in her car, she looked at the message. Rolled her eyes as she read, "*Good Morning, Baby. I know you're on your way to the gym to work it out. Sorry I didn't return your call last night but I was fuckin' around with Troy and Shiz tryna mix down some tracks. Love you.*"

"Lyin' Nigga," she murmured as she turned the key in the ignition of her car.

Immediately, Sharae turned up the car stereo to blast Philadelphia Rap artist Ms. Jade's single, *Why U Tell Me That*. She nodded her head to the beat as Jade heated up the track with a story of a woman's heart turned to stone. There'd probably be a nice note in her mailbox requesting that she keep her music down in the morning when she returned home from work. She sucked her teeth at the thought and backed out of her driveway.

Her cell phone rang as she shrieked her custom painted black on black 2009 Jaguar down the street of her quiet suburban block. She needed the hype music as she feared her worries would follow her to the gym and throughout the course of her day. She glanced down at the caller ID and saw that it was her best friend King. Sharae contemplated ignoring him but knew that he would call again if she didn't answer. Never mind the fact that he would see her in less than twenty minutes. He had no sense of time or respect for hers.

"Good morning, Beautiful," King's deep voice spoke in greeting. "Can you turn the music down?"

"What's up, King?" she responded, reaching to adjust the volume.

"Just wanted to let you know that I wil be late for our workout session," he explained to her as he rolled onto his back in his bed. The woman beside him stirred and snuggled into his side.

Sharae sighed. "What do you mean, you're going to be late?"

King cleared his throat. "Rae, I didn't get in until after twelve am this morning."

She ignored his excuses and went in on him. "How is this your job and you slacking?"

"I'm tired as shit—"

"It's cool," she said with disappointment. She had been looking forward to their kick boxing match to relieve some of the stress she'd been feeling. "I have my music, but know that you owe me two extra sessions this week."

"Naw. I will be there," he yawned sitting up. King dragged his hands over his face and glanced down at the woman lying beside him. He got out of the bed and moved around the darkened room. Kyrie was about to be pissed that she was going to be rudely awaken and sent home so he could meet Sharae at the gym.

"Where you going? I thought you said we was gonna sleep in," Kyrie purred as she sleepily looked up at him.

Kyrie knew that King thought she was sleeping but she had been listening since the moment she felt him reach for his phone in the dark. An instant pang of jealousy twisted in her stomach. She hated that she couldn't roll over to him when the sunlight crept through the blinds in the mornings because he was always rushing off to meet Sharae.

"I have meet Rae at the gym. Would you like to go then we can come back here and lounge 'til my next appointment."

Kyrie frowned, "I don't think so, King. You know what time it is?" She wanted to roll over and just get lost in the massive king sized bed but knew that he wasn't having any of that. King had a rule that all guests exited his house when he did. No one had a key to his place except for Sharae.

Kyrie was still trying to figure out if she'd ever used it for matters that extended beyond them being best friends. For the life of her, she couldn't figure out why the two of them weren't dating each other. When King had introduced her to Sharea as his best friend she had been surprised, she was beautiful and successful. They were comfortable in each other's personal space, had even completed one another's sentences. She assumed that since they'd known each other for over ten years that they were oblivious to their reactions to one another.

Kyrie frowned as she thought that Sharae must have been blind or completely happy with her man to not have been attempting to hook up with King. He was fine. His skin complexion reminded her of milk chocolate, the hair on his head was a dark set of waves, he'd let the hair on his face grow a little longer than a natural beard, resembling a Muslim man's beard. King stood six feet three inches tall, he was lean like a basketball player and his body was toned perfectly. It surprised her that King had been single and that there had been no drama with other women since they'd began dating six months before. Single black women were always on the lookout for handsome, heterosexual, and successful black men to snag as their own. With the way their relationship was going, this might be Kyrie's opportunity to get hers.

"I could have stayed home for all of this," she pouted as she climbed to the edge of the bed. She stood up on her knee in front of him.

King sent her a sideways glance with a bright smile that showed off his pearly white teeth. "And missed out on all this good dick this morning?" he smirked as he stepped closer to gather her up in his arms.

"Ummm. You bout to pass out some more?" She inquired as she let her arms settle around his neck. Her eyes sparkled in anticipation.

He glanced at the clock and grinned back at her. "I got a lil' bit of time," he murmured coaxing her onto her back.

ALSO

AVAILABLE 2013

You can read more about Briannah and Tyree in...
Love is Blind

You can read more about Alieas in...
Changing Stiles

Both will be available in 2013 on E-Book for electronic devices

ABOUT THE AUTHOR

I have been writing since I was fourteen years old and have enjoyed reading various genres of literature since then. I love romance and all of its ups and downs, all the joys, some of the pain, the heart lifting and heartbreaking, and let's not forget the funny and outrageous. I love creating characters that people can relate to and reflect back thinking that they know and love someone just like that. I hope to promote and build literacy in the African American community and to provide quality reading material in an entertaining way that reminds readers that everyone is human. I feel that real life is not black and white but filled with many colors in various shades so our literature should be as well.
I am the mother of two beautiful children. I work very hard to show them that they can have everything they dream of if they have enough drive, skill and ambition to make it happen.
So here's me making it happen....

I'm currently working on my next novel.
Visit: www.perfectperceptionspublishing.yolasite.com